ALSO BY ALAN FURST

Night Soldiers
Dark Star
The Polish Officer
The World at Night
Red Gold

KINGDOM OF SHADOWS

ALAN FURST

KINGDOM OF SHADOWS

A NOVEL

RANDOM HOUSE NEW YORK

Copyright © 2000 by Alan Furst

Map copyright © 2001 by Anita Karl and Jim Kemp

All rights reserved under International and Pan-American Copyright Conventions. Published in the United States by Random House, Inc., New York.

RANDOM HOUSE and colophon are registered trademarks of Random House, Inc.

This work was originally published by Victor Gollancz, a member of the Orion Publishing Group, London, in 2000.

Library of Congress Cataloging-in-Publication Data

Furst, Alan.
Kingdom of shadows: a novel / Alan Furst.
    p.   cm.
ISBN 0-375-50337-4 (alk. paper)
1. World War, 1939–1945—France—Fiction.   2. World War, 1939–1945—Hungary—Fiction.
3. France—Fiction.   4. Hungary—Fiction.   I. Title.
PS3556.U76 K56 2001
813'.54—dc21   00-032344

Random House website address: www.atrandom.com
Printed in the United States of America on acid-free paper
98765432
FIRST U.S. EDITION

Book design by Carole Lowenstein

This nation has already paid for its sins, past and future.
—HUNGARIAN NATIONAL ANTHEM

GERMANY

POLAND

Decin

SUDETENLAND

Prague

Marienbad

BOHEMIA

MORAVIA

INDEPENDENT
SLOVAKIA

Danube R.

Vienna

Bratislava

AUSTRIA
*(Annexed to Germany,
March 1938)*

Budapest

HUNGARY

Danube R.

ITALY

SLOVENIA

Szeged

Zagreb

CROATIA
*(Province of Austria~Hungary
before 1918)*

YUGOSLAVIA

Belgrad

Adriatic Sea

FIRST VIENNA AWARD *(Returne
to Hungary in November 1938)*

RUTHENIA
(Occupied by Hungary in March 193

Km.
0   100
0   100
Miles

SERBIA

Southeastern
EUROPE
1938~1939

N

UKRAINIAN
S. S. R.

ARPATHIAN
...od
...THENIA
...ny
Mukachevo

MOUNTAINS

...recen NORTHERN
Bistrita
TRANSYLVANIA
Cluj

TRANSYLVANIAN ALPS

ROUMANIA

Bucharest

Danube R.

Black
Sea

BULGARIA

©A·Karl/J·Kemp, 2000

IN THE
GARDEN
OF THE
BARONESS
FREI

ON THE TENTH OF MARCH 1938, THE NIGHT TRAIN FROM BUDAPEST pulled into the Gare du Nord a little after four in the morning. There were storms in the Ruhr Valley and down through Picardy and the sides of the wagon-lits glistened with rain. In the station at Vienna, a brick had been thrown at the window of a first-class compartment, leaving a frosted star in the glass. And later that day there'd been difficulties at the frontiers for some of the passengers, so in the end the train was late getting into Paris.

Nicholas Morath, traveling on a Hungarian diplomatic passport, hurried down the platform and headed for the taxi rank outside the station. The first driver in line watched him for a moment, then briskly folded his *Paris-Midi* and sat up straight behind the wheel. Morath tossed his bag on the floor in the back and climbed in after it. "L'avenue Bourdonnais," he said. "Number eight."

Foreign, the driver thought. *Aristocrat.* He started his cab and sped along the quai toward the Seventh Arrondissement. Morath cranked the window down and let the sharp city air blow in his face.

8, avenue de la Bourdonnais. A cold, *haut bourgeois* fortress of biscuit-colored stone block, flanked by the legations of small countries. Clearly, the people who lived there were people who could live anywhere, which was why they lived there. Morath opened the gate with a big key, walked across the courtyard, used a second key for the building entry. "*Bonsoir*, Séléne," he said. The black Belgian shepherd belonged to the concierge and guarded the door at night. A shadow in the darkness, she came to his hand for a pat, then sighed as she stretched back out on the tile. *Séléne*, he thought, *goddess of the moon*.

Cara's apartment was the top floor. He let himself in. His footsteps echoed on the parquet in the long hallway. The bedroom door was open, by the glow of a streetlamp he could see a bottle of champagne and two glasses on the dressing table, a candle on the rosewood chest had burned down to a puddle of golden wax.

"Nicky?"

"Yes."

"What time is it?"

"Four-thirty."

"Your wire said midnight." She sat up, kicked free of the quilts. She had fallen asleep in her lovemaking costume, what she called her *"petite chemisette,"* silky and black and very short, a dainty filigree of lace on top. She leaned forward and pulled it over her head, there was a red line across her breast where she'd slept on the seam.

She shook her hair back and smiled at him. "Well?" When he didn't respond she said, "We are going to have champagne, aren't we?"

Oh no. But he didn't say it. She was twenty-six, he was forty-four. He retrieved the champagne from the dressing table, held the cork, and twisted the bottle slowly until the air hissed out. He filled a glass, gave it to her, poured one for himself.

"To you and me, Nicky," she said.

It was awful, thin and sweet, as he knew it would be, the *caviste* in the rue Saint-Dominique cheated her horribly. He set his glass on the carpet, went to the closet, began to undress.

"Was it very bad?"

Morath shrugged. He'd traveled to a family estate in Slovakia where his uncle's coachman lay dying. After two days, he died. "Austria was a nightmare," he said.

"Yes, it's on the radio."

He hung his suit on a hanger, bundled up his shirt and underwear and put it in the hamper. "Nazis in the streets of Vienna," he said. "Truckloads of them, screaming and waving flags, beating up Jews."

"Like Germany."

"Worse." He took a fresh towel off a shelf in the closet.

"They were always so nice."

He headed for the bathroom.

"Nicky?"

"Yes?"

"Come sit with me a minute, then you can bathe."

He sat on the edge of the bed. Cara turned on her side, pulled her knees up to her chin, took a deep breath and let it out very slowly, pleased to have him home at last, waiting patiently for what she was showing him to take effect.

Oh well. Caridad Valentina Maria Westendorf (the grandmother) de Parra (the mother) y Dionello. *All five feet, two inches of her.* From one of the wealthiest families in Buenos Aires. On the wall above the bed, a charcoal nude of her, drawn by Pablo Picasso in 1934 at an atelier in the Montmartre, in a shimmering frame, eight inches of gold leaf.

Outside, the streetlamp had gone out. Through a sheer curtain, he could see the ecstatic gray light of a rainy Parisian morning.

Morath lay back in the cooling water of the bathtub, smoking a Chesterfield and tapping it, from time to time, into a mother-of-pearl soap dish. *Cara my love.* Small, perfect, wicked, slippery. "A long, long night," she'd told him. Dozing, sometimes waking suddenly at the sound of a car. "Like blue movies, Nicky, my fantasies, good and bad, but it was you in every one of them. I thought, he isn't coming, I will pleasure myself and fall dead asleep." But she didn't, said she didn't. *Bad* fantasies? About him? He'd asked her but she only laughed. Slavemaster? Was that it? Or naughty old Uncle Gaston, leering away in his curious chair? Perhaps something from de Sade—*and now you will be taken to the abbot's private chambers.*

Or, conversely, what? The "good" fantasies were even harder to imagine. The Melancholy King? *Until tonight, I had no reason to live.* Errol Flynn? Cary Grant? The Hungarian Hussar?

He laughed at that, because he had been one, but it was no operetta. A lieutenant of cavalry in the Austro-Hungarian army, he'd fought Brusilov's cossacks in the marshes of Polesia, in 1916 on the eastern front. Outside Lutsk, outside Kovel and Tarnopol. He could still smell the burning barns.

Morath rested his foot on the gold-colored spigot, staring down at the puckered pink-and-white skin that ran from ankle to knee. Shrapnel had done that—a random artillery round that blew a fountain of mud from the street of a nameless village. He had, before passing out, managed to shoot his horse. Then he woke in an aid station, looking up at two surgeons, an Austrian and a Pole, in blood-spattered leather aprons. "The legs come off," said one. "I cannot agree," said the other. They stood on either side of a plank table in a farmhouse kitchen, arguing while Morath watched the gray blanket turn brown.

The storm that had followed him across Europe had reached Paris, he could hear rain drumming on the roof. Cara came plodding into the bathroom, tested the water with her finger and frowned. "How can you stand it?" she said. She climbed in and sat facing him, rested her back against the porcelain, and turned the hot water on full blast. He handed her the Chesterfield and she took an elaborate puff—she didn't actually smoke—blowing out a dramatic stream of smoke as though she were Marlene Dietrich. "I woke up," she said. "Couldn't go back to sleep."

"What's wrong?"

She shook her head.

They'd certainly played long and hard—it was what they did best—night love and morning love tumbled up together, and when he'd left the bedroom she'd been out cold, mouth open, breathing sonorous and hoarse. Not snoring, because, according to her, she never snored.

In the light of the white bathroom he could see that her eyes were shining, lips pressed tight—*portrait of a woman not crying.* What was it? Sometimes women just felt sad. Or maybe it was something he'd said, or done, or not done. The world was going to hell, maybe it was that. Christ he hoped it wasn't that. He stroked the skin of Cara's legs where they wrapped around his, there wasn't anything to say and Morath knew better than to try and say it.

The rain slackened, that afternoon, Paris a little *triste* in its afternoon drizzle but accustomed to weather in the spring season and looking forward to the adventures of the evening. Count Janos Polanyi— properly von Polanyi de Nemeszvar but beyond place cards at diplomatic dinners it hardly ever appeared that way—no longer waited for evening to have his adventures. He was well into his sixties now, and the *cinq-à-sept affaire* suited the rhythm of his desire. He was a large, heavy man with thick white hair, almost yellow in lamplight, who wore blue suits cut by London tailors and smelled like bay rum, used liberally several times a day, cigar smoke, and the burgundy he drank with lunch.

He sat in his office in the Hungarian legation, crumpled up a cable and tossed it in the wastebasket. Now, he thought, it was actually going to happen. *A leap into hell.* The real thing, death and fire. He glanced at his watch, left the desk, and settled in a leather chair, dwarfed by immense portraits hanging high on the walls: a pair of Arpad kings, Geza II and Bela IV, the heroic general Hunyadi hung beside his son Matthias Corvinus, with customary raven. All of them dripping furs and bound in polished iron, with long swords and drooping mustaches, attended by noble dogs of breeds long vanished. The portraits continued in the hall outside his office, and there would have been more yet if they'd had room on the walls. A long and bloody history, and no end of painters.

5:20. She was, as always, subtly late, enough to stir anticipation. With the drapes drawn the room was almost dark, lit only by a single small lamp and firelight. Did the fire need another log? No, it would do, and he didn't want to wait while the porter climbed three flights of stairs.

Just as his eyes began to close, a delicate knock at the door, followed by the appearance of Mimi Moux—the chanteuse Mimi Moux as the gossip writers of the newspapers had it. Ageless, twittering like a canary, with vast eyes and carmine lipstick—a theatrical face—she bustled into his office, kissed him on both cheeks, and touched him, somehow, damned if he knew how she did it, in sixteen places at once. Talking and laughing without pause—you could enter the conversation or not, it didn't matter—she hung her afternoon Chanel in a closet and fluttered around the room in expensive and pleasantly exhilarating underwear.

"Put on the Mendelssohn, my dear, would you?"

Arms crossed over her breasts—a mock play on modesty—she twitched her way over to an escritoire with a Victrola atop it and, still talking—"you can imagine, there we were, all dressed for the opera, it was simply *insupportable,* no? Of course it was, one couldn't do such a thing in ignorance, or, at least, so we thought. Nonetheless"— put the First Violin Concerto on the turntable and set the needle down, returned to the leather chair, and curled herself up in Count Polanyi's commodious lap.

Eventually, just at the moment—of their several underappreciated virtues, he mused, the French possessed the purest sense of timing in all Europe—she settled on her knees in front of his chair, unbuttoned his fly with one hand and, at last, stopped talking. Polanyi watched her, the concerto came to an end, the needle hissed back and forth in an empty groove. He had spent his life, he thought, giving pleasure to women, now he had reached a point where they would give pleasure to him.

Later, when Mimi Moux had gone, the legation cook knocked lightly on his door and carried in a steaming tray. "A little something, your excellency," she said. A soup made from two chickens, with tiny dumplings and cream, and a bottle of 1924 Echézeaux. When he was done, he sat back in his chair and breathed a sigh of great contentment. Now, he noted, his fly was closed but his belt and pants button were undone. *Really just as good,* he thought. *Better?*

•

The Café Le Caprice lurked in the eternal shadows of the rue Beaujo-lais, more alley than street, hidden between the gardens of the Palais Royal and the Bibliothèque Nationale. His uncle, Morath had real-ized long ago, almost never invited him to the legation, preferring to meet in unlikely cafés or, sometimes, at the houses of friends. "Indulge me, Nicholas," he would say, "it frees me from my life for an hour." Morath liked the Le Caprice, cramped and grimy and warm. The walls had been painted yellow in the nineteenth century, then cured to a rich amber by a hundred years of cigarette smoke.

Just after three in the afternoon, the lunch crowd began to leave and the regulars drifted back in to take their tables. *The mad schol-ars,* Morath thought, who spent their lives in the Bibliothèque. They were triumphantly seedy. Ancient sweaters and shapeless jackets had replaced the spotted gowns and conical hats of the medieval al-chemists, but they were the same people. Morath could never come here without recalling what the waiter, Hyacinthe, had once said about his clientele: "God forbid they should actually ever *find* it." Morath was puzzled—"Find what?" Hyacinthe looked startled, al-most offended. "Why, *it,* monsieur," he said.

Morath took a table vacated by a party of stockbrokers who'd walked over from the Bourse, lit a cigarette, ordered a *gentiane,* and settled in to wait for his uncle. Suddenly, the men at the neighboring table stopped arguing, went dead silent, and stared out at the street.

A very grand Opel Admiral had pulled up in front of Le Caprice, the driver held the back door open, and a tall man in black SS uni-form emerged, followed by a man in a raincoat, followed by Uncle Janos. Who talked and gesticulated as the others listened avidly, ex-pectant half-smiles on their faces. Count Polanyi pointed his finger and scowled theatrically as he delivered what was obviously a punch line. All three burst into laughter, just faintly audible inside the café, and the SS man clapped Polanyi on the back—*that was a good one!*

They said good-bye, shook hands, and the civilian and the SS man returned to the Opel. Here's something new, Morath thought, you rarely saw SS men in uniform in Paris. They were everywhere in Ger-many, of course, and very much in the newsreels; marching, saluting, throwing books into bonfires.

Morath's uncle entered the café and took a moment to find him. Somebody at the next table made a remark, one of his friends snickered. Morath stood, embraced his uncle, and they greeted each other—as usual, they spoke French together in public. Count Polanyi took off his hat, gloves, scarf, and coat and piled them up on the empty chair. "Hmm, that went over well," he said. "The two Roumanian businessmen?"

"I haven't heard it."

"They run into each other on the street in Bucharest, Gheorgiu is carrying a suitcase. 'Where are you off to?' Petrescu asks. 'Cernauti,' his friend says. 'Liar!' Petrescu shouts. 'You tell me you're going to Cernauti to make me think you're going to Iasi, but I've bribed your office boy, and I know you're going to Cernauti!' "

Morath laughed.

"You know Von Schleben?"

"Which one was he?"

"Wearing a raincoat."

Hyacinthe appeared. Polanyi ordered a Ricon.

"I don't think so," Morath said. He wasn't completely sure. The man was tall, with pale, fading hair a little longer than it should be, and something about the face was impish; he had the sly grin of the practical joker. Quite handsome, he could have played the suitor—not the one who wins, the one who loses—in an English drawing-room comedy. Morath was sure he'd seen him somewhere. "Who is he?"

"He works in the diplomatic area. Not a bad sort, when all is said and done, I'll introduce you sometime."

The Ricon arrived, and Morath ordered another *gentiane*. "I never did get lunch," his uncle said. "Not really. Hyacinthe?"

"Monsieur?"

"What's for lunch today?"

"Tête de veau."

"How is it?"

"Not too bad."

"I think I'll have some. Nicholas?"

Morath shook his head. He placed a small packet on the table. The size of a hand, it was wrapped in very old, yellowed muslin, perhaps a piece cut from a curtain a long time ago. He unfolded the fabric, revealing a silver cross on a faded ribbon, black and gold, the colors of Austria-Hungary. "This he sent to you."

Polanyi sighed. "Sandor," he said, as though the coachman could hear him. He picked up the medal, let it lie flat on his open hand. "A Silver Cross of Valor. You know, Nicholas, I'm honored, but this is worth something."

Morath nodded. "I offered it to the daughter, with your kindest sympathies, but she wouldn't hear of it."

"No. Of course not."

"When is it from?"

Polanyi thought for a time. "The late eighties, as near as I can work it out. A Serbian rising, down in the Banat. Sandor was a sergeant, in the regiment raised in Pozsony. It was Pressburg then."

"Bratislava, now."

"The same place, before they gave it to the Slovaks. Anyhow, he used to talk about it, now and then. The Serbs gave them a hard time, they had snipers up in the caves, on the hillsides. Sandor's company spent a week dealing with that—some villages had to be burnt down—and he got the cross."

"He wanted you to have it."

Polanyi nodded that he understood. "Is anything left, up there?"

"Not much. They stripped the house, after the border moved. Doorknobs, windows, the good floors, fireplace brick, chimneys, whatever pipe they could get out of the walls. The livestock's long gone, of course. Some of the vineyard remains. The older fruit trees."

"*Nem, nem, soha,*" Polanyi said. No, no, never—the Hungarian rejection of Trianon, the treaty that took away two thirds of its land and people after the Austro-Hungarian army was defeated in the Great War. There was more than a touch of irony in Polanyi's voice when he said it, a shrug, *all we can do is whine,* but that wasn't all. In some sense, complex, possibly obscure, he meant it.

"One day, perhaps, it comes back."

The group at the next table had been attentive. One pugnacious little man, balding, nostrils flared, the reek of his mildewed room floating over their aperitifs, said *"Revanchiste."* He didn't say it to them, quite, or to his friends, perhaps he meant it for the world at large.

They looked at him. *Revanchist, irredentist Hungarian fascists,* he meant, seething with Red Front indignation. But Morath and Polanyi were not that, they were of the Hungarian Nation, as the nobility was called, Magyars with family histories that went back a thousand years, and they were quite prepared, with chair leg and wine bottle, to throw the whole crowd out into the rue Beaujolais.

When the group at the next table had returned, ostentatiously, to minding its own business, Polanyi carefully folded the medal back into its wrapping and put it in the inside pocket of his jacket.

"He spent a long time dying," Morath said. "Not in pain, and he wasn't sad—he just had a hardheaded soul, it didn't want to go."

From Polanyi, a tender little snort of pleasure as he tasted the veal.

"Also," Morath went on, "he wanted me to tell you something."

Polanyi raised his eyebrows.

"It had to do with the death of his grandfather, who was ninety-five, he thought, and who had died in the same bed. The family knew the time had come, they were all gathered around. Suddenly, the old man became agitated and started to talk. Sandor had to lean close in order to hear him. 'Remember,' he whispered, 'life is like licking honey . . .' He said it three or four times, and Sandor could tell there was more. At last, he managed—'licking honey off a thorn.' "

Polanyi smiled, acknowledging the story. "It's been twenty years," he said, "since I saw him. When it was no longer Hungary, I didn't want anything to do with it, I knew it would be destroyed." He took a sip of the wine, then more. "You want some, Nicholas? I'll have them bring a glass."

"No, thank you."

"I wouldn't go up there," Polanyi said. "That was weak. And I knew it." He shrugged, forgiving himself.

"He didn't hold it against you."

"No, he understood. His family was there?"

"All sorts. Daughters, a son, nieces and nephews, his brother."

"Ferenc."

"Yes, Ferenc. They had all the mirrors turned around. One old lady—immense, she cried, she laughed, she cooked me an egg—couldn't stop talking about it. When the soul leaves, it mustn't ever be allowed to see itself in the mirror. Because, she said, if it did, it might like looking at itself, and then it would be back, again and again."

"I don't think mine would. Did they put out the tub of water?"

"By the door. For death to wash his scythe. Otherwise, he would have to go all the way down to the creek, and somebody else in the house would die within the year."

Polanyi daintily ate a chunk of bread he'd soaked in the sauce. When he looked up, the waiter was just passing by. "Hyacinthe, *s'il vous plaît,* a glass for my nephew here. And, while you're at it, another carafe."

They walked in the Palais Royal gardens after lunch. A dark afternoon, perpetual dusk, Polanyi and Morath like two ghosts in overcoats, moving slowly past the gray branches of the winter parterre.

Polanyi wanted to hear about Austria—he knew that Wehrmacht units were poised on the borders, ready to march in to suppress the "riots" organized by the Austrian Nazis. "If Hitler gets his Anschluss, there will be war in Europe," he said.

"The trip was a nightmare," Morath said. A nightmare that began with an absurdity—a fistfight in the corridor of the first-class car between two German harmonica salesmen. "Imagine, two stout men, both with mustaches, screaming insults at each other and flailing away with their little white fists. By the time we got them separated, they were bright red. We made them sit down, gave them water. We were afraid one of them would drop dead, and the conductor would have to stop the train and call for the police. Nobody, *nobody* in the car wanted that."

"It started in Bucharest, no doubt," Polanyi said. Roumania, he explained, had been forced to sell its wheat harvest to Germany, and the Reich finance ministry refused to pay in marks. They would only barter. For, exclusively, aspirin, Leica cameras, or harmonicas.

"Well, that was just the beginning," Morath said. "We were still in western Hungary." While the train stood in the station in Vienna, a man approximately Morath's age, pale, trembling, had taken the seat across from him. When the family that occupied the rest of the compartment went off to the dining car, they had started to talk.

The man was a Viennese Jew, an obstetrician. He told Morath that the Jewish communities of Austria had been destroyed in a day and a night. It was, he said, sudden, chaotic, not like Berlin. By which he meant, Morath knew, a certain style of persecution—the slow, meticulous grinding of civil servants. *Schreibtischtäter,* he called them, "desk-murderers."

The mobs had run wild in the city, led by Austrian SS and SA, hauling Jews out of their apartments—identified by the building custodi-ans—and forcing them to scrub the walls free of slogans for Schuschnigg, the elected chancellor, in the plebiscite that Hitler re-fused to allow. In the wealthy Jewish suburb of Währing, they made the women put on their fur coats and forced them to clean the streets on their hands and knees, then stood over them and urinated on their heads.

Morath grew worried, the man was coming apart before his eyes. Would he care for a cigarette? No, he didn't smoke. Perhaps a brandy. Morath offered to go to the dining car and bring it back. The man shook his head—what was the point? "We are finished," he said. Eight hundred years of Jewish life, ended in one night. At the hospi-tal, an hour before he'd made a run for it, a woman with a newborn child had taken it in her arms and jumped out a window on the top floor. Other patients crawled from their beds and fled into the streets. A young intern said he'd seen a man standing at a bar, the night be-fore, who took a razor from his pocket and cut his throat.

"Was there no warning?" Morath said.

"Anti-Semites in political office," the man said. "But you don't sell your house because of that. A month ago, more or less, a few people left the country." Of course there were some, he added, who'd gotten out in 1933, when Hitler came to power. He'd said, in *Mein Kampf*, that he meant to unite Austria with Germany. *Ein volk, ein Reich, ein Führer!* But reading the political future was like reading Nos-tradamus. His wife and children he'd put on a Danube steamer to Bu-dapest, thank God, the last week in February. "It was her brother who did that. He came to the house, said we should leave, insisted. There was an argument, my wife in tears, bad feelings. In the end, I was so angry I let him have his way."

"But, you stayed on," Morath said.

"I had patients."

They were silent for a moment. Outside, boys with swastika flags were running down the platform, screaming some kind of rhymed chant, their faces wild with excitement.

Polanyi and Morath sat on a bench in the gardens. It seemed very quiet there. A few sparrows working at the crumbs of a baguette, a little girl in a coat with a velvet collar, trying to play with a hoop and a stick while a nursemaid watched her.

"In the town of Amstetten," Morath said, "just outside the station, they were waiting at a road crossing so they could throw rocks at the trains. We could see the police, standing around with their arms folded, they'd come to watch. They were laughing, it was a certain kind of joke. The whole thing had, more than anything, a terrible strangeness to it. I remember thinking, they've wanted this for a long time. Under all the sentiment and *Schlag*, was this."

"Their cherished *Wut*," Polanyi said. "You know the word."

"Rage."

"Of a particular kind, yes. The sudden burst of anger that rises from despair. The Germans believe it lies deep within their character; they suffer in silence, and then they explode. Listen to Hitler speak— it's always, 'How much longer must we endure . . . ,' whatever it is. He can't leave it alone." Polanyi paused for a moment. "And now, with Anschluss, we will have the pleasure of their company on *our* border."

"Will anything happen?"

"To us?"

"Yes."

"I doubt it. Horthy will be summoned to meet with Hitler, he'll bow and scrape, agree to anything. As you know, he has beautiful manners. Of course, what we actually do will not be quite what we've agreed to, but, even so, when it's all over, we won't keep our innocence. It can't be done. And we will pay for that."

For a time, they watched the people walking along the gravel paths, then Polanyi said, "These gardens will be lovely, in the spring. The whole city."

"Soon, I hope."

Polanyi nodded. "You know," he said, "they fight wars, the French, but their country, their Paris, is never destroyed. Do you ever wonder how they do that?"

"They are clever."

"Yes, they are. They are also brave. Foolish, even. But that's not, in the end, how they save what they love. That they do by crawling."

The eleventh of March, Morath thought. Too cold to sit in a garden, the air damp in a certain way, sharp, as though chilled in wet earth. When it began to sprinkle rain, Morath and Polanyi rose and walked in the covered arcade, past a famous milliner, a store that sold expensive dolls, a dealer in rare coins.

"And the Viennese doctor?" Polanyi said.

"Reached Paris, long after midnight. Although he did have trouble at the German border. They tried to send him back to Vienna, something not quite right with his papers. A date. I stood next to him throughout the whole filthy business. In the end, I couldn't keep out of it."

"What did you do, Nicholas?"

Morath shrugged. "Looked at them a certain way. Spoke to them a certain way."

"And it worked."

"This time."

4 April 1938.

Théâtre des Catacombes. 9:20 P.M.

"Know him? Yes, I know him. His wife makes love to my wife every Thursday afternoon."

"Really? Where?"

"In the maid's room."

Lines not spoken from the stage—*would that they had been,* Morath thought—but overheard in the lobby during intermission. As Morath and Cara worked their way through the crowd, they were noticed, the glances polite, covert. A dramatic couple. Cara's face was not her best feature—it was soft and plain, hard to remember. Her best feature was long, honey-gold hair, beautiful scarves, and the ways she found to make people want her. For an evening of avant-garde theatre she had added a Gypsy skirt, with appropriate hoop earrings, and soft leather boots with the tops folded over.

Morath seemed taller than he was. He had black hair, thick, heavy, combed back from the forehead, a certain tightness around the eyes, "green" on his passport but very close to black, and all that darkness made him seem pale, a fin-de-siècle decadent. He'd once met a film producer, introduced by a mutual friend at Fouquet. "I usually make gangster films," the man told him with a smile. "Or, you know, intrigue." But, at the moment, a costume epic was soon to go into production. A large cast, a new version of *Taras Bulba*. Had Morath ever acted? He could play, possibly, "a chieftain." The producer's friend, a scrawny little man who looked like Trotsky, added, "A khan, maybe."

But they were wrong. Morath had been eighteen years in Paris and the émigré life, with its appetizing privacy, and immersion in the city, all passion, pleasure, and bad philosophy, had changed the way he looked. It meant that women liked him more, meant that people didn't mind asking him for directions in the street. Still, what the producer had seen remained, somewhere, just below the surface. Years earlier, toward the end of a brief love affair, a French woman said to him, "Why, you're not at all cruel." She had sounded, he thought, slightly disappointed.

Act II. *A Room in Purgatory—The Following Day.*

Morath shifted his weight, a pointless effort to get comfortable in the diabolical chair. Crossed his legs, leaned the other way. Cara clutched his arm—*stop it*. The row of seats, fixed on a wooden frame, went twelve across. Where did Montrouchet get them, he wondered. From some long-dead institution, no doubt. A prison? A school for horrible children?

On stage, the Seven Deadly Sins were harassing a gloomy Everyman. Poor soul, seated on a stool, wearing a gray shroud. "Ahh, but you slept through her funeral." This well-meaning woman, no longer young, was probably Sloth—though Morath had been wrong two or three times when he'd actually tried watching the play. They had soft edges, the Sins. Either the playwright's fault or Satan's—Morath wasn't sure. Pride was greedy, it seemed to him, and Greed upstaged Envy every chance he got. But then, Greed.

On the other hand, Gluttony wasn't so bad. A plump young man, come to Paris from the provinces, trying for a career in theatre or the movies. Trouble was, the playwright hadn't given him much to do. What could he say to poor, dead Everyman? You ate too much! Well, he made the best of what had been given him. Perhaps a prominent director or producer would come to watch the play, one never knew.

But one did know. Morath looked down at the program in his lap, the only permissible distraction to the white fog that rolled in from the stage. The back cover was given over to promotion—the critic from *Flambeau Rouge,* red torch, had found the play "Provocative!" Below that, a quote from Lamont Higson of *The Paris Herald.* "The Théâtre des Catacombes is the only Parisian theatre in recent memory to present plays of both Racine and Corneille in the nude." There followed a list of sponsors, including one Mlle. Cara Dionello. Well, he thought, why not. At least a few of those poor beasts in Argentina, trudging down the ramp to the abattoir, added more to life than roast beef.

The theatre lay deep in the heart of the Fifth Arrondissement. Originally, there'd been a plan for Montrouchet to stage his performances at the catacombs themselves, but the municipal authority had been mysteriously cool to the possibility of actors capering about in the dank bone-rooms beneath the Denfert Rochereau Métro stop. In the end, he had had to make do with a mural in the lobby: piles of clown-white skulls and femurs sharply picked out in black.

"What? You forgot? That night by the river?" Morath returned from dreamland to find Lust, typecast, maybe seventeen, whispering her line as she slithered on her belly across the stage. Cara took his arm again, gentle this time.

Morath did not sleep at the avenue Bourdonnais that night, he returned to his apartment in the rue Richelieu, then left early the following morning to catch the Nord Express up to Antwerp. This was a no-nonsense train, the conductors brisk and serious, the seats filled with soldiers of commerce on the march along the ancient trade route. Besides the rhythm of the wheels on the track, the only sound in Morath's compartment was the rustle of newsprint as a turned-over page of *Le Figaro* was snapped into place.

In Vienna, he read, the Anschluss was to be formalized by a plebiscite—the Austrian voter now prone to say *Ja* in order not to get his nose broken. This was, Hitler explained in a speech on 9 April, God's work.

There is a higher ordering, and we are all nothing else than its agents. When on 9 March Herr Schuschnigg broke his agreement then in that second I felt that now the call of Providence had come to me. And that which then took place in three days was only conceivable as the fulfillment of the wish and will of Providence. I would now give thanks to Him who let me return to my homeland in order that I might now lead it into the German Reich! Tomorrow may every German recognize the hour and measure its import and bow in humility before the Almighty, who in a few weeks has wrought a miracle upon us.

So, Austria ceased to exist.

And the Almighty, not quite satisfied with His work, had determined that the fuddled Doktor Schuschnigg should be locked up, guarded by the Gestapo, in a small room on the fifth floor of the Hotel Metropole.

For the moment, Morath couldn't stand any more. He put the paper down and stared out the window at tilled Flemish earth. The reflection in the glass was Morath the executive—very good dark suit, sober tie, perfect shirt. He was traveling north for a meeting with Monsieur Antoine Hooryckx, better known, in business circles, as *Hooryckx, the Soap King of Antwerp.*

In 1928, Nicholas Morath had become half-owner of the Agence Courtmain, a small and reasonably prosperous advertising agency. This was a sudden, extraordinary gift from Uncle Janos. Morath had been summoned to lunch on one of the restaurant-boats and, while cruising slowly beneath the bridges of the Seine, informed of his elevated status. "You get it all eventually," Uncle Janos said, "so you may as well have the use of it now." Polanyi's wife and children would be provided for, Morath knew, but the real money, the thousand kilometers of wheat field in the Puszta with villages and peasants, the small bauxite mine, and the large portfolio of Canadian railroad stock, would come to him, along with the title, when his uncle died.

But Morath was in no hurry, none of that *race you up the stairs, grampa* stuff for him. Polanyi would live a long time, that was fine with his nephew. The convenient part was that, with steady income assured, if Count Polanyi needed Nicholas to help him out, he was available. Meanwhile, Morath's share of the profits kept him in aperitifs and mistresses and a slightly shabby apartment at a reasonably *bonne adresse.*

The Agence Courtmain had a very *bonne adresse* indeed but, as an advertising agency, it had first of all to advertise its own success.

Which it did, along with various lawyers, stock brokerages, and Lebanese bankers, by renting an absurdly expensive suite of offices in a building on the avenue Matignon. More than likely owned, Courtmain theorized—the title of the *société anonyme* gave no indication—"by an Auvergnat peasant with goatshit in his hat."

Sitting across from Morath, Courtmain lowered his newspaper and glanced at his watch.

"On time?" Morath said.

Courtmain nodded. He was, like Morath, very well dressed. Emile Courtmain was not much over forty. He had white hair, thin lips, gray eyes, and a cold, distant personality found magnetic by virtually everybody. He smiled rarely, stared openly, said little. He was either brilliant or stupid, nobody knew, and it didn't seem terribly important. What sort of life he may have had after seven in the evening was completely unknown—one of the copywriters claimed that after everybody left the office, Courtmain hung himself up in the closet and waited for daylight.

"We aren't going to the plant, are we?" Morath said.

"No."

Morath was grateful. The Soap King had taken them to his plant, a year earlier, just making sure they didn't forget who they were, who he was, and what made the world go 'round. They didn't forget. Huge, bubbling vats of animal fat, moldering piles of bones, kettles of lye boiling gently over a low flame. The last ride for most of the cart and carriage horses in northern Belgium. "Just give your behind a good wash with that!" Hooryckx cried out, emerging like an industrial devil from a cloud of yellow steam.

They arrived in Antwerp on time and climbed into a cab outside the station. Courtmain gave the driver complicated instructions—Hooryckx's office was down a crooked street at the edge of the dockside neighborhood, a few rooms in a genteel but crumbling building. "The world tells me I'm a rich man," Hooryckx would say. "Then it snatches everything I have."

In the back of the cab, Courtmain rummaged in his briefcase and produced a bottle of toilet water called Zouave, a soldier with fierce mustaches stared imperiously from the label. This was also a

Hooryckx product, though not nearly so popular as the soap. Courtmain unscrewed the cap, splashed some in his hand, and gave the bottle to Morath. They rubbed it on their faces and reeked like country
boys in the city on Saturday night. "Ahh," said Courtmain, as the
heavy fragrance filled the air, "the finest peg-house in Istanbul."

Hooryckx was delighted to see them. "The boys from Paris!" He
had a vast belly and a hairstyle like a cartoon character that sticks his
finger in a light socket. Courtmain took a colored drawing from his
briefcase. Hooryckx, with a wink, told his secretary to go get his advertising manager. "My daughter's husband," he said. The man
showed up a few minutes later, Courtmain laid the drawing on a
table, and they all gathered around it.

In a royal-blue sky, two white swans flew above the legend *Deux
Cygnes* . . . This was something new. In 1937, their magazine advertising had presented an attractive mother, wearing an apron, showing
a bar of *Deux Cygnes* to her little girl.

"Well," said Hooryckx. "What do the dots mean?"

"Two swans . . ." Courtmain said, letting his voice trail away. "No
words can describe the delicacy, the loveliness of the moment."

"Shouldn't they be swimming?" Hooryckx said.

Courtmain reached into his briefcase and brought out the swimming version. His copy chief had warned him this would happen.
Now the swans made ripples in a pond as they floated past a clump of
reeds.

Hooryckx compressed his lips.

"I like them flying," the son-in-law said. "More chic, no?"

"How about it?" Hooryckx said to Morath.

"It's sold to women," Morath said.

"So?"

"It's what they feel when they use it."

Hooryckx stared, back and forth, from one image to the other. "Of
course," he said, "swans sometimes fly."

After a moment, Morath nodded. *Of course.*

Courtmain brought forth another version. Swans flying, this time
in a sky turned aquamarine.

"Phoo," Hooryckx said.

Courtmain whipped it away.

The son-in-law suggested a cloud, a subtle one, no more than a wash in the blue field. Courtmain thought it over. "Very expensive," he said.

"But an excellent idea, Louis," Hooryckx said. "I can see it."

Hooryckx tapped his fingers on the desk. "It's good when they fly, but I miss that curve in the neck."

"We can try it," Courtmain said.

Hooryckx stared for a few seconds. "No, better this way."

After lunch, Courtmain went off to see a prospective client, and Morath headed for the central commercial district—to a shop called Homme du Monde, man about town, its window occupied by suave mannequins in tuxedos. Much too warm inside, where a clerk was on her knees with a mouthful of pins, fitting a customer for a pair of evening trousers.

"Madame Golsztahn?" Morath said.

"A moment, monsieur."

A curtain at the rear of the shop was moved aside, and Madame Golsztahn appeared. "Yes?"

"I came up from Paris this morning."

"Oh, it's you," she said. "Come in back."

Behind the curtain, a man was pressing pants, working a foot pedal that produced a loud hiss and a puff of steam. Madame Golsztahn led Morath down a long rack of tuxedos and tailcoats to a battered desk, its cubbyholes packed with receipts. They had never met before, but Morath knew who she was. She'd been famous for love affairs, in her younger days in Budapest, the subject of poems in little journals, the cause of two or three scandals and a rumored suicide from the Elizabeth Bridge. He felt it, standing next to her. *Like the current in a river.* A ruined face and stark, brick-red hair above a dancer's body in a tight black sweater and skirt. She gave him a tart smile, read him like a book, wouldn't have minded, then swept the hair back off her forehead. There was a radio playing, Schumann maybe, violins, something exceptionally gooey, and, every few seconds, a loud hiss from the steam press. "So then," she said, before anything actually happened.

"Should we go to a café?"

"Here would be best."

They sat side by side at the desk, she lit a cigarette and held it between her lips, squinting as the smoke drifted into her eyes. She found
one of the receipts, turned it over, and smoothed it flat with her
hands. Morath could see a few letters and numbers, some circled.
"Mnemonics," she said. "Now all I have to do is remember how it
works."

"All right," she said at last, "here is your uncle's friend in Budapest, to be known as 'a senior police official.' He states that 'as of
10 March, evidence points to intense activity among all sectors of the
nyilas community.' " *Neelosh*—her voice was determinedly neutral. It
meant the Arrow Cross, pure Hitlerite fascists; the E.M.E., which spe-
cialized in bomb attacks against Jewish women; the *Kereszteny
Kurzus,* Chritian Course, which meant so much more than "Christ-
ian"; and various others, great and small.

"On the fifth of March," she said, "a fire in a shed in the Eighth
District, *Csikago*"—Chicago, as in factories and gangsters—"police
inspectors were called when rifles and pistols were found to have been
stored there."

She coughed, covering her mouth with the back of her hand, and
rested the cigarette among a line of brown scars on the edge of the
desk. "An Arrow Cross member, by trade a cabinetmaker, detained
for defacing public property, was found in possession of the home
telephone number of the German economic attaché. A police in-
former in Szeged, murdered on the sixth of March. Eight young men,
members of the *Turul* student association, observed carrying out a
surveillance of the army barracks at Arad. A furniture-mover's truck,
parked in an alley by the south railroad station, was searched by police on information received from the estranged wife of the driver. A
Berthier heavy machine gun was found, with eighty-five belts of ammunition."

"I'm going to have to make notes," Morath said.

Golsztahn's eyes met his. "You aren't going anywhere, are you?"
She paused. "East?"

Morath shook his head. "Just to Paris. Tonight."

She handed him an unused rental receipt. "Use the back. The police official notes that a report of these events has been routed, in the
customary way, to the office of Colonel Sombor in the Hungarian
legation in Paris."

"A minute," Morath said. He was almost caught up. Sombor had something to do with security at the legation—the same name as the head of the secret police, taken from a town in the south of Hungary. This usually meant Hungarians of German, Saxon, ancestry.

When he looked up, she continued. "An Arrow Cross informant reports that several of his colleagues are preparing to send their families out of the city the first week in May. And . . ." She peered closely at the top of the receipt. "What?" she said, then, "Oh. Two known agents of the German intelligence service, the SD, had in their room at the Hotel Gellert photographs of the architectural blueprints of the Water District police station and the Palace of Justice. The police official states finally that there are further instances of this kind of activity, some three dozen, that point to a political action in the near future."

It was quiet on the evening train to Paris. Courtmain worked, jotting notes on a tablet, and Morath read the newspaper. The leading stories continued to focus on Austria and the Anschluss. The British politician Churchill, a member of the Tory opposition, was quoted by a political columnist on the editorial page, from a speech given in parliament at the end of February: "Austria has now been laid in thrall, and we do not know whether Czechoslovakia will suffer a similar fate."

Well, somebody will.

Morath touched the receipt in his pocket. Golsztahn had burned hers in a coffee cup, then poked the ashes apart with the end of a pencil.

Of all the cities, Otto Adler loved Paris the most. He had arrived in the winter of 1937, installed his life—a wife, four children, two cats, and an editorial office—in a big, drafty old house in Saint Germain-en-Laye, where, from a window in his study, he could look out over miles of Parisian rooftops. *Paris—the best idea mankind ever had.*

"Third time lucky!" was the way his wife put it. Otto Adler had grown up in Königsberg, the capital of East Prussia, in the Baltic German community. After university in Berlin, he came home a Marxist, then spent the decade of his thirties becoming a Social Democrat, a journalist, and a pauper. "When you are that poor," he'd say, "the only thing left for you is to start a little magazine." So, *Die Aussicht,* The Outlook, was born. Not so popular, it turned out, in the tight, *Volksdeutsch* world of Königsberg. "This failed postcard painter from Linz will destroy German culture," he said of Hitler in 1933. Two broken windows, for that, his wife cursed in the butcher shop, and, soon enough, a big, drafty old apartment in Vienna.

Otto Adler fitted in much better there. "Otto, darling, I think you were born to be Viennese," his wife said. He had a round, hairless, rosy face, a beaming smile, he wished the world well—one of those bighearted people who can be benign and angry at once and laugh at himself in the bargain. Somehow, he kept publishing the magazine. "We should probably call it *The Ox,* it plods along in all weathers." And in time, a little Viennese money—from progressive bankers, Jewish businessmen, union leaders—began to come his way. As *Die Aussicht* gained credibility, he managed to obtain an article by one of the gods of German literary culture, Karl Kraus, the savage, brilliant satirist whose disciples—his readers, his students—were known as *Krausianer.*

In 1937, *Die Aussicht* published a brief *reportage* by an Italian journalist, the wife of a diplomat, who'd been present at one of Hermann Goering's infamous dinners at Schorfheide, his hunting lodge. The usual Nazi merriment, with the soup and the fish, but before the main course arrived Goering left the table and returned wearing a rawhide shirt, with a bearskin thrown over his shoulders—a warrior costume from the old Teutonic tribes. Not nearly, of course, enough. Goering was armed with a spear and led a pair of hairy bison, harnessed in chains, around and around the room while the guests roared. Still, not enough. The entertainment concluded with the mating of the bison. "A party to remember," it said in *Die Aussicht.* Adler's children were expelled from school, a swastika chalked on his door, the maid quit, the neighbors ceased to say *"Gruss Gott."*

It was a big, drafty old house they found in Geneva. But nobody was very happy there. What the *Volksdeutsch* and the Austrians did with party operatives, the Swiss did with clerks. Nobody actually said anything about the magazine—he could, apparently, publish whatever he wanted in Democratic Switzerland, but life was a spiderweb of rules and regulations that controlled mailing permits, alien residence, and, it seemed to Adler, the very air they breathed.

It was a little quiet around the dinner table when Adler informed the family they had to move. "A necessary adventure," he said, beaming away. Under the table, his wife put her hand on his knee. So, December of '37, Paris. Saint Germain-en-Laye was a classic of the exile's geography, it turned out, a time-honored refuge for princes unwelcome in many lands. There was a grand Promenade Anglais where one could walk for hours, just right for a bittersweet contemplation of the lost crown, castle, or homeland. Adler found a sympathetic printer, made contacts in the community of liberal German émigrés, and went back to work hammering the fascists and the Bolsheviks. Such was the destiny of the Social Democrat, and who was that man in the raincoat by the newspaper kiosk.

Meanwhile, Adler fell in love with the public gardens of Paris. "What sort of lunatic takes a train to go to the park?" The kind who filled his briefcase with books; Schnitzler, Weininger, Mann, maybe von Hoffmansthal, two pens, and a cheese sandwich, then sat in the Jardin du Luxembourg and watched the dappled light of the plane trees playing on the gravel path. A few centimes to the old dragon who kept watch on the chairs, and one could spend the afternoon in a painting.

At first he went in nice weather, later in light rain. It became his habit. As time went by, as the spring of 1938 worked its way toward whatever summer had in store, Otto Adler, fountain pen scratching out a new editorial or, for a moment, just snoozing, was almost always to be found in the park.

The note from the baroness Frei invited *My dearest Nicholas* to call at her house at five in the afternoon on the sixteenth of April. Morath took a taxi to the Sèvres-Babylone Métro stop and from there walked to the rue de Villon.

Buried deep in a maze of narrow lanes that crisscrossed the border between the Sixth and Seventh Arrondissements, it was, like paradise everywhere, damned hard to find. Taxi drivers thumbed through their city directories, then sped off to the rue François-Villon, named for the medieval robber poet, in a distant neighborhood where, on arrival, it was immediately clear to both driver and patron that this was not the right street *at all*.

The one true rue de Villon could be entered only through a vaulted alley—the impasse Villon—a tunnel of perpetual dusk that dared the courageous *automobiliste* to try his luck. It could sometimes be done, depending on the model and year of the machine, and was always a matter of centimeters, but it did not *look* like it could be done. The alley gave no indication of what lay beyond it, the casual passerby tended to do exactly that, while the truly self-confident tourist peered defiantly down the tunnel and then went away.

On the other side, however, light from heaven poured down on a row of seventeenth-century houses, protected by wrought-iron palings, that dead-ended at a garden wall: 3, rue de Villon, to 9, rue de Villon, in a sequence whose logic was known only to God and the postman. In the evening, the tiny street was lit by Victorian gas lamps, which made soft shadows of a vine that twisted its way along the top of the garden wall. The garden belonged to number three—a faint impression of the number could be found on a rusty metal door, the width of a carriage—which was owned by the baroness Lillian Frei. She did not know her neighbors. They did not know her.

A maid answered the door and led Morath to the garden. Sitting at the garden table, the baroness put her cheek up to be kissed. "Dearest love," she said. "I am so happy to see you." Morath's heart warmed, he smiled like a five-year-old and kissed her with pleasure.

The baroness Frei was possibly sixty. She was bent over in a lifelong crouch, and one side of her back humped far above her shoulder. She had shimmering blue eyes and soft, snow-white hair and a radiance like the sun. She was, at the moment, as always, surrounded by a pack of vizsla dogs—not one of which could Morath distinguish from another but which, as the baroness liked to tell her guests, belonged to a vast, capricious, bumptious family who lived out an unending romantic epic in the house and garden. Korto, bred to Fina, loved Malya, his daughter by the gallant and long-departed Moselda. Of course, for the integrity of the line, they could never "be together," so, in heat, the exquisite Malya was sent to live in the kitchen whilst poor Korto lay about on the garden gravel with his chin slumped atop his forepaws or stood on his hind legs, peered myopically through the windows, and barked until the maid threw a rag at him.

Now they stormed around Morath's legs and he bent to run his hands along the satin skin of their sides.

"Yes," said the baroness, "here's your friend Nicholas."

The vizslas were fast, Morath got a wet kiss on the eye and never saw it coming.

"Korto!"

"No, no. I'm flattered."

The dog smacked his forepaws against the ground.

"What, Korto, you want to hunt?"

Morath roughed him up a little and he mewed with pleasure.

"Go to the forest?"

Korto danced sideways—*chase me.*

"A bear? That would be best?"

"He would not run away," the baroness said. Then, to the dog, "Would you?"

Korto wagged his tail, Morath stood up, then joined the baroness at the table.

"Pure courage," she said. "And the last five minutes of his life would be the best." The maid approached, pushing a glass-topped cart with a squeaky wheel. She set a tray of pastries on the table, poured a cup of tea and set it down by Morath. Silver tongs in hand, the baroness looked over the pastries. "Let's see . . ."

A doughy roll, folded over itself, with walnuts and raisins. The lightly sugared crust was still warm from the oven.

"And so?"

"Like the Café Ruszwurm. Better."

For that lie, a gracious nod from the baroness. Below the table, many dogs. "You must wait, darlings," the baroness said. Her smile was tolerant, infinitely kind. Morath had once visited at midmorning and counted twenty pieces of buttered toast on the baroness's breakfast tray.

"I was in Budapest last week," she said.

"How was it?"

"Tense, I should say. Underneath all the usual commotion. I saw your mother and sister."

"How are they?"

"In good health. Teresa's oldest girl may go to school in Switzerland."

"Maybe for the best."

"Maybe. They send you their love. You will write to them."

"I will."

"Your mother told me that Eva Zameny has left her husband." She and Morath had, long ago, been engaged to marry.

"I am sorry."

The baroness's expression indicated she wasn't. "For the best. Her husband was a hound. And he gambled terribly."

A bell—the kind worked by pulling a cord—rang in the house. "That will be your uncle."

There were other guests. The women in hats with veils, bolero jackets, and the black and white polka-dot dresses that were popular in spring-time. Former citizens of the Dual Monarchy, the guests spoke the Austrian dialect with High German flourishes, Hungarian, and French, shifting effortlessly between languages when only a very particular expression would say what they meant. The men were well barbered and used good cologne. Two of them wore decorations, one a black and gold ribbon beneath a medal marked K.u.K.—*Kaiser und Königlich,* meaning "Imperial and Regal," the Dual Monarchy; the other awarded for service in the Russo-Polish war of 1920. A refined group, very courteous, it was hard to tell who was rich and who wasn't.

Morath and Polanyi stood by a large boxwood at a corner of the garden wall, holding their cups and saucers.

"Christ, I'd like a drink," Polanyi said.

"We can go somewhere, after this."

"I'm afraid I can't. I have cocktails with the Finns, dinner with the Venezuelan foreign minister, Flores, up in the sixteenth."

Morath nodded, sympathetic.

"No, not Flores." Polanyi compressed his lips, annoyed at the lapse. "Montemayor, I should've said. Flores is, pfft."

"Any news of home?"

"It's what you passed along to me, when you came back from Antwerp. And worse."

"Another Austria?"

"Not the same way, certainly. We are not '*Ein volk,*' one people. But the pressure is growing—*be our allies, or else.*" He sighed, shook his head. "Now comes the real nightmare, Nicholas, the one where you see the monster but you can't run away, you're frozen in place. I think, more and more, that these people, this German aggression, will finish us, sooner or later. The Austrians pulled us into war in 1914— perhaps some day somebody will tell me precisely *why* we had to do all that. And now, it begins again. In the next day or so, the newspapers will announce that Hungary has come out in favor of the Anschluss. In return, Hitler will guarantee our borders. Quid pro quo, very tidy."

"You believe it?"

"No." He took a sip of tea. "I'll amend that. To 'maybe.' Hitler is intimidated by Horthy, because Horthy is everything Hitler always wanted to be. Old nobility, aide-de-camp to Franz Josef, war hero, polo player, married into the cream of society. And they both paint. In fact, Horthy has now lasted longer than any other leader in Europe. That has to count for something, Nicholas, right?"

Polanyi's face showed exactly what it counted for.

"So the current unrest . . . will be dealt with?"

"Not easily, and maybe not at all. We're facing insurrection. Conservatives out, fascists in, liberals *au poteau.*" The phrase from 1789—to the guillotine.

Morath was surprised. In Budapest, when the Arrow Cross men dressed up in their uniforms and strutted about the city, the police forced them to strip and sent them home in their underwear. "What about the police? The army?"

"Uncertain."

"Then what?"

"If Daranyi means to stay in as premier, he'll have to give them something. Or there will be blood in the streets. So, at the moment, we find ourselves negotiating. And we will be forced, among other things, to do favors."

"For who?"

"Important people."

Morath felt it coming. Polanyi, no doubt, meant him to feel it. He set his cup and saucer on a table, reached in his pocket, took a cigarette from a tortoiseshell case and lit it with a silver lighter.

·

The last nights of April, but no sign of spring. The weather blew hard across the Métro staircase, wind and rain and fog with a taste of factory smoke. Morath held his overcoat closed and walked next to the buildings. Down a dark street, down another, then a sharp left and a blinking blue neon sign, *Balalaika*. The Cossack doorman, with sheepskin vest and fierce mustache, peered out from the shelter of the doorway, in his hand a black umbrella in the final hours of life on a windy night.

The doorman growled good evening, Russian accent thick and melodramatic. "Welcome, sir, to Balalaika, the show is now just starting."

Inside, thick air; cigarettes glowed in the darkness. Red plush walls and a stunning hatcheck girl. Morath gave her a generous tip and kept his coat. Here, too, they wore their decorations. The maitre d', six and a half feet tall with a sash and high boots, had a bronze medal pinned to his blouse, earned in service as mercenary and palace guardsman to King Zog of Albania.

Morath went to the bar and sat at the far end. From there he caught a glimpse of the stage. The Gypsy trio was sawing away in sentimental agonies, a dancer in sheer pantaloons and halter showed, in the blue klieg lights, just exactly what her faithless lover was giving up, while her partner stood to one side, hands clasped in fruitless longing, a red lightbulb in his pants going on and off in time to the music.

The barman came over, Morath ordered a Polish vodka, and, when it arrived, offered the barman a cigarette and lit it for him. He was a short, compact man with narrow eyes deeply lined at the corners, from laughing, maybe, or squinting into the distance. Beneath his red jacket he wore a shirt washed so often it was the pastel of an unknown color.

"Are you Boris?" Morath said.

"Now and then."

"Well, Boris, I have a friend . . ." A little cloud of irony hung over the phrase and the barman smiled appreciatively. "He was in trouble, he came to you for help."

"When was that?"

"Last year, around this time. His girlfriend needed a doctor."

The barman shrugged. A thousand customers, a thousand stories. "I can't say I remember."

Morath understood, a bad memory was a good idea. "Now, it's another friend. A different kind of problem."

"Yes?"

"A passport problem."

The barman used his rag to wipe down the zinc surface, then paused, and had a good look at Morath. "Where are you from, if you don't mind my asking."

"Budapest."

"Emigré?"

"Not really. I came here after the war. I'm in business here."

"You were in the war?"

"Yes."

"Where was that?"

"Galicia. Up into Volhynia for a time . . ."

"Then back to Galicia." The barman was laughing as he finished Morath's sentence. "Oh yes," he said, "*that* shithouse."

"You were there?"

"Mm. Likely we shot at each other. Then, fall of '17, my regiment took a walk. Same again?"

"Please."

The clear liquor came exactly to the rim.

"Will you join me?"

The barman poured himself a vodka and raised his glass. "To poor shooting, I guess." He drank in the Russian manner—with grace, but all gone.

From the nightclub tables, rhythmic clapping, growing louder as the patrons grew bolder, some of them yelling "Hey!" on the beat. The male dancer, squatting on the stage with his arms folded across his chest, was kicking his legs out.

"Passports," the barman said, suddenly gloomy. "You can get into real trouble, fooling with that. They lock you up, here, if they catch you. It goes on, of course, mostly among the refugees, the Jews and the political exiles. Once you get run out of Germany, you aren't legal anywhere, unless you've got a visa. That takes time, and money—you can't afford to be in a hurry. But you are—with the Gestapo after you, you have to do whatever it takes. So you sneak out. Now, you're a 'Stateless Person.' You slip into Czechoslovakia or Switzerland, hide out for a week if you know the right rooming house, then they catch you and send you across the Austrian border. After a week or two in jail, the customs officers walk you back across the frontier, at night, in the woods, and the whole thing starts again. Here it's a little better. If you stay out of trouble, the *flics* don't care that much, unless you try to work." He shook his head slowly, in sorrow.

"How did you manage?"

"Nansen. We were lucky. Because we were the first wave, we got the League of Nations passports, we got the work permits, we got the jobs the French didn't want. That was 1920 or so. Revolution over, civil war winding down, then the Cheka comes around—'We hear you were a friend of Ivanov.' So, time to run. Next, when Mussolini's boys got to work, came the Italians. Their luck was pretty much the same as ours—you used to be a professor of theoretical physics, now you're a real waiter. Now, *thank God* you're a waiter. Because, starting in '33, here come the Germans. They have passports, most of them, but no work permits. They peddle, sell needles and thread from little suitcases on the boulevards, work the tourists, starve, beg, sit in the offices of the refugee organizations. It's the same for the Spaniards, running from Franco, and now we're getting the Austrians. No papers, no work permits, no money."

"This friend, Boris, has money."

The barman had known that all along. After a time he said, "You're a detective, right?"

"With my accent?"

"Well, maybe you are, maybe you aren't. Either way, I'm not the man you want. You have to go where the refugees are, to the Café Madine, the Grosse Marie, places like that."

"A question? Personal question?"

"I'm an open book."

"Why did *you* run?"

"Because they were chasing me," he said, laughing again.

Morath waited.

"I was a poet. Also, to be honest, a criminal. When they came after me, I was never really sure which one it was."

The Café Madine was in the 11th Arrondissement, just off the place de la Republique, between a butcher that sold *halal* meat to Arabs and kosher meat to Jews, and a repair shop for musical instruments called Szczwerna. It was easy, maybe too easy, to make contact at Madine. He showed up in the late afternoon, stood at the counter, ordered a beer, stared out at the throbbing street life of the quarter. A man tried to sell him a ring, Morath looked it over—he was there to buy, let them see a buyer. A small, red stone set in gold, University of Heidelberg, 1922.

"How much?"

"Worth three hundred, more or less."

"I'll think about it. Actually, I'm here because a friend of mine in Paris lost his passport."

"Go to *préfecture.*"

From Morath a look, *if only one could.* "Or?"

"Or nothing."

Back the next day. Ten in the morning, deserted, silent. A shaft of sunlight, a sleeping cat, the *patron* wore his glasses down on his nose. He took his time with Morath's café au lait, there was no skin on the boiled milk, the coffee was powerful and fresh, and he sent his little boy off to the bakery to get fresh bread for a *tartine.*

The contact was a tough old bird, once upon a time a timber merchant in the Ukraine, though Morath had no way of knowing that. He tipped his hat, asked Morath to join him at a table. "You're the fellow with the passport difficulties?"

"Friend of mine."

"Naturally."

"What's the market like, these days?"

"Seller's market, obviously."

"He needs the real thing."

"The real thing." Maybe in other times he would have found it funny enough to laugh at. Morath got it, he thought. *Borders, papers, nations*—made-up stuff, politicians' lies.

"As much as possible."

"A man who buys the best."

Morath agreed.

"Twenty-five hundred francs. A figure like that scares you, perhaps."

"No. For good value, you pay."

"Very reasonable, this gentleman." He spoke to an invisible friend. Then he told Morath where to be, and when.

Two days later, now it was Friday. A busy afternoon at the Louvre. Morath had to work to find the right room—up the stairs here in order to go down the stairs there, past Napoleon's swag from Egypt, past rooms of small, puzzling Roman things, around a corner and down an endless corridor of British schoolboys. At last, *the room with the Ingres portrait*. A luminous nude, seated at a table, her back curved and soft.

A man rose from a bench against the wall, smiled, and spread his hands in welcome. He knew who Morath was, had probably looked him over at the café. A handsome gentleman, portly, with a Vandyke beard and a tweed suit. Something like, Morath thought, the owner of a prosperous art gallery. He had, apparently, a colleague, standing on the other side of the room and staring at a painting, hands clasped behind his back. Morath saw them exchange a glance. White as chalk, this man, as though missing a lifelong beard, he wore a black homburg set square on a shaved head.

The man who looked like an art dealer sat next to Morath on the wooden bench. "I'm told that you are seeking a document of the finest quality," he said. He spoke French like an educated German.

"I am."

"That would be a corpse."

"All right."

"You are buying from the family of the deceased, naturally, and they will want twenty-five hundred francs. For our work, for the change of identity, it is another thousand francs. Can we agree?"

"Yes."

The art dealer opened a newspaper, revealing a report of a polo match in the Bois de Boulogne and a passport in a cardboard folder. "The family wishes to sell immediately. The nationality of the passport is Roumanian, and has seventeen months to run." The head in the identification photograph was of a man in middle years, formal, self-satisfied, his dark mustache carefully clipped and groomed. Below it, the name *Andreas Panea*.

"I will pay you now, if you like."

"Half now. Half when we give you the finished product. Your photo goes in place of the deceased, the raised lettering on the photo is provided by the technician. The physical description is washed out and your own put in. The one thing that can't be changed is the place of birth—that's on the seal. So, the bearer of the document will be called this name, is of Roumanian nationality, and was born in Cluj."

"What happened to him?"

The art dealer stared for a moment. *Why are you concerned with that?* Then he said, "Nothing dramatic." And, a moment later, "He came to the end of caring. It is quite common."

"Here's the photograph," Morath said.

The art dealer was mildly surprised. It wasn't Morath. A man in his twenties, a hard, bony face made even more severe by steel-rimmed spectacles and hair cut back to a colorless inch and brushed flat. A student, perhaps. At best, that. Given a passing grade by his professors whether he attended the lectures or not. The art dealer turned the photo over. Stamped on the back was the name of the photography studio, in Serbo-Croatian, and the word *Zagreb.*

The art dealer signaled to his friend, who joined them on the bench, took the photograph, and studied it for a long minute, then said something in Yiddish. Morath, who spoke fluent German, would ordinarily have gotten the sense of it but this was argot of some kind, spoken rapidly, the tone sarcastic.

The art dealer nodded, almost smiled.

"Can the bearer work?" Morath asked.

"In Roumania. Not here. Here he could apply to work, but . . ."

"And, if it should be checked with the Roumanian authority?"

"Why would it be checked?"

Morath didn't answer.

The man wearing the homburg took a stub of pencil from his pocket and asked a question, again in Yiddish.

"He wants to know, how tall, how much does he weigh?"

Morath gave him the numbers—lean, shorter than average.

"Eyes?"

"Gray. The hair is blond."

"Identifying marks?"

"None."

"Profession?"

"Student."

The photograph was put away. The art dealer turned a page of the newspaper to reveal an envelope. "Take this to the washroom down the hall. Put seventeen hundred and fifty francs in here, tuck the newspaper under your arm, and leave the museum. Use the exit on the rue Coligny. Stand on the top step and wait for a few minutes. Then, tomorrow at noon, go back there. You'll see somebody you recognize, follow that person, and the exchange will be made someplace where you can have a good look at what you're buying."

Morath did as he was told—counted hundred-franc notes into the envelope, then waited at the entrance. Ten minutes later, a woman waved and came toward him, smiling, trotting up the museum steps. She was well dressed, wore pearl earrings and white gloves. She kissed him lightly on the cheek, slid the newspaper from beneath his arm, and left in a waiting taxi.

The night before the train.

It had become something of a tradition for Nicky and Cara, a *Kama Sutra* evening—farewell my love, something to remember. They sat around the bedroom in candlelight and drank a bottle of wine. Cara wore black underwear, Morath a dressing gown. Sometimes they played records—Morath owned two kinds, Ellington and Lee Wiley— or listened to *"les beeg bands"* on the radio. One night they'd journeyed up to Pigalle, where Cara waited in a taxi while Morath bought picture books. Then they'd hurried back to the avenue Bourdonnais and looked at the pictures. Sepia couples, trios, quartets, heavy women with wide hips and sweet smiles, the book printed in Sofia.

Cara teased him, sometimes, with Tales of the Convent School. She'd spent three years in such a place, on a grand estate outside Buenos Aires. "It was just as you would suppose, Nicky," she'd say, a little breathless and wide-eyed. "All these girls, beauty of every type. Dark. Fair. Passionate, shy, some of them so naive they knew, *nothing,* not even what to *touch.* And all of them locked up together at night. Imagine!"

He did.

But, closer to the truth, he suspected, were the daylight recollections of "cold hands and smelly feet" and the diabolical nuns who forced them to learn, among other things, French. It was the only language she and Morath had in common, but Cara couldn't forgive. "God, how they terrified us," she'd say. Would clap her hands— as the teaching nun apparently did—and sing out, *"Traduction, les jeunes filles!"* Next they would be confronted by some unfathomable horror, a grammar monster, and allowed only five minutes for translation.

"I remember once," Cara told him, "who was it? Sister Modeste. She wrote on the board: *What if they should never have united themselves in that, over there?*" Cara had started to laugh, remembering the moment. "Panic! *Se joindre,* a homicidal verb. It's much simpler in Spanish. And then my friend Francesca, after the sister wrote out the answer, leaned across the aisle and whispered, 'Well, I'm certainly glad I know how to say *that!*' "

Morath poured out the last of the wine, Cara finished hers, put the glass on the floor and wound herself around him. He kissed her, reached over and undid her bra, she shrugged her shoulders, he tossed it on a chair. Some time later, he hooked a finger in the waistband of her panties and slid them down her legs, slow and easy, until she pointed her feet so he could get them off. He could feel her breath on the side of his face, it always changed at that moment.

Then, for a time, they lay still. She took his hand and held it against her breast—she wouldn't let him move—as though this was sufficient, no need to go further. He wondered what might be nice to do, his mind wandering idly through the repertoire. Was she thinking about that? Or something else? *He loves me?* Morath opened his eyes and saw that she was smiling.

All very good to think about, in the morning, cast adrift in the cold world. She didn't wake up when he left, sleeping with her mouth open, a hand trapped under the pillow. Somehow he could look at her and know she'd made love the night before. He almost dozed, as the train left the empty streets and moved through the countryside. *Her tits, her ass, looking up at her, looking down, fucking.* She whispered sometimes, talking to herself. He could never actually hear what she was saying.

It was a very slow train, that left at dawn. Going east, it crawled, as if it really didn't want to get there. It would go through Metz and Saarbrucken, then on to Würzburg, where passengers could change for the train to Prague, with connections to Brno, to Kosice, and to Uzhorod.

Eastern France, a lost season, not winter, not spring. The sky low and heavy, the wind colder than it should have been, the train crawling through dead, weedy fields.

A pleasant countryside, once upon a time, small farms and villages. Then 1914 came along and war turned it into gray mud. It would never really heal, people said. A few years earlier, when the snow melted, a farmer had come upon what had, evidently, once been a trench, where a squad of French soldiers, heading into battle, had been suddenly buried by the explosion of an enormous artillery shell. Then, with that spring's thaw, the farmer saw a dozen bayonet points thrust out of the earth, still in marching order.

Morath lit a cigarette and went back to reading—Nicholas Bartha's *Land of the Kazars,* published in Hungarian in 1901.

> The sovereign stag should not be disturbed in its family affairs. What is a Ruthenian compared with it? Only a peasant. The hunting period lasts two weeks. For this pastime, 70,000 Ruthenians must be doomed to starvation by the army of the officials. The deer and the wild boar destroy the corn, the potatoes and the clover of the Ruthenians (the whole harvest of his tiny lot of half an acre). Their whole yearly work is destroyed. The people sow and the deer of the estate harvest. It is easy to say the peasant should complain. But where and to whom? Those who have the power he sees always together. The village chief, the deputy sheriff, the sheriff, the district judge, the tax-officer, the forester, the steward and the manager, all are men of the same education, of the same social pleasures, and of the same standard. From whom could he hope for justice?

When he'd learned he'd be going up into Ruthenia, he'd borrowed the book from the baroness Frei's enormous library—purchased by the Baron from universities that fell, after 1918, within the borders of other nations. "Saved from the fire," he'd say. Morath smiled at the memory of him. A short, fat man with muttonchops who never knew himself just how much money he made with his "schemes." For Morath's sixteenth birthday, the Baron had taken him on an "educational ramble" to the casino at Monte Carlo, bought him a pair of diamond cuff links and a cadaverous blonde.

He'd sat by the baron's side at the chemin de fer table and watched him write, at four in the morning, a check with an alarming number of zeros. Pale but smiling, the baron stood, lit a cigar, winked at Morath, and headed off toward the marble staircase. Ten minutes later, a black-suited *fonctionnaire* floated to his side, cleared his throat, and said, "The baron Frei has gone into the garden." Morath hesitated, then stood and went quickly into the casino garden, where the baron was discovered urinating on a rosebush. He would die, ten years later, of a tropical disease contracted in the jungles of Brazil, where he'd gone to buy industrial diamonds.

Morath glanced up at the luggage rack above the seat, making sure of his leather satchel. Inside, a passport he'd received at the Louvre, now sewn into the lining of a wool jacket. *Pavlo,* Polanyi called the man, a man he said he'd never met. *The student.* Who had gotten himself into the town of Uzhorod and couldn't get out. "A favor for a friend," Polanyi said.

In midafternoon, the train slowed for the Moselle bridges and the station at Metz, the buildings dark with soot from the mills. Most of Morath's fellow passengers got off—not many people traveling into Germany just then. Morath took a walk on the platform and bought a newspaper. At twilight, the train halted for the French border control. No problem for Morath, officially a *résident* of France.

Two hours later, the train crossed the frontier at Saarbrucken. No problem there either. The officer who knocked on the door of Morath's compartment was pleased to see the Hungarian passport. "Welcome to the Reich," he said. "I know you will enjoy your stay."

Morath thanked him graciously and tried to settle down for the night. The border station was floodlit a brilliant white; wire strung on stanchions, officials, sentries, machine guns, dogs. This is for you, it said, and Morath didn't like it. It recalled a certain Hungarian saying: "One should never voluntarily enter a room or a country the door of which cannot be opened from the inside."

Somewhere down the line, he was joined by a pair of SS officers and spent the night drinking cognac and discussing the old Europe, the new Germany, and how to lay Hungarian women. The two young officers—political intellectuals who'd gone to university together in Ulm—had a fine time. They talked and laughed, polished their spectacles, got drunk, and fell asleep. Morath was relieved to arrive in Würzburg, where he slept overnight at the railroad hotel and left the next morning on the train to Prague.

The Czech border police weren't quite so happy to see him. Hungary ran espionage networks in several cities and the Czechs knew it.

"How long," the border guard asked him, "do you plan to stay in Czechoslovakia?"

"A few days."

"Your business here, sir?"

"To buy woodland, if possible, on behalf of a group of investors in Paris."

"Woodland."

"In Ruthenia, sir."

"Ah. Of course. You are traveling to . . . ?"

"Uzhorod."

The guard nodded and tapped Morath's passport with the end of a pencil. "I will stamp a one-week visa for you. Please apply at the Uzhorod prefecture if you need to extend that."

He ate a ghastly *blutwurst* in the dining car, finished Bartha, managed to buy a copy of *Est,* the evening edition brought in from Budapest, at the station buffet in Brno. Clearly, political life was heating up. Two members of parliament had come to blows. At a workers' march in the Tenth District, bricks thrown, people arrested. *To the Editor. Sir: How can we let these liberal pansies run our lives?* An editorial called for "strength, firmness, singleness of purpose. The world is changing, Hungary must change with it." A coffeehouse by the university had burned down. TENS OF THOUSANDS CHEER HITLER SPEECH IN RE- GENSBURG. With photograph, on page one. *Here they come,* Morath thought.

Outside the window, a strange countryside. Low hills, pine forest. Sudden rivers at spring flood, the sound of the locomotive sharpening as it passed through an open gorge. At the station in the Slovakian town of Zvolen, the train stood between Warsaw to the north and Budapest to the south. Next stop, Košice, a border town before 1918. On the platform, women holding straw baskets, their heads covered with black kerchiefs. The train climbed through snow-patched meadows, came to a village with domed churches painted lime green. In the late afternoon haze, Morath could see the Carpathians on the far horizon. An hour later he got off in Uzhorod.

The stationmaster told him there was a place he could stay in Krolevska Street. It turned out to be a yellow brick building with a sign that said HOTEL. The proprietor had a white eye, wore a greasy silk vest and a knitted yarmulke. "Our finest room," he said. "The finest." Morath sat on the straw mattress, picked the stitching from the lining of his wool jacket, and extracted the passport. *Andreas Panea.*

Late in the afternoon, he walked to the post office. The Czech postal clerks wore blue uniforms. On an envelope he had written *Malko, Poste Restante, Uzhorod.* Inside, a meaningless note—a sister had been ill, now she was better. The actual message was the address: the same as "Malko's", with a different name.

Now, to wait.

Morath lay on the bed and stared out the cloudy window. The finest room was bent at a strange angle; a low ceiling of wooden boards, whitewashed long ago, went in one direction, then another. When he stood up, it was only a few inches above his head. In the street, the steady sound of horses' hooves on cobblestone. Ruthenia. Or, affectionately, Little Russia. Or, technically, Sub-Carpathian Ukraine. A Slavic nibble taken by the medieval kings of Hungary, and ever since a lost land in the northeast corner of the nation. Then, after the world war, on a rare day when American idealism went hand in hand with French diplomacy—what Count Polanyi called "a frightening convergence"—they stuck it onto Slovakia and handed it to the Czechs. Somewhere, Morath speculated, in a little room in a ministry of culture, a Moravian bureaucrat was hard at work on a little song. "Merry old Ruthenia / Land we love so well."

At dinner, the proprietor and his wife served him jellied calf's foot, buckwheat groats with mushrooms, white cheese with scallions, and thin pancakes with red-current jam. A bottle of cherry brandy stood on the plank table. The proprietor nervously rubbed his hands.

"Very good," Morath said, pretending to wipe his mouth with the napkin—it had certainly been a napkin, once—and pushed his chair away from the table. He'd meant the compliment, however, and the proprietor could see that.

"Another blini, sir? Uhh, *Pfannkuchen? Crêpe? Blintz?*"

"Thank you, but no."

Morath paid for the dinner and returned to his room. Lying there in the darkness, he could sense the countryside. There was a stable attached to the hotel, and sometimes the horses whickered and moved around in their stalls. The aroma, manure and rotted straw, drifted up to Morath's room. Still cold, at the end of April. He wrapped himself up in the thin blanket and tried to sleep. Out on Krolevska Street, somebody got drunk in a tavern. Singing at first, then the argument, then the fight. Then the police, then the woman, crying and pleading, as her man was taken away.

Two days later, a letter at the post office, an address on the edge of Uzhorod, he had to take a droshky. Down streets of packed dirt lined with one-story log houses, each with a single window and a thatched roof. A woman answered his knock on the door. She was dark, with black, curly hair, wore crimson lipstick and a tight, thin dress. Perhaps Roumanian, he thought, or Gypsy. She asked him a question in a language he didn't recognize.

He tried her in German. "Is Pavlo here?"

She'd expected him, he could sense that; now he'd arrived and she was curious, looked him over carefully. Morath heard a door slam in the house, then a man's voice. The woman stood aside and Pavlo came to the door. He was one of those people who look very much like their photograph. "Are you the man from Paris?" The question was asked in German. Not good, but serviceable.

"Yes."

"They took their time, getting you here."

"Yes? Well, now I'm here."

Pavlo's eyes swept the street. "Maybe you'd better come inside."

The room was crowded with furniture, heavy chairs and couches covered in various patterns and fabrics, much of it red, some of the fabric very good, some not. Morath counted five mirrors on the walls. The woman spoke quietly to Pavlo, glanced over at Morath, then left the room and closed the door.

"She is packing her suitcase," Pavlo said.

"She's coming with us?"

"She thinks she is."

Morath did not show a reaction.

Pavlo took that for disapproval. "Try it sometime," he said, his voice a little sharp, "life without a passport." He paused, then, "Have you money for me?"

Morath hesitated—maybe somebody was supposed to give Pavlo money, but it wasn't him. "I can let you have some," he said, "until we get to Paris."

This wasn't the answer Pavlo wanted, but he was in no position to argue. He was perhaps a few years older than Morath had thought, in his late twenties. He had on a stained blue suit, colorful tie, and scuffed, hard-worn shoes.

Morath counted out a thousand francs. "This should tide you over," he said.

It was much more than that, but Pavlo didn't seem to notice. He put eight hundred francs in his pocket and looked around the room. Under a shimmering aquamarine vase with a bouquet of satin tulips in it was a paper doily. Pavlo slid two hundred-franc notes beneath the doily so the edges of the bills were just visible.

"Here's the passport," Morath said.

Pavlo looked it over carefully, held it up to the light, squinted at the photograph, and ran a finger over the raised lettering on the edge. Then he shrugged. "It will do," he said. "Why Roumanian?"

"That's what I could get."

"Oh. Well, I don't speak it. I'm Croatian."

"That won't be a problem. We're going across the Hungarian border. At Michal'an. Are you carrying another passport? I don't think we have to worry about it, but still . . ."

"No. I had to rid of it."

He left the room. Morath could hear him, talking to the woman.

When he reappeared, he was carrying a briefcase. Walking behind him, the woman held a cheap valise in both hands. She'd put on a hat, and a coat with a ragged fur collar. Pavlo whispered something to her and kissed her on the forehead. She looked at Morath, her eyes suspicious but hopeful, and sat on a couch, the valise between her feet.

"We're going out for an hour or so," Pavlo said to the woman. "Then we'll be back."

Morath wanted no part of it.

Pavlo closed the door. Out in the street, he grinned and cast his eyes to heaven.

They walked for a long time before they found a droshky. Morath directed the driver back to the hotel, then Pavlo waited in the room while Morath went to see the proprietor in a tiny office behind the kitchen where he was laboring over a bookkeeper's ledger. As Morath counted out Czech koruny to pay the bill, he said, "Do you know a driver with a car? As soon as possible—I'll make it worthwhile."

The proprietor thought it over. "Are you going," he said delicately, "some distance away from here?"

He meant, *borders*.

"Some."

"We are, as you know, blessed with many neighbors."

Morath nodded. Hungary, Poland, Roumania.

"We are going to Hungary."

The proprietor thought it over. "Actually, I do know somebody. He's a Pole, a quiet fellow. Just what you want, eh?"

"As soon as possible," Morath said. "We'll wait in the room, if that's all right with you." He didn't know who was looking for Pavlo, or why, but railroad stations were always watched. Better, a quiet exit from Uzhorod.

The driver appeared in the late afternoon, introduced himself as Mierczak, and offered Morath a hand like tempered steel. Morath sensed a powerful domesticity. "I'm a mechanic at the flour mill," he said. "But I also do this and that. You know how it is." He was ageless, with a receding hairline and a genial smile and a British shooting jacket, in houndstooth check, that had somehow wandered into this region in an earlier age.

Morath was actually startled by the car. If you closed one eye it didn't look so different from the European Fords of the 1930s, but a second look told you it wasn't anything like a Ford, while a third told you it wasn't anything. It had lost, for example, all its color. What remained was a shadowy tone of iron, maybe, that faded or darkened depending on what part of the car you looked at.

Mierczak laughed, jiggling the passenger-side door until it opened. "Some car," he said. "You don't mind, do you?"

"No," Morath said. He settled down on the horse blanket that had, a long time ago, replaced the upholstery. Pavlo got in the back. The car started easily and drove away from the hotel.

"Actually," Mierczak said, "it's not mine. Well, it's partly mine. Mostly it is to be found with my wife's cousin. It's the Mukachevo taxi, and, when he's not working at the store, he drives it."

"What is it?"

"What is it," Mierczak said. "Well, some of it is a Tatra, built in Nesseldorf. After the war, when it became Czechoslovakia. The Type II, they called it. Some name, hey? But that's that company. Then it burned. The car, I mean. Though, now that I think about it, the factory also burned, but that was later. So, after that, it became a Wartburg. We had a machine shop in Mukachevo, back then, and somebody had left a Wartburg in a ditch, during the war, and it came back to life in the Tatra. But—we didn't really think about it at the time—it was an *old* Wartburg. We couldn't get parts. They didn't make them or they wouldn't send them or whatever it was. So, it became then a Skoda." He pressed the clutch pedal to the floor and revved the engine. "See? Skoda! Just like the machine gun."

The car had used up the cobblestone part of Uzhorod and was now on packed dirt. "Gentlemen," Mierczak said. "We're going to Hungary, according to the innkeeper. But, I must ask if you have a particular place in mind. Or maybe it's just 'Hungary.' If that's how it is, I perfectly understand, believe me."

"Could we go to Michal'an?"

"We could. It's nice and quiet there, as a rule."

Morath waited. "But . . . ?"

"But even quieter in Zahony."

"Zahony, then."

Mierczak nodded. A few minutes later, he turned a sharp corner onto a farm road and shifted down to second gear. It sounded like he'd swung an iron bar against a bathtub. They bumped along the road for a time, twenty miles an hour, maybe, until they had to slow down and work their way around a horse cart.

"What's it like there?"

"Zahony?"

"Yes."

"The usual. Small customs post. A guard, if he's awake. Not any traffic, to speak of. These days, most people stay where they are."

"I imagine we can pick up a train there. For Debrecen, I guess, where we can catch the express."

Pavlo kicked the back of the seat. At first, Morath couldn't believe he'd done it. He almost turned around and said something, then didn't.

"I'm sure there's a train from Zahony," Mierczak said.

They drove south in the last of the daylight, the afternoon fading away to a long, languid dusk. Staring out the window, Morath had a sudden sense of home, of knowing where he was. The sky was filled with torn cloud, tinted red by the sunset over the Carpathian foothills, empty fields stretched away from the little road, boundary lines marked by groves of birch and poplar. The land turned to wild meadow, where the winter grass hissed and swayed in the evening wind. It was very beautiful, very lost. *These blissful, bloodsoaked valleys,* he thought.

A tiny village, then another. It was dark now, cloud covered the moon, and spring mist rose from the rivers. Midway through a long, slow curve, they caught sight of the bridge over the Tisza and the Zahony border station. Pavlo shouted, "Stop." Mierczak stamped on the brake as Pavlo hung over the top of the seat and punched the button that turned off the lights. "The bitch," he said, his voice ragged with fury. He was breathing hard, Morath could hear him.

In the distance they could see two khaki-colored trucks, river fog drifting through the beams of their lights, and a number of silhouettes, possibly soldiers, moving about. In the car it was very quiet, the idling engine a low rumble, the smell of gasoline strong in the air.

"How can you be sure it was her?" Morath asked.

Pavlo didn't answer.

"Maybe they are just there," Mierczak said.

"No," Pavlo said. For a time, they watched the trucks and the soldiers. "It's my fault. I knew what to do, I just didn't do it."

Morath thought the best thing would be to drive south to Berezhovo, find a rooming house for a day or two, and take a train into Hungary. Or, maybe better, drive west into the Slovakian part of the country—away from Ruthenia, land of too many borders—and then take the train.

"You think they saw our lights?" Mierczak said. He swallowed once, then again.

"Just turn around and get out of here," Pavlo said.

Mierczak hesitated. He hadn't done anything wrong, but if he ran away, that changed.

"Now," Pavlo said.

Reluctantly, Mierczak yanked the gearshift into reverse and got the car turned around. He drove a little way in the darkness, then turned the lights back on. Pavlo watched through the rear window until the border post disappeared around the curve. "They're staying put," he said.

"How far is it to Berezhovo?" Morath said. "Maybe the best thing now is to take the train."

"An hour. A little more at night."

"I'm not getting on a train," Pavlo said. "If your papers don't work, you're trapped."

Stay here, then.

"Is there another way across?" Pavlo said.

Mierczak thought it over. "There's a footbridge, outside the village of Vezlovo. It's used at night, sometimes."

"By who?"

"Certain families—for avoiding the import duties. A trade in cigarettes, mostly, or vodka."

Pavlo stared, couldn't believe what he'd heard. "So why didn't you take us there in the first place?"

"We didn't ask him to do that," Morath said. Even in the cool night air, Pavlo was sweating. Morath could smell it.

"You have to go through a forest," Mierczak said.

Morath sighed, he wasn't sure what he wanted to do. "At least we can take a look," he said. *Maybe the trucks just happened to be there.* He was wearing a sweater, a tweed jacket, and flannels—dressed for a country hotel and a train. Now he was going to have to crawl around in the woods.

They drove for an hour, the moon rose. There were no other cars on the road. The land, field and meadow, was dark, empty. At last they came upon a village—a dozen log houses at the edge of the road, windows lit by oil lamps. A few sheds and barns. The dogs barked at them as they went past. "It's not far from here," Mierczak said, squinting as he tried to peer into the night. The car's headlights gave off a dull amber glow. Just as the countryside turned to forest, Mierczak stopped the car, got out, and walked up the road. A minute later, he returned. He was grinning again. "Believe in miracles," he said. "I found it."

They left the car, Morath carrying a satchel, Pavlo with his briefcase, and the three of them started walking. The silence was immense, there was only the wind and the sound of their footsteps on the dirt road.

"It's right there," Mierczak said.

Morath stared, then saw a path in the underbrush between two towering beech trees.

"About a kilometer or so," Mierczak said. "You'll hear the river."

Morath opened his wallet and began to count out hundred-koruna notes.

"That's very generous of you," Mierczak said.

"Would you agree to wait here?" Morath asked him. "Maybe forty minutes. Just in case."

Mierczak nodded. "Good luck, gentlemen," he said, clearly relieved. He hadn't realized what he was getting himself into—the cash in his pocket proved that he'd been right to be scared. He waved as they walked into the forest, glad to see them go.

•

Mierczak was right, Morath thought. Almost from the moment they entered the forest they could hear the river, hidden, but not far away. Water dripped from the bare branches of the trees, the earth was soft and spongy underfoot. They walked for what seemed like a long time, then got their first view of the Tisza. About a hundred yards wide and running at spring flood, heavy and gray in the darkness, with plumes of white foam where the water surged around a rock or a snag.

"And where is this bridge?" Pavlo said. *This supposed bridge.*

Morath nodded his head—just up the path. They walked for another ten minutes, then he saw a dry root at the foot of a tree, sat down, gave Pavlo a cigarette and lit one for himself. Balto, they were called, he'd bought them in Uzhorod.

"Lived in Paris a long time?" Pavlo asked.

"A long time."

"I can see that."

Morath smoked his cigarette.

"You seem to forget how life goes, over here."

"Take it easy," Morath said. "We'll be in Hungary soon enough. Find a tavern, have something to eat."

Pavlo laughed. "You don't believe the Pole is going to wait for us, do you?"

Morath looked at his watch. "He's there."

Pavlo gave Morath a sorrowful look. "Not for long. He'll be going home to his wife any minute now. And on the way he'll stop and have a word with the police."

"Calm down," Morath said.

"Over here, it's about one thing, and one thing only. And that is money."

Morath shrugged.

Pavlo stood. "I'll be right back," he said.

"What are you doing?"

"A few minutes," he said, over his shoulder.

Christ! Morath heard him for a minute or so, heading back the way they'd come, then it was quiet. Maybe he'd gone, really gone. Or he was going back to check on Mierczak, which made no sense at all. *Well, he must have value to somebody.* When Morath was growing up, his mother went to Mass every day. She often told him that all people were good, it was just that some of them had lost their way.

Morath stared up at the tops of the trees. The moon was in and out, a pale slice among the clouds. A long time since he'd been in a forest. This was an old one, probably part of a huge estate. Prince Esterhazy had three hundred thousand acres in Hungary, with eleven thousand people in seventeen villages. Not so unusual, in this part of the world. The nobleman who owned this property no doubt intended his grandchildren to cut the slow-growing hardwood, mostly oak and beech.

It occurred to Morath that, when all was said and done, he hadn't actually lied to the Czech customs officer. He'd said he was going to look at woodland; well, here he was, looking at it. In the distance, two pops, and, a moment later, a third.

When Pavlo returned, he said only, "Well, we should be getting on our way." What needed to be done was done, why talk about it. The two of them walked in silence, and, a few minutes later, they saw the bridge. A narrow, rickety old thing, the water sucked into deep eddies around the wooden poles that held it up, the surface maybe ten feet below the walkway. As Morath watched the bridge, it moved. The far end was sharp against the sky—a broken shard of railing thrust out toward the Hungarian side of the river. And, by moonlight, he could just make out the blackened char pattern on the wood, where the part that had been set on fire—or dynamited, or whatever it was—had fallen into the water.

Morath was already so sickened inside at what Pavlo had done that he hardly cared. He'd seen it in the war, a dozen times, maybe more, and it brought always the same words, never spoken aloud. *Pointless* was the important one, the rest never mattered that much. *Pointless, pointless.* As though anything in the world might happen as long as somebody, somewhere, could see the point of it. A rather black joke, he'd thought at the time. The columns riding through the smoking villages of Galicia, a cavalry officer saying *pointless* to himself.

"They'll have a way to get across," Pavlo said.

"What?"

"The people who go back and forth across the border at night. Will have a way to do it."

He was probably right, Morath thought. A boat, another bridge, something. They worked their way toward the bank of the river, were within a few meters of it when they heard the voice. A command. In Russian, or maybe Ukrainian. Morath didn't speak the language but, even so, the intention was clear and he started to stand up. Pavlo grabbed him by the shoulder and forced him down, into the high reeds along the riverbank. "Don't do it," Pavlo whispered.

Again the voice, mock polite, wheedling. *We wouldn't hurt a fly.*

Pavlo tapped his lips with his forefinger.

Morath pointed behind them, at the relative safety of the forest. Pavlo thought it over, and nodded. When they started to crawl backward, somebody shot at them. A yellow spark in the woods, a report that flattened out over the water. Then a shout in Russian, followed, rather thoughtfully, by a version in Hungarian, *fuck you, stand up* being the general idea, followed by a snicker.

Pavlo picked up a stone and threw it at them. At least two guns responded. Then a silence, then the sound of somebody lurching through the underbrush, a crash, an oath, and a raucous bellow that passed for laughter.

Morath never saw where it came from—the briefcase?—but a heavy, steel-colored revolver appeared in Pavlo's hand and he squeezed off a round in the general direction of the noise.

That *wasn't* funny. That was unconscionably rude. Somebody screamed at them, and Morath and Pavlo went flat as a fusillade whizzed over the reeds. Morath made a hand sign, stay still. Pavlo nodded, he agreed. From the darkness, a challenge—*come out and fight, you cowards.* Followed by shouted dialogue between two, then three voices. All of them drunk, mean, and very angry.

But that was it. Pavlo's single shot had made an eloquent statement, had altered the social contract: sorry, no free killing tonight. It took a long time, thirty minutes, of yelling, shooting, and what Morath guessed were meant to be intolerable insults. Still, Pavlo and Morath managed to tolerate them, and, when the gang went away, knew enough to wait the requisite fifteen minutes for the final shot, when they sent somebody back to ruin the victory celebration.

•

4:40 A.M. The light pearl gray. The best moment to see and not to be easily seen. Morath, wet and cold, could hear birds singing on the Hungarian side of the river. He and Pavlo had walked upstream for a half hour, soaked by the heavy mist, looking for a boat or another way across, found nothing, and returned to the bridge.

"Whatever they use, they've hidden it," Pavlo said.

Morath agreed. And this was not the morning for two strangers to walk into an isolated village. The Czech police would be interested in the murder of a Polish taxi driver, the Ukrainian gang more than curious to know who'd been shooting at them the night before. "Can you swim?" Morath said.

Very slowly, Pavlo shook his head.

Morath was a strong swimmer, and this would not be the first time he'd been in a fast river. He'd done it in his teens, with daring friends. Jumped into spring current holding a piece of log, floated downstream until he could fight his way to the far shore. But, this time of year, you had only fifteen minutes. He'd seen that too, during the war, in the Bzura and the Dniester. First an agonized grimace at the cold, next a silly smile, then death.

Morath would take his chances; the problem was what to do with Pavlo. It didn't matter what he felt—he had to get him across. *Strange, though, a lot of folklore on this issue.* Endless foxes and roosters and frogs and tigers and priests and rabbis. A river to be crossed—why was it always the cunning one that couldn't swim?

And there weren't any logs. Maybe they could break off a piece of the burnt railing, but they'd know that only when they got to the far end of the bridge. Morath decided to abandon his satchel. He was sorry to lose the copy of Bartha, he would find a way to replace it. For the rest, razor and socks and shirt, good-bye. The Ukrainians could have it. As for Pavlo, he unbuckled his belt and looped it through the handle of the briefcase. "Put your passport in your mouth," Morath said.

"And money?"

"Money dries."

Flat on his belly, Morath worked his way across the bridge. He could hear the water as it rushed past, ten feet below, could feel it—

the damp, chill air that rose from heavy current. He did not look back, Pavlo would either find the nerve to do this or he wouldn't. Crawling over the weathered planks, he realized that a lot more of it had burned than was evident from the shore. It smelled like old fire, and his lamb's-wool sweater from a shop on the rue de la Paix—"Not that green, Nicky, this green"—already caked with mud, was now smeared with charcoal.

Long before he reached the end, he stopped. The support poles had burned, part of the way anyhow, leaving black sticks to hold up the bridge. Morath realized he would be going into the river a little earlier than he'd planned. The bridge trembled and swayed each time he moved, so he signaled back to Pavlo to stay where he was and went ahead on his own.

He reached a bad place, hung on, felt himself start to sweat in the cold air. Would it be better to dive in here? No, it was a long way to the other shore. He waited for the bridge to stop wobbling, then curled his fingers around the edge of the next board and slid forward. Waited, reached out, pulled, and slid. Resting his face against the wood, he saw a pair of white egrets flying toward him, just above the water, then heard the beating of their wings as they passed above him.

By the time he reached the end—or as close as he could get to it, beyond a certain point the wood was so burned away it wouldn't hold a cat—he had to take a minute to catch his breath. He motioned for Pavlo to come along. As he waited, he heard voices over the water. He turned, saw two women, black skirts held above their knees, standing in the river shallows and staring at him.

When Pavlo arrived, they studied the far bank—a good forty yards away. In the growing daylight, the water was brown with earth swept down from the mountain streams. Lying next to him, Pavlo was the color of chalk.

"Take off your tie," Morath said.

Pavlo hesitated, then, reluctantly, pulled the knot apart.

"I'm going into the water, you follow. You hold on to one end of the tie, I'll swim across and pull you with me. You do the best you can—kick your feet, paddle with your free arm. We'll manage."

Pavlo nodded.

Morath looked down at the water, ten feet below him, dark and swirling. The far shore seemed a long distance away, but at least the bank was low.

"Wait a minute," Pavlo said.

"Yes?"

But there was nothing to say, he just didn't want to go into the water.

"We'll be fine," Morath said. He decided to try for the next pole, something he could hang on to while he coaxed Pavlo to jump in after him. He pulled himself along, felt the planks beneath him quiver, then shift. He swore, heard a beam snap, was turned on his side and dropped. He fought the air, then landed with a shock that knocked him senseless. It wasn't the icy jolt of the water, he was waiting for that. It was the rock. Smooth and dark, about two feet below the surface. Morath found himself on his hands and knees, no pain yet but he could feel it coming, the river churning around him. *Hidden causeway.* The oldest trick in the world.

Pavlo came crawling toward him, tie held in his hand, passport clenched in his teeth, steel spectacles askew, and laughing.

They walked to Zahony. Following first the river, then a cart track through the woods that turned into a road. It took all morning but they didn't care. Pavlo was pleased not to be drowned, and his money wasn't all that wet—he peeled the bills apart, Austrian, Czech, French, blew gently on the various kings and saints, then put it away in his briefcase.

Morath had hurt his wrist and knee, but not as badly as he'd feared, and had a bruise by his left eye. A plank, most likely, he never felt it happen. In time, the sun came out and light sparkled on the river. They passed a woodcutter, a tramp, and two boys fishing for the small sturgeon that ran in the Tisza. Morath spoke to the boys in Hungarian: "Any luck?" A little, yes, not too bad. They seemed not very surprised when two men in muddy clothes walked out of the forest. That's what came from living on a frontier, Morath thought.

They found a little restaurant in Zahony, ate cabbage stuffed with sausage and a plate of fried eggs, and got on a train that afternoon. Pavlo fell asleep, Morath stared out the window at the Hungarian plain.

Well, he'd kept his word. Promised Polanyi he would bring this, this whatever-he-was to Paris. *Pavlo.* Certainly an alias—nom de guerre, code name, impersonation. Something. He claimed he was a Croat and that, Morath thought, just might be true. Perhaps a Croatian Ustachi. Which meant terrorist in some neighborhoods and patriot in others.

Croatia, a province of Hungary for centuries and her access to the sea—which was how Miklos Horthy came to be Admiral Horthy— had stewed up quite a bit of political history since becoming part of a manufactured kingdom, Yugoslavia, in 1918. The founder of the Ustachi, Ante Pavelic, had found celebrity by turning to a political opponent in the Croatian Chamber of Deputies and shooting him in the heart. Six months later, Pavelic returned from hiding, walked into the lobby of the chamber carrying a shotgun, and killed two more.

Under Mussolini's protection, Pavelic moved to a villa in Turin, where he kept a guiding hand on the political philosophy of his organization: over forty train wrecks in ten years, numberless public buildings bombed, hand grenades thrown into soldiers' cafés, and five thousand Croatian and Serbian officials murdered. The money came from Mussolini, the assassins from IMRO, Internal Macedonian Revolutionary Organization, with headquarters in Bulgaria. It had been IMRO operatives who assassinated King Alexander of Yugoslavia in 1934, in Marseilles. They had been trained in camps in Hungary which, in service of an alliance with Italy, also provided military instructors and false papers. Papers issued, quite often, in the name of Edouard Benes, the hated president of Czechoslovakia. A certain sense of humor at work there, Morath thought.

"Balkan, Balkan," they said in France of a pimp slapping a whore or three kids beating up a fourth—anything barbarous or brutal. In the seat across from Morath, Pavlo slumbered away, arms crossed protectively over his briefcase.

The passport formalities at the Austrian border were, mercifully, not too drawn out. For *Andreas Panea,* the Roumanian, that particular masked rudeness of central Europe—you practically had to be Austrian to know you'd been insulted. For everybody else, it took a day or two, and by then you'd left the country.

A long time on the train, Morath thought, anxious to be back in the life he'd made in Paris. Hungarian plain, Austrian valley, German forest, and, at last, French fields, and the sun came out in Morath's heart. By evening, the train chugged through the Ile-de-France, wheatfields and not much else, then the conductor—who was all French train conductors, broad and stocky with a black mustache— announced the final stop, just the edge of a song in his voice. Pavlo grew attentive, peering out the window as the train slowed for the villages outside the city.

"You've been to Paris?"

"No."

On the tenth of May 1938, the night train from Budapest pulled into the Gare du Nord a little after 9:20 P.M. It was, on the whole, a quiet evening in Europe, cloudy and warm for the season, rain expected toward dawn. Nicholas Morath, traveling on a Hungarian diplomatic passport, stepped slowly from the first-class car and headed for the taxi rank outside the station. Just as he left the platform he turned, as though he was about to say something to a companion, but, on looking back, he discovered that whoever he'd been with had disappeared into the crowd.

VON
SCHLEBEN'S
WHORE

THE BAR OF THE BALALAIKA, A LITTLE AFTER THREE, THE DUSTY, TIRED air of a nightclub on a spring afternoon. On the stage were two women and a man, dancers, in tight black clothing, harassed by a tiny Russian wearing a pince-nez, hands on hips, stricken with all the hopelessness in the world. He closed his eyes and pressed his lips together, a man who'd been right about everything since birth. "To leap like a Gypsy," he explained, "is to leap like a Gypsy." Silence. All stared. He showed them what he meant, shouting "Hah!" and throwing his arms into the air. He thrust his face toward them. "You, *love,* life!"

Boris Balki was leaning on his elbows, the stub of a blunt pencil stuck behind his ear, a half-completed crossword puzzle in a French newspaper spread out on the bar. He looked up at Morath and said, "Ça va?"

Morath sat on a stool. "Not too bad."

"What can I get for you?"

"A beer."

"Pelforth all right?"

Morath said it was. "Have one with me?"

Balki's eyebrow raised a fraction as he got the bottles from beneath the counter. He opened one and poured the beer into a tilted glass.

Morath drank. Balki filled his own glass, looked down at his puzzle, flipped the page, took a look at the headlines. "Why I keep buying this rag I don't know."

Morath read the name upside down. It was one of the friskier Parisian weeklies: sexy gossip, risqué cartoons, photos of lurid chorus girls, pages of racing news from Auteuil and Longchamps. His name had once, to his shame and horror, appeared in it. Just before he met Cara he'd been going around with a second-rank movie star, and they'd called him "the Hungarian playboy Nicky Morath." There'd been neither a duel nor a lawsuit but he'd considered both.

Balki laughed. "Where do they get this stuff? 'There are currently twenty-seven Hitlers locked up in Berlin insane asylums.' "

"And one to go."

Balki flipped the page, took a sip of his beer, read for a few moments. "Tell me, you're Hungarian, right?"

"Yes."

"So, it says here, now you have a law against the Jews."

The last week in May, the Hungarian parliament had passed a law restricting Jewish employment in private companies to twenty percent of the workforce.

"Shameful," Morath said. "But the government had to do something, something symbolic, or the Hungarian Nazis would have staged a coup d'état."

Balki read further. "Who is Count Bethlen?"

"A conservative. Against the radical right." Morath didn't mention Bethlen's well-known definition of the anti-Semite as "one who detests the Jews more than necessary."

"His party fought the law," Balki said. "Alongside the liberal conservatives and the Social Democrats. 'The Shadow Front,' they call it here."

"The law is a token," Morath said. "Nothing more. Horthy

brought in a new prime minister, Imredy, to get a law passed and quiet the lunatics, otherwise—"

From the stage, a record of Gypsy violins. One of the woman dancers, a ginger blonde, raised her head to a haughty angle, held a hand high, and snapped her fingers. "Yes," the tiny Russian cried out. "That's good, Rivka, that's *Tzigane!*" He made his voice husky and dramatic and said, "What man will dare to take me." Morath, watching the dancer, could see how hard she was trying.

"And the Jews?" Balki said, raising his voice above the music. "What do they think?"

"They don't like it. But they see what's going on in Europe, and they can look at a map. Somehow the country has to find a way to survive."

Disgusted, Balki flipped back to the crossword and took the pencil from behind his ear. "Politics," he said. Then, "a wild berry?"

Morath thought it over. "Maybe *fraise des bois?*"

Balki counted the spaces. "Too long," he said.

Morath shrugged.

"And you? What do you think?" Balki said. He was back to the new law.

"Of course I'm against it. But one thing we all know is that if the Arrow Cross ever takes power, then it *will* be like Germany. There will be another White Terror, like 1919. They'll hang the liberals, the traditional right, *and* the Jews. Believe me, it will be like Vienna, only worse." He paused a moment. "Are you Jewish, Boris?"

"I sometimes wonder," Balki said.

It wasn't an answer Morath expected.

"I grew up in an orphanage, in Odessa. They found me with the name 'Boris' pinned to a blanket. 'Balki' means ditch—that's the name they gave me. Of course, Odessa, almost everybody's *something*. Maybe a Jew or a Greek or a Tartar. The Ukrainians think it's in the Ukraine, but people in Odessa know better."

Morath smiled, the city was famously eccentric. In 1920, when French, Greek, and Ukrainian troops occupied Odessa during the civil war, the borders of the zones of occupation were marked by lines of kitchen chairs.

"I basically grew up in the gangs," Balki said. "I was a Zakovitsa.

Age eleven, a member of the Zakovits gang. We controlled the chicken markets in the Moldavanka. That was mostly a Jewish gang. We all had knives, and we did what we had to do. But, for the first time in my life, I had enough to eat."

"And then?"

"Well, eventually the Cheka showed up. Then *they* were the only gang in town. I tried going straight, but, you know how it is. Zakovits saved my life. Got me out of bed one night, took me down to the dock, and put me on a Black Sea freighter." He sighed. "I miss it sometimes, bad as it was."

They drank their beer, Balki working on the puzzle, Morath watching the dance rehearsal.

"It's a hard world," Morath said. "Take, for instance, the case of a friend of mine."

Balki looked up. "Always in difficulties, your friends."

"Well, that's true. But you have to try and help them out, if you can."

Balki waited.

"This one friend of mine, he has to do business with the Germans."

"Forget it."

"If you knew the whole story, you'd be sympathetic, believe me." He paused, but Balki was silent. "You lost your country, Boris. You know what that feels like. We're trying not to lose ours. So it's what you just said, we're doing what we have to do. I'm not going to be a *conard* and offer you money, but there is money in this, for somebody. I can't believe you won't put them in the way of it. At least, find out what the offer is."

Balki softened. Everybody he knew needed money. There were women, out in Boulogne where the Russian émigrés lived, going blind from doing contract embroidery for the fashion houses. He gestured with his hands, helpless. *Je m'en fous—I'm fucked no matter what happens.*

"Old story. German officer in Paris, needs girlfriend."

Balki was offended. "Someone told you I was a pimp?"

Morath shook his head. *It's not like that.*

"Tell me," Balki said. "Who are you?" He meant, *what are you?*

"Nicholas Morath. I'm in the advertising business. You can look me up in the telephone book."

Balki finished his beer. "Oh, all right." He gave in, more to some fate he thought he had than to Morath. "What's the rest of it."

"Pretty much as I said."

"Monsieur Morath—Nicholas, if you don't mind—this is Paris. If you want to fuck a camel, all it takes is a small bribe to the zookeeper. Whatever you want to do, any hole you can think of and some you can't, it's up in Pigalle, out in Clichy. For money, anything."

"Yes, I know. But, remember what happened to Blomberg and Fritsch"—two generals Hitler had gotten rid of, one accused of a homosexual affair, the other married to a woman rumored to have been a prostitute. "This officer can't be seen to have a mistress. Boris, I don't know the man, but my friend tells me he has a jealous wife. They both come from stodgy old Catholic families in Bavaria. He can be ruined. Still, here he is in Paris, it's everywhere, it's all around him, in every café, on every street. So he's desperate to arrange something, a liaison. But it must be discreet. For the woman, for the woman who, tells absolutely nobody and understands what's at stake without being told too much and makes him happy in the bargain, there's a monthly arrangement. Five thousand francs a month. And, if everybody's satisfied, more over time."

That was a lot of money. A schoolteacher earned twenty-five hundred francs a month. Balki's face changed, Morath saw it. No more Boris the bartender. Balki the Zakovitsa.

"I don't handle the money."

"No."

"Then maybe," Balki said. "Let me think it over."

Juan-les-Pins, 11 June.

Her breasts, pale in the moonlight.

Late at night, Cara and her friend Francesca, holding hands, laughing, rising naked from the sea, shining with water. Morath sat on the sand, his pants rolled to midcalf, feet bare. Next to him, Simon something, a British lawyer, said, "My God," awed at the Lord's work running up the beach toward them.

They came down here every year, around this time, before the people showed up. To what they called "Juan." Where they lived by the sea in a tall, apricot-colored house with green shutters. In the little village where you could buy a Saint-Pierre from the fishermen when the boats returned at midday.

Cara's crowd. Montrouchet from the Théâtre des Catacombes, accompanied by Sloth. A handsome woman, ingeniously desirable. Montrouchet called her by her proper name, but to Morath she was Sloth and always would be. They stayed at the Pension Helga, up in the pine forest above the village. Francesca was from Buenos Aires, from the Italian community in Argentina, the same as Cara, and lived in London. Then there was Mona, known as Moni, a Canadian sculptor with an apartment in Paris, and the woman she lived with, Marlene, who made jewelry. Shublin, a Polish Jew who painted fire, Ilsa, who wrote small novels, and Bernhard, who wrote poems about Spain. And others, a shifting crowd, friends of friends or mysterious strangers, who rented little cabins in the pines or took cheap rooms at the Hôtel de la Mer or slept under the stars.

Morath loved the Cara of Juan-les-Pins, where the warm air heated her excessively. "We will be up very late tonight," she would say, "so we will have to rest this afternoon." A wash in the sulphurous, tepid water that trickled into the rust-stained tub, then sweaty, inspired love on the coarse sheet. Half asleep, they lay beneath the open window, breathing the pine resin on the afternoon wind. At dusk, the cicadas started, and went on until dawn. Sometimes they would take a taxi up to the restaurant on the *moyenne* corniche above Villefranche, where they brought you bowls of garlicky *tapenade* and pancakes made of chickpea flour and then, finding you at peace with the world and unable to eat another bite, dinner.

Too proud and Magyar for beach sandals, Morath ran to the sea at noon, burning his feet on the hot pebbles, then treading water and staring out at the flat horizon. He would stay there a long time, numb as a stone, as happy as he ever got, while Cara and Francesca and their friends stretched out on their towels and glistened with coconut oil and talked.

"Half past eight in Juan-les-Pins, half past nine in Prague." You heard that at the Bar Basque, where people went in the late afternoon to drink white rum. So the shadow was there, darker on some days, lighter on others, and if you didn't care to take measurements for yourself, the newspapers would do it for you. Going to the little store for a *Nice Matin* and a *Figaro,* Morath joined the other addicts, then went to a café. The sun was fierce by nine in the morning, the shade of the café umbrella cool and secret. "According to Herr Hitler," he read, " 'The Czechs are like bicycle racers—they bow from the waist but down below they never stop kicking.' " In June, that was the new, the fashionable, place for the war to start, Czechoslovakia. The *Volksdeutsch* of the old Austrian provinces, Bohemia and Moravia—the Sudetenland—demanded unification with the Reich. And the *incidents,* the fires, the assassinations, the marches, were well under way.

Morath turned the page.

Spain was almost finished now—you had to go to page three. The Falange would win, it was only a matter of time. Off the coast, British freighters, supplying Republican ports, were being sunk by Italian fighter planes flying from bases in Majorca. *Le Figaro* had reproduced a British editorial cartoon: Colonel Blimp says, "Gad sir, it is time we told Franco that if he sinks another 100 British ships, we shall retire from the Mediterranean altogether."

Morath looked out to sea, a white sail in the distance. The fighting was heavy seventy kilometers north of Valencia, less than a day's drive from the café where he drank his coffee.

Shublin had gone to Spain to fight, but the NKVD kicked him out. "The times we live in," he said at the Bar Basque one evening. "The rule of the invertebrates." He was in his thirties, with curly blond hair, a broken nose, and tobacco-stained fingers with oil paint under the nails. "And King Adolf will sit on the throne of Europe."

"The French will smash him." Bernhard was German. He had marched in a Communist demonstration in Paris and now he couldn't go home.

"Still," said Simon the lawyer. The others looked at him, but he wasn't going to make a speech. A sad smile, that was it.

The table was at the edge of the dance floor, which was liberally dusted with sand and pine needles brought in by the wind. It blew hard off the sea, smelled like a jetty at low tide, and fluttered the tablecloths. The little band finished playing "Le Tango du Chat" and started up on "Begin the Beguine."

Bernhard turned to Moni. "You have danced this 'Beguine'?"

"Oh yes."

"You have?" Marlene said.

"Yes."

"When was that?"

"When you weren't there to see."

"Oh yes? And when was *that*?"

"Dance with me, Nicky," Sloth said and took him by the arm. They did something not unlike a fox-trot, and the band—*Los Tres Hermanos* was printed in script on the bass drum—slowed down to accomodate them. She leaned against him, heavy and soft. "Do you stay up late, when you're here?"

"Sometimes."

"I do. Montrouchet drinks at night, then he sleeps like the dead." They danced for a time.

"You're lucky to have Cara," she said.

"Mm."

"She must be, exciting, to you. I mean, she just is that way, I can feel it."

"Yes?"

"Sometimes I think about the two of you, in your room." She laughed. "I'm terrible, aren't I?"

"Not really."

"Well, I don't care if I am. You can even tell her what I said."

Later, in bed, Cara sat back against the wall, sweat glistening between her breasts and on her stomach. She took a puff of Morath's Chesterfield and blew out a long stream of smoke. "You're happy, Nicky?"

"Can't you tell?"

"Truly?"

"Yes, truly."

Outside, the fall of waves on the beach. A rush, a silence, then the crash.

The moon was down, hazy gold, waning, in the lower corner of the window, but not for long. Cautiously, careful not to wake Cara, he reached for his watch on a chair by the bed. Three-fifty. *Go to sleep.*

"That knits up the raveled sleeve of care." Well, it would take some considerable knitting.

Cara was on to him, but that was just too bad. He was doomed to live with a certain heaviness of soul, not despair, but the tiresome weight of pushing back against it. It had cost him a wife, long ago, an engagement that never quite led to marriage, and had ended more than one affair since then. If you made love to a woman it had better make you happy—or else.

Maybe it was the war. He was not the same when he came back—he knew what people could do to each other. It would have been better not to know that, you lived a different life if you didn't know that. He had read Remarque's book, *All Quiet on the Western Front,* three or four times. And, certain passages, again and again. *Now if we go back we will be weary, broken, burnt out, rootless, and without hope. We will not be able to find our way anymore. . . . Let the months and the years come, they bring me nothing, they can bring me nothing. I am so alone and so without hope that I can confront them without fear.*

A German book. Morath had a pretty good idea what Hitler was mining in the hearts of the German veterans. But it was not only about Germany. They had all, British, French, Russian, German, Hungarian, and the rest, been poured into the grinding machine. Where some of them died, and some of them died inside themselves. Who, he wondered, survived?

But who *ever* did? He didn't know. The point was to get up in the morning. To see what might happen, good or bad, a red/black wager. But, even so, a friend of his used to say, it was probably a good idea that you couldn't commit suicide by counting to ten and saying *now.*

Very carefully, he slid out of bed, put on a pair of cotton pants, crept downstairs, opened the door, and stood in the doorway. A silver line of wave swelled, then rolled over and vanished. Somebody laughed on the beach, somebody drunk, who just didn't care. He could see, barely, if he squinted, the glow of a dying fire and a few silhouettes in the gloom. A whispered shout, another laugh.

Paris. 15 June.

Otto Adler settled in a chair in the Jardin du Luxembourg, just across from the round pool where children came with their sailboats.

He folded his hands behind his head and studied the clouds, white and towering, sharp against the clear sky. Maybe a thunderstorm by late afternoon, he thought. It was hot enough, unseasonal, and he would have looked forward to it but for the few centimes it would cost him to seek refuge in the café on the rue de Médecis. He couldn't afford a few centimes.

This would be his first full summer in France, it would find him poor and dreamy, passionate for dark, lovely corners—alleys and churches—full of schemes and opinions, in love with half the women he saw, depressed, amused, and impatient for lunch. In short, Parisian.

Die Aussicht, like all political magazines, didn't quite live and didn't quite die. The January issue, out in March, had featured an article by Professor Bordeleone, of the University of Turin, "Some Notes on the Tradition of the Fascist Aesthetic." It hadn't quite the elevated depth his readers expected, but it did have the epic sweep—reaching back into imperial Rome and snaking forward past nineteenth-century architecture to d'Annunzio. A gentle, twinkling sort of man, Bordeleone, now professor emeritus of the University of Turin, after a night of interrogation and castor oil at the local police station. But, thank God, at least Signora Bordeleone was rich, and they would survive.

For the winter issue, Adler had grand ambitions. He had received a letter from an old Königsberg friend, Dr. Pfeffer, now an émigré in Switzerland. Dr. Pfeffer had attended a lecture in Basel, and at the coffee hour following the talk the lecturer had mentioned that Thomas Mann, himself an émigré since 1933, was considering the publication of a brief essay. For Mann, that could mean eighty pages, but Adler didn't care. His printer, down in Saclay, was—to date, anyhow—an idealist in matters of credit and overdue bills, and, well, *Thomas Mann.* "I wondered aloud," said Pfeffer in his letter, "ever so gently, whether there was any indication of a *topic,* but the fellow simply coughed and averted his eyes—would you ask Zeus what he had for breakfast?" Adler smiled, remembering the letter. Of course, the topic was completely beside the point. To have that name in *Die Aussicht* he would have published the man's laundry bill.

He unbuckled his briefcase and peered inside: a copy of Schnitzler's collected plays, a tablet of cheap writing paper—the good stuff stayed in his desk back in Saint Germain-en-Laye—yesterday's *Le Figaro,* gathered, he thought of it as *rescued,* on the little train that brought him to Paris, and a cheese sandwich wrapped in brown paper. *"Ah, mais oui, monsieur, le fromage de campagne!"* The lady who owned the local *crémerie* had quickly figured out that he had no money, but, French to the bone, had a small passion for seedy intellectuals and sold him what she called, with a curious mixture of pride and cruelty, *cheese of the countryside.* Nameless, yellow, plain, and cheap. But, Adler thought, bless her anyhow for keeping us alive.

He took the tablet from his briefcase, hunted around until he found a pencil, and began to compose. *"Mein Herr Doktor Mann."* Could he do better with the honorific? Should he try? He let that sit, and went on to strategy. *"Mein Herr Doktor Mann:* As I have a wife and four children to feed and holes in my underwear, I know you will want to publish an important essay in my little magazine." Now, how to say that without saying it. "Perhaps not widely known but read in important circles?"

Phooey. "The most substantive and thoughtful of the émigré political magazines?"

Limp. "Makes Hitler shit!" Now, he thought, there he was on to something. What if, he thought, for one manic second, he actually came out and said such a thing?

His gaze wandered up from the paper to the deep green of chestnut trees on the other side of the pool. No children this morning, of course, they would be suffering through a June day in a schoolroom.

A stroller in the park came toward him. A young man, clearly not at work, perhaps, sadly, unemployed. Adler looked back down at his tablet until the man stood beside his chair. *"Pardon, monsieur,"* he said. "Can you tell me the time?"

Adler reached inside his jacket and withdrew a silver pocket watch on a chain. The minute hand rested precisely on the four.

"It is just . . ." he said.

M. Coupin was an old man who lived on a railroad pension and went to the park to read the newspaper and look at the girls. He told his story to the *flics* standing just outside the Jardin du Luxembourg, then to the detectives at the *préfecture*, then to a reporter from the *Paris-Soir*, then to two men from the Interior Ministry, and, finally, to another reporter, who met him at his local café, bought him a *pastis*, then another, seemed to know more about the event than any of the others, and asked him a number of questions he couldn't answer.

He told them all the same story, more or less. The man sitting across from the sailboat pond, the man in the blue suit and the steel-rimmed spectacles who approached him, and the shooting. A single shot and a coup de grâce.

He did not see the first shot, he heard it. "A sharp report, like a firecracker." That drew his attention. "The man looking at his watch dropped it, then leapt to his feet, as though he had been insulted. He swayed for a moment, then toppled over, taking the chair with him. His foot moved once, after that he was still. The man in the blue suit leaned over him, aimed his pistol, and fired again. Then he walked away."

M. Coupin did not shout, or give chase, or anything else. He stayed where he was, motionless. Because, he explained, "I could not believe what I had seen." And further doubted himself when the assassin "simply walked away. He did not run. He did not hurry. It was, it was as though he had done nothing at all."

There were other witnesses. One described a man in an overcoat, another said there were two men, a third reported a heated exchange between the assassin and the victim. But almost all of them were farther away from the shooting than M. Coupin. The exception was a couple, a man and a woman, strolling arm in arm on a gravel path. The detectives watched the park for several days but the couple did not reappear, and, despite a plea in the story that ran in the newspapers, did not contact the *préfecture*.

"Extraordinary," Count Polanyi said. He meant a soft waffle, folded into a conical shape so that a ball of vanilla ice cream rested on top. "One can eat it while walking."

Morath had met his uncle at the zoo, where a *glacier* by the restaurant offered the ice cream and waffle. It was very hot, Polanyi wore a silk suit and a straw hat. They strolled past a llama, then a lion, the zoo smell strong in the afternoon sun.

"Do you see the papers, Nicholas, down there?"

Morath said he did.

"The Paris papers?"

"Sometimes *Figaro,* when they have it."

Polanyi stopped for a moment and took a cautious taste of the ice cream, holding his pocket handkerchief under the small end of the waffle so that it didn't drip on his shoes. "Plenty of politics, while you were away," he said. "Mostly in Czechoslovakia."

"I read some of it."

"It felt like 1914—events overtaking politicians. What happened was this: Hitler moved ten divisions to the Czech border. At night. But they caught him at it. The Czechs mobilized—unlike the Austrians, who just sat there and waited for it to happen—and the French and British diplomats in Berlin went wild. *This means war!* In the end, he backed down."

"For the time being."

"That's true, he won't give it up, he hates the Czechs. Calls them 'a miserable pygmy race without culture.' So, he'll find a way. And he'll pull us in with him, if he can. And the Poles. The way he's going to sell it, we're simply three nations settling territorial issues with a fourth."

"Business as usual."

"Yes."

"Well, down where I was, nobody had any doubts about the future. War is coming, we're all going to die, there is only tonight . . ."

Polanyi frowned. "It seems a great indulgence to me, that sort of thing." He stopped to have some more ice cream. "By the way, have you had any luck, finding a companion for my friend?"

"Not yet."

"As long as you're at it, it occurs to me that the lovebirds will need a love nest. Very private, of course, and discreet."

Morath thought it over.

"It will have to be in somebody's name," Polanyi said.

"Mine?"

"No. Why don't you ask our friend Szubl?"

"Szubl and Mitten."

Polanyi laughed. "Yes." The two men had shared a room, and the hardships of émigré life, for as long as anyone could remember.

"I'll ask them," Morath said.

They walked for a time, through the Ménagerie, into the gardens.

They could hear train whistles from the Gare d'Austerlitz. Polanyi finished his ice cream. "I've been wondering," Morath said, "what became of the man I brought to Paris."

Polanyi shrugged. "Myself, I make it a point not to know things
like that."

It wasn't hard to see Szubl and Mitten. Morath invited them to lunch.
A Lyonnais restaurant, he decided, where a *grand déjeuner* would
keep you going for weeks. They were famously poor, Szubl and Mitten. A few years earlier, there'd been a rumor that only one of them
could go out at night, since they shared ownership of a single, ash-
black suit.

Morath got there early, Wolfi Szubl was waiting for him. A heavy
man, fifty or so, with a long, lugubrious face and red-rimmed eyes
and a back bent by years of carrying sample cases of ladies' founda-
tion garments to every town in Mitteleuropa. Szubl was a blend of nationalities—he never said exactly which ones they were. Herbert
Mitten was a Transylvanian Jew, born in Cluj when it was still in
Hungary. Their papers, and their lives, were like dead leaves of the
old empire, for years blown aimlessly up and down the streets of a
dozen cities. Until, in 1930, some good soul took pity on them and
granted them Parisian residence permits.

Morath ordered aperitifs, then chatted with Szubl until Mitten returned, the skin of his face ruddy and shining, from the WC. Good
God, Morath thought, he hadn't *shaved* in there, had he? "Ah,
Morath," Mitten said, offering a soft hand and a beaming theatrical
smile. A professional actor, Mitten had performed in eight languages
in the films of five nations and played always the same character—
best defined by his most recent appearance as Mr. Pickwick in a Hungarian version of *The Pickwick Papers*. Mitten had the figure of a
nineteenth-century cartoon, wide at the middle and tapering on either
end, with hair that stood out from his head like a clown wig.

They ordered. Copiously. It was a family restaurant—thick china
bowls and heavy platters. Bearing sausage, some of it in oil, slices of
white potato fried in butter, fat roasted chickens, salads with *haricots
blancs* and salads with lardoons of bacon. Mont d'Or cheese. And
strawberries. Morath could barely see the tablecloth. He spent money

on the wine—the '26 burgundies—exciting the red-faced *patron* to smiles and bows.

They walked afterward, down the dark streets that ran from the back of the 5th to the river. "An apartment," Morath said, "for a clandestine love affair."

Szubl thought it over. "A lover who won't rent his own apartment."

"Very romantic," Mitten said.

"Very clandestine, anyhow," said Szubl.

Mitten said, "What are they, prominent?"

"Cautious," Morath said. "And rich."

"Ah."

They waited. Morath said, "Two thousand a month for the love nest. Five hundred for you. One of you signs the lease. If they need a maid, you hire her. The concierge knows you, only you, the friend of the lovers."

Szubl laughed. "For the five hundred, do we have to believe this?"

"For the five hundred, you know better."

"Nicholas," Mitten said, "people like us don't get away with spying."

"It isn't spying."

"We get put against a wall."

Morath shook his head.

"So, God willing, it's only a bank robbery."

"Love affair," Morath said.

"Six hundred," Mitten said.

"All right. Six hundred. I'll give you money for the furniture."

"Furniture!"

"What kind of love affair is this?"

They were, to Morath's surprise, good at it. Quite good. Somehow, in a week's time, they managed to unearth a *selection* of love nests. To start, they took him up to Mistress Row, the avenue Foch area, where gorgeous shop girls luxuriated on powder-puff sofas, behind windows draped in pink and gold. In the apartment they took him to, the most recent *affaire* had evidently ended abruptly, an open tin of caviar and a mossy lemon left in the little refrigerator.

Next, they showed him a large room, formerly servant's quarters, up in the eaves of an *hôtel particulier* in the Fourth Arrondissement, where nobody ever went. "Six flights of stairs," Mitten said.

"But very private."

And for an actual love affair, Morath thought, not the worst choice. A quiet neighborhood, last popular in 1788, and deserted streets. Next, a taxi up to Saint Germain-des-Prés, to a painter's atelier on the rue Guénégaud, with a pretty blue slice of the Seine in one of the windows. "He paints, she models," Szubl said.

"And then, one afternoon, Fragonard!"

Morath was impressed. "It's perfect."

"For a Parisian, I'm not so sure. But if the lovers are, perhaps, *foreign*, well, as you can see, it's pure MGM."

"*Très chic*," Szubl said.

"And the landlord's in prison."

Their final choice was, obviously, a throwaway. Perhaps a favor for a friend—another Szubl, a different Mitten, penniless and awash in a Gallic sea. Two rooms, barely, at the foot of the Ninth Arrondissement, near the Chaussée d'Antin Métro stop, halfway down the side street—the rue Mogador—just behind the Galeries Lafayette department store. The streets were full of people, shopping at the Galeries or working there. At Christmas, children were brought here to see the mechanical père Noël in the window.

The apartment was on the third floor of a nineteenth-century tenement, the exterior dark with soot and grime. Inside, brown walls, a two-burner stove, toilet in the hall, limp net curtains, yellow with age, a table covered with green oilcloth, a couch, and a narrow bed with a page of an illustrated Hungarian calendar tacked to the wall above the pillow—*Harvest in Esztergom*.

"Well, Morath, here it is!"

"Gives you a stiff pencil just to *see* this bed, right?"

"*Ma biche, ma douce*, that army blanket! That coat rolled up for a pillow! Now is our moment! Undress—if you dare!"

"Who's your friend?"

"Laszlo."

"Nice Hungarian name."

"Nice Hungarian man."

"Thank him for me—I'll give you some money to take him to dinner."

"So then, it's the first one, right? The pink boudoir?"

"Or the atelier. I have to think it over."

They left the apartment and walked downstairs. Morath headed toward the street door but Mitten took his elbow. "Let's go the other way."

Morath followed, through a door at the opposite end of the hallway, across a narrow courtyard in perpetual shadow, then through another door and down a corridor where several men and women were talking and smoking cigarettes.

"Where the hell are we?"

"The Galeries. But not the part the public sees. It's where the clerks go for a cigarette. Sometimes it's used for deliveries."

They came to another door, Szubl opened it and they were on the street floor of the department store, amid crowds of well-dressed people carrying packages.

"Need anything?" Szubl said.

"Maybe a tie?"

"*Salauds!*" Morath was smiling.

"Laszlo wants twenty-five hundred."

Balki called him a week later.

"Perhaps you'd like to meet a friend of mine."

Morath said he would.

"So tomorrow. At the big café on the rue de Rivoli, by the Palais Royal Métro. Around four. She'll be wearing flowers—you'll know who she is."

"Four o'clock."

"Her name is Silvana."

"Thank you, Boris," Morath said.

"Sure," Balki said, his voice hard. "Any time."

The café was exceptionally neutral ground; tourists, poets, thieves, anybody at all could go there. On a steaming day in July, Silvana wore a dark suit with a tiny corsage pinned to the lapel. Back straight, knees together, legs angled off to one side, face set in stone.

Morath had very good manners—not once in his life had he remained seated when a woman came to a table. And a very good heart, people tended to know that about him right away. Even so, it did not go easily between them. He was pleased to meet her, he said, and went on a little, his voice quiet and cool and far more communicative than whatever words it happened to be saying. *I know how hard life can be. We all do the best we can. There is nothing to fear.*

She was not unattractive—that was the phrase that occurred to him when he first saw her. Thirty-five or so, with brass-colored hair that hung limp around her face, an upturned nose, generous lips, and olive, slightly oily skin. Not glamorous particularly, but sulky, that kind of looks. Prominent breasts, very pert in a tight sweater, narrow waist, hips not too wide. From somewhere around the Mediterranean, he guessed. Was she *Marseillaise*? Maybe Greek, or Italian. But cold, he thought. Would Von Schleben actually make love to her? For himself, he wouldn't, but it was impossible to know what other people liked in bed.

"Well then," he said. "An aperitif? A Cinzano—would that be good? With *glaçons*—we'll drink like Americans."

She shook a stubby Gauloise Bleue loose from its packet and tapped the end on her thumbnail. He lit a match for her, she cupped the back of his hand with hers, then blew out the flame. "Thank you," she said. She inhaled eagerly, then coughed.

The drinks came—there was no ice. Looking over Silvana's shoulder, he happened to notice that a little man seated at a corner table was watching her. He had thin hair combed flat and wore a bow tie, which made him look like—Morath had to search for it—the American comedian Buster Keaton. He met Morath's eyes for a moment, then went back to reading his magazine.

"My friend is German," Morath said. "A gentleman. From the nobility."

She nodded. "Yes, Balki told me."

"He would like you to join him for dinner, tomorrow night, at the Pré Catalan. At 8:30. Of course he'll send his car for you."

"All right. I stay at a hotel on the rue Georgette, in Montparnasse." She paused. "It's just the two of us?"

"No. A large dinner party, I believe."

"And where did you say?"

"Pré Catalan. In the Bois de Boulogne. It's very fin-de-siècle. Champagne, dancing till dawn."

Silvana was amused. "Oh," she said.

Morath explained about Szubl and Mitten, the apartment, the money. Silvana seemed a little detached, watching the smoke rise from the end of her cigarette. They had another Cinzano. Silvana told him she was Roumanian, from Sinaia. She'd come to Paris in the winter of '36 with "a man who made a living playing cards." He'd gotten into some sort of trouble, then disappeared. "I expect he's dead," she said, then smiled. "Of course, with him you never know." A friend found her a job in a shop, selling candy in a *confiserie,* but it didn't last. Then, down on her luck, she'd been hired as the hatcheck girl at the Balalaika. She shook her head ruefully. *"Quelle catastrophe."* She laughed, exhaling Gauloise smoke. "I couldn't do it at all, and poor Boris got the blame."

It was the end of the afternoon, cool and dark beneath the arches that covered the rue de Rivoli. The café was jammed with people and very loud. A street musician showed up and started to play the concertina. "I think I'll go home," Silvana said. They stood and shook hands, then she unchained a bicycle from the lamppost on the corner, climbed on, waved to Morath, and pedaled away into traffic.

Morath ordered a scotch.

An old woman came around, selling newspapers. Morath bought a *Paris-Soir* to see what was at the movies. He was going to spend the evening by himself. The headlines were thick and black: GOVERNMENT DECLARES COMMITMENT TO DEFEND CZECHOSLOVAKIA "INDISPUTABLE AND SACRED."

The little man who looked like Buster Keaton left the café, giving Morath a glance as he went. Morath thought, for a moment, that he'd nodded. But, if it happened at all, it was very subtle, or, more likely, it was just his imagination.

Juillet, Juillet. The sun hammered down on the city and the smell of the butcher shops hung like smoke in the dead air.

Morath retreated to the Agence Courtmain, not the first time he'd sought refuge there. On the run from summer, on the run from Uncle Janos and his politics, on the run from Cara, lately consumed by vacation manias. The sacred *mois d'Août* approached—one either went to the countryside or hid in one's apartment and didn't answer the phone. What troubled Cara was, should they go to the baroness Frei up in Normandy? Or to her friend Francesca and her boyfriend, in Sussex? It wasn't the same, not at all, and one had to shop.

At Agence Courtmain they had big black fans that blew the heat around, and sometimes a breeze from the river worked its way up avenue Matignon and leaked in the window. Morath sat with Courtmain and his copy chief in her office, staring at a tin of cocoa.

"They have plantations in Africa, at the southern border of the Gold Coast," the copy chief said. Her name was Mary Day—a French mother and an Irish father. She was close to Morath's age and had never married. One line of gossip had it that she was religious, formerly a nun, while another speculated that she made extra income by writing naughty novels under a pen name.

Morath asked about the owner.

"It's a big provincial family, from around Bordeaux. We deal with the general manager."

"A Parisian?"

"Colonial," Courtmain said. "*Pied-noir,* with barbered whiskers."

The tin had a red label with CASTIGNAC printed in black across the top. Down below it said CACAO FIN. Morath pried up the metal cap, touched a finger to the powder and licked it. Bitter, but not unpleasant. He did it again.

"It's supposedly very pure," Mary Day said. "Sold to *chocolatiers,* here and in Turin and Vienna."

"What do they want us to do?"

"Sell cocoa," Courtmain said.

"Well, new art," Mary Day said. "Posters for bakeries and grocery stores. And he told us that now, with the war winding down, they want to sell in Spain."

"Do Spaniards like chocolate?"

She leaned forward to say *of course,* then realized she didn't know.

"Can't get enough," Courtmain said. *They do in this agency.*

Morath held the tin up to the window. Outside, the sky was white, and there were pigeons cooing on a ledge. "The label's not so bad."

There was a decorative strand of intertwined ivy leaves around the border, nothing else.

Courtmain laughed. "It's perfection," he said. "We'll sell it back to them in ten years."

Mary Day took several sheets of art paper from a folder and pinned them up on the wall. "We're going to give them Cassandre," she said. A. M. Cassandre had done the artwork for the popular *Dubo/Dubon/Dubonnet* image in three panels.

"In-house Cassandre," Courtmain said.

The art was sumptuous, suggesting the tropics. Backgrounds in renaissance ochres and chrome yellows, with figures—mostly tigers and palm trees—in a span of Venetian reds.

"Handsome," Morath said, impressed.

Courtmain agreed. "Too bad about the name," he said. He made a label in the air with his thumb and index finger. "*Palmier,*" he suggested, meaning palm tree. "*Cacao fin!*"

"*Tigre?*" Morath said.

Mary Day had a very impish smile. "*Tigresse,*" she said.

Courtmain nodded. He took an artist's chalk from a cup on the desk and stood to one side of the drawings. "That's the name," he said. "With this tree," it curved gently, with three fronds on top, "and this tiger." A front view. The animal sat on its haunches, revealing a broad expanse of white chest.

Morath was excited. "Do you think they'll do it?"

"Not in a thousand years."

He was at Cara's when the telephone rang, three-thirty in the morning. He rolled out of bed, managed to fumble the receiver free of the cradle. "Yes?"

"It's Wolfi." Szubl was almost whispering.

"What is it?"

"You better go to the apartment. There's big trouble."

"I'll be there," Morath said, and hung up the phone.

What to wear?

"Nicky?"

He'd already put on a shirt and was trying to knot his tie. "I have to go out."

"*Now?*"

"Yes?"

"What's going on?"

"A friend in trouble."

After a silence, "Oh."

He buttoned his pants, shrugged a jacket on, forced his feet into his shoes while smoothing his hair back with his hands.

"What friend?" Now the note was in her voice.

"A Hungarian man, Cara. Nobody you know."

Then he was out the door.

The streets were deserted. He walked quickly toward the Métro at Pont d' Alma. The trains had stopped running two hours earlier, but there was a taxi parked by the entrance. "Rue Mogador," Morath told the driver. "Just around the corner from the Galeries."

The street door had been left open. Morath stood at the foot of the staircase and peered up into the gloom. Thirty seconds, nothing happened, then, just as he started up the stairs, he heard the click of a closing door, somewhere above him. *Trying not to make a noise.* Again he waited, then started to climb.

On the first floor landing, he stopped again. "Szubl?" He said it in a low voice—not a whisper, just barely loud enough to be heard on the floor above.

No answer.

He held his breath. He thought he could hear light snoring, a creak, then another. Normal for a building at four in the morning. Again he climbed, slowly, standing for a moment on every step. Halfway up, he touched something sticky on the wall. What was *that*? Too dark to see, he swore and rubbed his fingers against his trousers.

On the third floor, he went to the end of the hall and stood in front of the door. The smell was not at all strong—not yet—but Morath had fought in the war and knew exactly what it was. *The woman.* His heart sank. He had known this would happen. Somehow, mysteriously, he'd known it. And he would settle with whoever had done it. Von Schleben, somebody else, it didn't matter. His blood was racing, he told himself to calm down.

Or, maybe, Szubl. No, why would anyone bother.

He put his index finger on the door and pushed. It swung open. He could see the couch, the bed, a dresser he didn't remember. He smelled paint, along with the other smell, stronger now, and the burnt, bittersweet odor of a weapon fired in a small room.

He stepped inside. Now he could see the tiny stove and the table covered with oilcloth. At one end, a man was sitting in a chair, his legs spread wide, his head hanging, almost upside down, over the back, his arms dangling at his sides.

Morath lit a match. Boots and trousers of a German officer's uniform. The man was wearing a white shirt and suspenders, his jacket hung carefully on the chair and now pinned in place by his head. A gray face, well puffed up, one eye open, one eye shut. The expression—and he had seen this before—one of sorrow mixed with petty irritation. The hole in the temple was small, the blood had dried to brown on the face and down the arm. Morath knelt, the Walther sidearm had dropped to the floor beneath the hand. On the table, the wallet. A note? No, not that he could see.

The match started to burn his fingers. Morath shook it out and lit another. He opened the wallet: a photograph of a wife and grown children, various Wehrmacht identity papers. Here was Oberst—Colonel—Albert Stieffen, attached to the German general staff at the Stahlheim barracks, who'd come to Paris and shot himself in the kitchen of Von Schleben's love nest.

A soft tap at the door. Morath glanced at the pistol, then let it lay there. "Yes?"

Szubl came into the room. He was sweating, red-faced. "Christ," he said.

"Where were you?"

"Over at the Gare Saint-Lazare. I used the phone, then I stood across the street and watched you come inside."

"What happened?"

Szubl spread his hands apart, *God only knows.* "A man called, about two-thirty in the morning. Told me to come over here and take care of things."

" 'Take care of things.' "

"Yes. A German, speaking German."

"Meaning, it happened here, so it's our problem." Morath looked at his watch, it was almost five.

"Something like that."

They were silent for a time. Szubl shook his head, slow and ponderous. Morath exhaled, a sound of exasperation, ran his fingers through his hair, swore in Hungarian—mostly to do with fate, shitting pigs, saints' blood—and lit a cigarette. "All right," he said, more to himself than to Szubl. "So now it disappears."

Szubl looked glum. "It will cost plenty, that kind of thing."

Morath laughed and waved the problem away. "Don't worry about that," he said.

"Really? Well, then you're in luck. I have a friend."

"*Flic*? Undertaker?"

"Better. A desk man at the Grand Hotel."

"Who is he?"

"One of us. From Debrecen, a long time ago. He was in a French prisoner-of-war camp in 1917, somehow managed to get himself to the local hospital. Long story short, he married the nurse. Then, after the war, he settled in Paris and worked in the hotels. So, about a year ago, he tells me a story. Seems there was a symphony conductor, a celebrity, staying in the luxury suite. One night, maybe two in the morning, the phone at the desk rings. It's the maestro, he's frantic. My friend rushes upstairs—the guy had a sailor in the room, the sailor died."

"Awkward."

"Yes, very. Anyhow, it was taken care of."

Morath thought it over. "Go back to Saint-Lazare," he said. "Call your friend."

Szubl turned to leave.

"I'm sorry to put you through this, Wolfi. It's Polanyi, and his . . ."

Szubl shrugged, adjusted his hat. "Don't blame your uncle for intrigue, Nicholas. It's like blaming a fox for killing a chicken."

From Morath, a sour smile, Szubl wasn't wrong. *Although*, he thought, *"blaming" isn't what's usually done to a fox*. The stairs creaked as Szubl went down, then Morath watched him through the window. The dawn was gray and humid, Szubl trudged along, head down, shoulders hunched.

•

The desk man was tall and handsome, *dashing*, with a cavalry mustache. He arrived at 6:30, wearing a red uniform with gold buttons. "Feeling better?" he said to the corpse.

"Two thousand francs," Morath said. "All right?"

"Could be a little more, by the time it's done, but I trust Wolfi for it." For a moment, he stared at the dead officer. "Our friend here is drunk," he said to Morath. "We're going to get his arms around our shoulders and carry him downstairs. I'd ask you to sing, but something tells me you won't. Anyhow, there's a taxi at the door, the driver is in on it. We'll put our friend here in the backseat, I'll get in with the driver, and that's that. The jacket, the gun, the wallet, you find a way to get rid of those. If it was me, I'd burn the papers."

Eventually, Morath and the desk man had to carry Stieffen downstairs—the pantomime played out only from the street door to the taxi, and they barely made it that far.

A blue car—later he thought it was a big Peugeot—pulled to the curb in front of him. Slowly, the back window was lowered and the little man in the bow tie stared out at him. "Thank you," he said. The window was rolled back up as the car pulled away, following the taxi.

Morath watched as they drove off, then returned to the apartment where Szubl, stripped to his underwear, was scrubbing the floor and whistling a Mozart aria.

Polanyi outdid himself, Morath thought, when he chose a place to meet. A nameless little bar in the quarter known as the *grande truanderie*, the thieves' palace, buried in the maze of streets around Montorgueil. It reminded Morath of something Emile Courtmain had once told him: "The truth of lunch is in the choice of the restaurant. All that other business, eating, drinking, talking, that doesn't mean very much."

Polanyi sat there, looking very sorrowful and abused by the gods. "I'm not going to apologize," he said.

"Do you know who he was? Colonel Stieffen?"

"No idea. And no idea why it happened. To do with honor, Nicholas—if I had to bet, I'd bet on that. He puts his wallet on the table, meaning this was who I was, and does it in a secret apartment, meaning this is where I failed."

"Failed at what?"

Polanyi shook his head.

They were sitting at one of the three tables in the room. The fat woman at the bar called out, "Say, boys, let me know when you're ready for another."

"We will," Polanyi said.

"Who's the little man with the bow tie?"

"He is called Dr. Lapp."

"Dr. Lapp."

"A name. Certainly there are others. He is an officer in the Abwehr."

"Oh well, that explains it then. I've become a German spy. Should we stay for lunch?"

Polanyi took a sip of wine. He was like, Morath thought, a man going to work. "They're going to get rid of him, Nicholas. It's dangerous for me to tell you that, and dangerous for you to know it, but this Colonel Stieffen has opened a door and now I have, against my better judgment, believe me, to let you inside."

"To get rid of who?"

"Hitler."

No answer to that.

"If they fail, we will have war, and it will make the last one look like a tea party. The fact is, if you hadn't called me, I was going to call you. I believe it's time for you to think seriously about how to get your mother and your sister out of Hungary."

It had a life of its own, the war, like an immense rumor, that wound its way through the newspapers, the cafés, and the markets. But somehow, in Polanyi's voice, it was fact, and Morath, for the first time, believed it.

Polanyi leaned forward, his voice confidential. "Hitler is going to *settle,* as he puts it, with the Czechs. The Wehrmacht will invade, probably in the fall—the traditional time, when the harvest is in and the men from the countryside become soldiers. Russia is pledged to defend Czechoslovakia if France does. The Russians will march through Poland, with or without the Poles' permission, but she'll invade us. You know what that means—Mongolian cavalry and the Cheka and all the rest of it. France and England will invade Germany through Belgium—this is no different than 1914. Given the structure of treaties in Europe, the alliances, that is exactly what is going to happen. Germany will bomb the cities, fifty thousand casualties every night. Unless they use phosgene gas, then it's more. Britain will blockade the ports, central Europe will starve. The burning and the starving will go on until the Red Army crosses the German border and destroys the Reich. Will they stop there? 'God lives in France,' as the Germans like to say—perhaps Stalin will want to go and see Him."

Morath looked for contradictions. He couldn't find them.

"This is what worries me, this is what ought to worry you, but this means very little to the OKW, the Oberkommando Wehrmacht, the army's general staff. Those people—the map people, the logistics people, the intelligence people—have always been accused, by operational commanders, of thinking more than is good for them, but this time they've got it right. If Hitler attacks Czechoslovakia—which is easy for Germany because, since the Anschluss, they surround the Czechs on three sides—England, France, and Russia will come into the war. Germany will be destroyed. But, more important to the OKW, the *army* will be destroyed. Everything they've worked for, since the ink dried on the treaties in 1918, will be torn to pieces. Everything. They can't let that happen. And they know, with Hitler protected by the SS, that only the army has the strength to remove him."

Morath thought for a time. "In a way," he said, "this is the best thing that could happen."

"If it happens, yes."

"What can go wrong?"

"Russia fights only if France does. France and England will fight only if Germany invades and the Czechs resist. Hitler can be removed only for starting a war he can't win."

"Will the Czechs fight?"

"They have thirty-five divisions, about 350,000 men, and a defensive line of forts that runs along the Sudetenland border. Said to be good—as good as the Maginot Line. And, of course, Bohemia and Moravia are bordered by mountains, the Shumava. For the German tanks, the passes, especially if they are defended, will be difficult. So, certain people in the OKW are making contact with the British and the French, urging them to stand firm. Don't give Hitler what he wants, make him fight for it. Then, when he fights, the OKW will deal with him."

"Making contact, you said."

Polanyi smiled. "You know how it's done, Nicholas, it's not a lone hero, crawling through the desert, trying to save the world. It's various people, various approaches, various methods. Connections. Relationships. And when the OKW people need a quiet place to talk, away from Berlin, away from the Gestapo, they have an apartment in the rue Mogador—where that rogue Von Schleben sees his Roumanian girlfriend. Who knows, it might even be a place to meet a foreign colleague, over from London for the day."

"A setting provided by their Hungarian friends."

"Yes, why not?"

"And, similarly, the man we brought into Paris."

"Also for Von Schleben. He has many interests, many projects."

"Such as . . ."

Polanyi shrugged. "He didn't explain, Nicholas. I didn't insist."

"And Colonel Stieffen?" Now they'd ridden the merry-go-round back to where they'd started. Morath might have gotten the brass ring, he wasn't sure.

"Ask Dr. Lapp," Polanyi said. "If you feel you have to know."

Morath, puzzled, stared at his uncle.

"If you should happen to see him, I meant to say."

On Saturday mornings, Cara and Nicky went riding in the Bois de Boulogne, on the Chemin des Vieux Chênes, or around the Lac Inferieur. They rode big chestnut geldings, the sweat white and foamy above the horses' hocks in the midsummer heat. They rode very well; they both came from countries where horseback riding was part of life, like marriage or religion. Sometimes Morath found the bridle paths boring, too sedate—he had galloped into machine-gun positions and jumped horses over barbed wire—but the feel of it brought him a peace he could find no other way.

They nodded to the other couples, everyone smart in their jodhpurs and handmade boots, and trotted along at a good, stiff pace in the shade of the oak trees.

"I have a letter from Francesca," Cara told him. "She says the house in Sussex is lovely, but small."

"If you'd prefer something grand, we'll go up to the baroness's place."

"That's what you'd like, right, Nicky?"

"Well," Morath said. He really didn't care but pretended in order to please Cara. "Maybe Normandy's better. Cool at night, and I like to swim in the sea."

"Good. I'll write this afternoon. We can see Francesca when she comes in the fall. For the clothes."

Boris Balki telephoned and asked him to come to the nightclub. The Balalaika was closed for the August vacation, the tables covered with old bedsheets. There was no beer to drink, so Balki opened a bottle of wine. "They won't miss it," he said. Then, "So, you must be leaving soon."

"A few days. The great migration."

"Where do you go?"

"Normandy. Just outside Deauville."

"That must be nice."

"It's all right."

"I like the time off," Balki said. "We have to paint, fix the place up, but at least I don't have to make jokes." He reached in a pocket, unfolded a page of cheap writing paper covered with small Cyrillic characters. "It's from a friend of mine, in Budapest. He writes from Matyas Street."

"Not much there. The prison."

From Balki, a grim smile.

"Oh."

"He's an old friend, from Odessa. I thought, maybe, if somebody knew somebody . . ."

"Matyas is the worst—in Budapest, anyhow."

"He says that, as much as he can get it past the censor."

"Is he in for a long time?"

"Forty months."

"Long enough. What'd he do?"

"Bonds."

"Hungarian?"

"Russian. Railroad bonds. The 1916 kind."

"Somebody *buys* that?"

Balki nodded, then, despite himself, started laughing. "Poor Rashkow. He's tiny. 'Look at me,' he used to say. 'If I tried to hold somebody up they'd stuff me in a drawer.' So he sells things. Sometimes jewelry, sometimes paintings, even manuscripts. Tolstoy! His unfinished novel! But, lately, it's railroad bonds."

They both laughed.

"You see why I love him," Balki said.

"They're not actually *worth* anything, are they?"

"Well, Rashkow would say, not *now*. But think of the future. 'I sell hope,' he used to say. 'Hope for tomorrow. Think how important that is, hope for tomorrow.' "

"Boris," Morath said, "I'm not sure I can help."

"Well, anyhow, you'll try." The *after all, I tried for you* was unspoken but not difficult to hear.

"Of course."

"Before you go away?"

"Even if I can't do that, I won't wait for September. They have telephones in Deauville."

"Semyon Rashkow." Balki held the letter up to the light and squinted. Morath realized he needed glasses. "Number 3352-18."

"Just out of curiosity, who wrote Tolstoy's unfinished novel?"

Balki grinned. "Wasn't bad, Morath. Really. It wasn't."

The last place he wanted to be, in Colonel Sombor's office on the top floor of the Hungarian legation. Sombor sat erect at his desk, reading a dossier, using the end of a pencil to guide his eyes along a typewritten line. Morath stared out the open window. Down below, in the garden, a porter, an old man in a gray uniform and a gray peaked cap, was raking the gravel. The sound was sharp in the silent courtyard.

He had to help; he felt he had to help. Balki wasn't an affable barman, Balki was him, Morath, just in the wrong country, in the wrong year, forced to live the wrong life. A man who hated having to be grateful for a job he hated.

Morath had tried his uncle first, was told he was not in Paris, then reached Sombor at his office. "Of course, come tomorrow morning." Sombor was the man who could help, so Morath went to see him, knowing it was a mistake every step of the way. Sombor had a title, something innocuous, but he worked for the secret police, and everybody knew it. There was an official spy at the legation, Major Fekaj, the military attaché, and there was Sombor.

"I don't see you enough," he complained to Morath, closing the dossier. Morath found it hard to look at him. He was one of those people whose hair looks like a hat—a polished, glossy black hat—and with his sharp, slanted eyebrows, he suggested a tenor made up to play the devil in a comic opera.

"My uncle keeps me busy."

Sombor acknowledged Polanyi's position with a gracious nod. Morath certainly wanted it to be gracious.

"Yes, I can believe it," Somber said. "Also, I'm sure, this wonderful city. And its opportunities."

"That too."

Sombor touched his lips with his tongue, leaned forward, lowered his voice. "We're grateful, of course."

From a man who'd been forced, in 1937, to remove a portrait of Julius Gombos from his wall—Gombos was widely credited with having invented the philosophies of Adolf Hitler—not necessarily what Morath wanted to hear. "Good of you to say it." *Grateful for what?*

"Not the kind of thing you can allow," Sombor said.

Morath nodded. What in hell's name had Polanyi told this man? And why? For his own good? Morath's? Some other reason? What he did know was that this conversation was not, not if he could help it, going to turn frank and open.

"Someone who has done a favor for me, for us"—Morath smiled, so did Sombor—"needs a favor in return."

"Favors . . ."

"Well, what is one to do."

"Quite."

A contest of silence. Sombor ended it. "So, exactly what sort of favor are we talking about?"

"An old friend. Locked up in Matyas."

"For?"

"Selling worthless bonds."

"*Beszivargo?*" Infiltrator. Which meant, for Sombor and others, Jew.

Morath thought it over. Rashkow? "I don't think so," he said. "Not from the name."

"Which is?"

"Rashkow."

Sombor took a tablet of white paper and unscrewed the cap of his pen and carefully wrote the name down on the paper.

The *month in the country* gathered momentum, preparation on the avenue Bourdonnais proceeded at a fever pitch. The baroness had been written, then telephoned, then telephoned again. Cara's MG had been washed, waxed, and filled with water, oil, and gasoline, the seats rubbed with saddle soap, the walnut dashboard polished to a soft glow. The picnic hamper was ordered from Pantagruel, then Delbard, then Fauchon. Did Morath like sliced beef tongue in aspic? No? Why not? The tiny folding table purchased, taken back to the store, replaced with a green horse blanket, then a fine wool blanket, brown with a gray stripe, which could also be used on the beach. Cara brought home a bathing suit this little, then this little, and then this little; the last one springing a seam as Morath whipped it off. And she should be damned glad, he thought, that there weren't toothmarks in it—take *that* back to Mademoiselle Ninette on the rue Saint-Honoré.

Saturday morning, Morath had a long list of errands, carefully saved up as a pretext to escape from Cara's packing. He stopped at Courtmain, at the bank, at the *tabac*, at the bookstore, where he bought Freya Stark's *The Valleys of the Assassins* and Hemingway's *A Farewell to Arms*, both in French translation. He already had a Gyula Krudy novel. Krudy was in essence the Hungarian Proust—"Autumn and Budapest were born of the same mother"—and Morath had always liked him. In fact, the baroness's houses were stacked to the ceilings with books, and Morath knew he would fall in love with some exotic lost masterpiece and never turn a page of whatever he'd brought with him.

When he got back to the avenue Bourdonnais, he discovered there'd been a blizzard of underwear and shoes and crinkly pink paper. On the kitchen table was a vase with a dozen yellow roses. "These are not from you, Nicky, are they?"

"No."

"I didn't think so."

"Is there a card?"

"Yes, but it's in Hungarian. I can't read it."

Morath could read it. A single word written in black ink on a florist's card. *Regrets.*

Three-thirty when Cara's phone rang and a man's voice asked him, very politely, if it would be altogether too much trouble to walk to the newspaper kiosk by the Pont D'Alma Métro.

"I'm going to get the paper," he said to Cara.

"What? *Now?* For God's sake, Nicky, I—"

"Back in a minute."

Dr. Lapp was in a black Mercedes. His suit was blue, his bow tie green, his face as sad as Buster Keaton's. There was really nothing to discuss, he said.

This was a privilege, not a sacrifice.

Still, Morath felt terrible. Perhaps if he'd been able to say something, to explain, maybe it wouldn't have been so bad.

"Messieurs et mesdames."

The conductor had opened the door of the compartment and the rhythmic hammering of the wheels on the track grew suddenly louder. Morath rested the Freya Stark book on his knee.

The conductor held the first-class passenger list in his hand. "*'Sieurs et 'dames,* the dining car will open in thirty minutes, you may reserve for the first or second seating."

He went around the compartment: businessman, middle-aged woman, mother and little boy—possibly English, then Morath. "Second, please," Morath said.

"And that would be?"

"Monsieur Morath."

"Very good, sir."

"Can you tell me, what time we expect to be in Prague?"

"The timetable says four-thirty, monsieur, but, of course, these days . . ."

2 August 1938. Marienbad, Czechoslovakia.

Six-twenty in the evening, Morath came down the marble staircase and walked across the lobby. Grand hotels in spa towns were all of a type and the Europa was no different—miles of corridors, chandeliers, everywhere mahogany. Frayed carpets, frayed respectability, the former much rewoven, the latter a faint but detectable presence in the air, like the smell of the kitchen.

Two women in leather chairs smiled at him, widow and unmarried daughter, he guessed, come husband-hunting in Marienbad. Morath had been at the Europa for only a night and a day and they had flirted with him twice. They were handsome and well fleshed. *Good appetites,* he thought, *of all sorts.* Not unusual in that part of the world. The Czechs felt life owed them a little pleasure; they happily embraced the Protestant virtues but just as happily embraced each other. If a proposal of marriage was not forthcoming then, mother or daughter, rolling around in a creaky hotel bed might not be the worst thing in the world.

Morath walked out the entrance, into a genteel lane lit with gas lamps. There were mountains in the distance, dark shapes in the failing light. He walked for a long time, glancing at his watch every few minutes. He had once, dragged off to Evian-les-Bains by Cara's predecessor, actually tried the treatment—packed in mud by laughing girls, then hosed down by a stern woman wearing a hair net. Victorian medicine. Victorian eroticism? Victorian *something.*

He reached the edge of the town, a black, dense forest of pine rolling up a hillside above the street. Down below, the gas lamps twinkled. There were several orchestras at work and he could hear, when the wind was right, the violins. It was very romantic. Through the trees, a glimpse of the toy train that puffed its way up the mountain to the station called Marianske Lazne. Marienbad, in the Austro-Hungarian days. Hard to think of it any other way. The wind shifted, the distant violins floated up to him. Along with a faint smell of gunnery.

Now it was 7:10. There were candles on the tables of the tearoom in Otava Street. Morath studied the menu, mounted in a brass frame on a stand by the door. Inside, a Czech army officer watched him for a moment, then rose from his chair, leaving an uneaten pastry on his plate. To get to his feet, the officer used a stick, a good one, Morath saw, with a brass tip and an ivory head. He was not far from Morath's age, with a soldier's face and a neatly trimmed beard, blond and gray and red.

They shook hands in the street. "Colonel Novotny," the officer said, with a motion of the head somewhere between a nod and a bow.

"Morath."

An exchange of pleasantries. We are like, Morath thought, two provincial officials, meeting in the sleepy days of the old empire.

Novotny had a military car: the least expensive Opel, something like a Parisian taxicab, painted olive green. "We are going up toward Kreslice," he said. "About forty kilometers from here."

Morath opened the passenger door. On the seat was a holstered automatic pistol in a leather belt. "Oh, just put that on the floor," Novotny said. "We're in the Sudetenland here—it's wiser to have something in the car."

They drove on mountain roads, darker as they climbed, the beams of the headlights alive with moths. Novotny squinted through the windshield, the narrow dirt path twisted and turned and disappeared into the night. Twice they had to put branches under the wheels, and when they crossed bridges over mountain streams—built for wagons and oxen—Morath got out and walked ahead of the car with a flashlight. They passed one house only, a woodcutter's hut. Up on the crest, something ran away from them; they could hear it, crashing through the underbrush.

"I brought my dog along once," Novotny said, "coming up here. She went crazy. Ran around and around the car, scratching the windows with her paws."

"What do you have?"

"Pointer bitch."

"I've had them—couldn't wait to go to work."

"That's her. She was crying because I wouldn't let her out of the car. I've seen bear up here, and stag. Wild boar. The peasants say there's lynx—kills their animals."

Novotny slowed to a crawl, worked the car carefully around a hairpin curve. Morath could hear a stream a long way below them. "A shame, really," Novotny said. "When we start fighting here, well, you know what happens to the game."

"I know. I was in the Carpathians, in '15."

"This is, of course, where we want them."

"In the mountains."

"Yes. We watched them mobilize, back in May. Very educational. Tanks, trucks, cars, motorcycles. Big gasoline tankers. It's not a secret, what they mean to do—read Guderian's book, and Rommel's. Everything's motorized, that's the sharp edge of the ax. After the first wave, of course, it's all horses and artillery limbers, like everyone else. So, the logic goes, run them up the mountains, or make them go through the valleys."

"Enfilade."

"Yes. With registered mortars. And machine guns on the hillsides."

"When will it start?"

"In the fall. We hold them two months, it starts to snow." Up ahead, the road was cut into wagon ruts. Then it grew steeper, and Novotny shifted into a whining first gear. "What did you do, last time?"

"Hussars. The Sixteenth Corps, in the Second Army."

"Magyar."

"Yes, that's right."

"I was in the Seventh. First under Pflanzer, then Baltin."

"Down in Moldavia."

"To start with. Eventually—I'm an artillery officer—they sent me up to Russian Poland. Lemberg and Przemysl."

"The forts."

"Twenty-eight months," Novotny said. "Lost them, got them back."

Morath had never fought alongside the Czechs. The Austrian army spoke ten languages—Czech, Slovak, Croatian, Serbian, Slovene, Ruthenian, Polish, Italian, Hungarian, and German—and was normally divided into regiments based on nationality. But the history of the soldiers who defended the forts was well known. Twice they'd been surrounded and cut off, but the hundred and fifty thousand men in the blockhouses and bunkers had held out for months, while Russian dead piled up beneath their guns.

It was well after nine when they reached the Kreslice barracks—a set of long, low buildings in the imperial style, built of the honey-colored sandstone so loved by Franz Josef's architects. "We can probably get something for dinner," Novotny said, sounding hopeful. But there was a feast laid on for Morath in the officers' mess. Roast goose, red cabbage with vinegar, beer from a small brewery in Pilsen, and a lieutenant general at the head of the table.

"To friendship between our nations!"

"To friendship!"

Many of the officers were bearded, the style among artillerymen, and many had served on the eastern front in 1914—Morath saw all the medals. Most decorated of all, the general: short and thick and angry. And fairly drunk, Morath thought, with a flushed face and a loud voice. "It gets harder and harder to read the goddamn newspapers," he said. "Back in the winter, they couldn't love us enough, especially the French. Czechoslovakia—new hope! Liberal democracy—example for Europe! Masaryk and Benes—statesmen for the ages! Then something happened. Back in July, I think it was, there was Halifax, in the House of Lords, talking about 'impractical devotion to high purpose.' *Oh shit,* we said, now look what's happened."

"And it continues," Novotny said. "The little minuet."

The general took a long drink of beer and wiped his mouth with an olive-green napkin. "It encourages him, of course. The Reichsführer. The army's the only thing he ever liked, now he's gotten tired of watching it march. Now he wants to see it fight. But he's coming to the wrong neighborhood."

"Because you'll fight back."

"We'll give him a good Czech boot up his Austrian ass, is what we'll do. This Wehrmacht, we have films of their maneuvers; they're built to roll across the plains of Europe. It's the Poles who ought to worry, and the Russians. Down here, we'll fight in the mountains. Like the Swiss, like the Spaniards. He can beat us—he's *bigger* than we are, no way to change that—but it will take everything he has. When he does that, he leaves the Siegfried Line wide open, and the French can march in with a battalion of café waiters."

"If they dare." There was laughter at the table.

The general's eyes glowed. Like Novotny's pointer bitch, he couldn't wait to get at the game. "Yes, if they dare—*something's* gone wrong with them." He paused for a moment, then leaned toward Morath. "And what about Hungary? It's all plains, just like Poland. You don't even have a river."

"God only knows," Morath said. "We barely have an army. For the moment, we depend on being smarter than they are."

"Smarter," the general said. He thought it over: it didn't seem like much. "Than all of them?"

"Hitler killed off the really smart ones, or chased them out of the country. So, for the moment, that's what we have."

"Well then, may God watch over you," the general said.

They gave him a room of his own—above the stables, the horses restless down below—a hard bed, and a bottle of plum brandy. At least, he thought, they didn't send along "the stableman's daughter." He drank some of the brandy, but still he couldn't sleep. It was thunder that kept him awake, from a storm that never rained yet never moved away. He looked out the window now and then, but the sky was all stars. Then he realized that the Czechs were working at night. He could feel it in the floor. Not thunder, dynamite, the explosions rolling back and forth across the valleys. It was the engineers who kept him awake, blowing the faces off their mountains, building fortifications.

2:30. 3:00. Instead of sleeping, he smoked. He had felt, since he came to the barracks, a certain, familiar undercurrent. *Together we live, together we die, and nobody cares which way it goes.* He hadn't felt it for a long time. It wasn't that he liked it, but thinking about it kept him awake.

·

Just after dawn they were back on the mountain roads, this time in an armored car, accompanied by the general and a pale, soft civilian in a black suit, quite sinister, with tinted eyeglasses and very little to say. *A spy*, Morath thought. At least, a spy in a movie.

The road was newly made, ripped out of the forest with bulldozers and explosives then surfaced with sawn tree trunks at the low spots. It would break your back but it wouldn't stall your car. To make matters worse, the armored car rode as though it were sprung with steel bars. "Better keep your mouth closed," Novotny said. Then added, "No offense meant."

Morath never saw the fort until they were almost on top of it—cement walls, broken by firing slits, built into the mountainside, and independent blockhouses hidden in the natural sweep of the terrain. The general, clearly proud of the work, said, "Now you see it, now you don't."

Morath was impressed and showed it.

The spy smiled, pleased with the reaction.

Inside, the raw smell of new cement and damp earth. As they went down endless flights of stairs, Novotny said, "They have elevators in the Maginot Line. For people, elevators. But here, only the ammunition gets to ride." A shaft had been carved out of the rock, Morath could see, with a steel platform on cables that could be operated electrically or cranked by hand.

The spy's German was atrocious. "So many forts are blown up from their own magazines. It need not happen."

Novotny was joined by a group of officers who manned the fort. As they moved down a long corridor, the general put out a hand so that Morath stayed back from the group. "How do you like my engineer?"

"Who is he?"

"A fortification expert—artist is a better word. From the Savoy. They've been building these things since the renaissance—tradition of Leonardo, all that."

"He's Italian?"

The general spread his hands. "French by passport, Italian by culture, though he would say Savoyard, and a Jew by birth." The Savoy, a mountain country between France and Italy, had managed to keep its independence until 1860. "They've always permitted Jews to serve as officers," the general said. "This one was a major. Now he works for me."

At the end of a cement chamber, under a six-foot ceiling, an embrasure opened out above a forest valley. The Czech officers stood apart, hands clasped behind their backs, as the general and the spy and Morath approached the opening.

"Find a river," the spy said.

This took time. A pale summer sky, then a ridge top dense with trees, then a green mountainside and a narrow valley that led to the upward slope where the fort had been built. Finally, Morath caught sight of a blue ribbon that wound through the pine trees.

"You have it?"

"Yes."

"Here. Take."

He handed Morath a fist-sized wad of cotton. Two soldiers rolled a 105-millimeter mountain gun up to the opening and ran a shell into the breech. Morath tore pieces of cotton from the wad and stuffed his ears, then covered them with his hands. Everyone in the room did the same. Finally, the general mouthed the word *ready?* Morath nodded and the floor trembled as a tongue of flame leapt from the barrel of the cannon. Even with the cotton, the report was deafening.

Downrange, a flash and a drift of dirty gray smoke. In the river, Morath thought, though he didn't actually see it happen. Other guns began firing, some from the floor below them, some from the blockhouses, and puffs of smoke floated over the mountainside. The general handed Morath a pair of binoculars. Now he could see fountains of dirt blown forty feet in the air, trees torn from the ground or sheared in two. There was, in fact, a small road that led down to the river. As he watched, a cloud of orange tracers floated past his vision and churned up a storm of dirt spouts on the road.

The spy pointed to his ears. Morath took the cotton out, the room still rang with concussion. "Do you see?" the spy said.

"Yes."

"All the firing lines intersect, and the forts cover each other, so an attempt to storm will be very costly." He reached into the inside pocket of his jacket and produced a few sheets of paper and a sharpened pencil. "Please," he said. "Do best you can."

The general said, "I can't give you blueprints, of course, but we don't mind if you sketch."

The spy smiled. "My father always wanted to teach the espionage drawing. 'So terrible,' he would say."

They left him to work, only Novotny stayed behind. "Well, now you've met our expert."

"He seems a little—odd, maybe."

"Yes. He is very odd. But a genius. An architect, a mathematician, a gunnery expert. Also he knows geology and mining science." Novotny shook his head. "Likely there's more, we just haven't found out about it."

Morath sketched, he wasn't very good. He concentrated on showing how the fort and its independent firing points were fitted tight into the mountainside. They would be hard to bomb, he realized. Even a Stuka would have to fly directly at them, with machine guns tracking it the minute it appeared over the crest of the mountain.

"Draw the room," Novotny said. "Don't forget the elevator for the shells."

His day had barely begun. They drove him to other forts. At one of them, overlooking a paved road that ran south from Dresden, the spy took a stick and drew semicircles in the dirt to show overlapping fields of fire. Morath crawled into two-man pillboxes, sighted along machine guns aimed down mown strips of cornfield, saw tank traps to fall in and tank traps made of cement posts, "dragon's teeth," wound in generous tangles of barbed wire. He squinted through Swiss sniperscopes fitted to Steyr rifles and fired a ZGB 33, the Czech machine gun made in Brno—used as the model for the British Bren, Brno/Enfield—assassinating eight feather pillows gathering for an attack at the far end of a wheatfield. "Good shooting," Novotny said.

After Morath reloaded, the curved-box magazine locked in place with a loud metallic snap.

"When you talk about your trip to the mountains," Novotny said, "don't forget to mention that Europe would be better off if Adolf did not have control of the Czech machine shops."

Morath agreed. "Of course," he said, "if it should come to that, I imagine the workers here would be—prone to error."

But his conspiratorial smile was not returned. "Just between us," Novotny said, "if it should happen that we are betrayed by those who claim to be our friends, we may not be so quick to give our lives in their service. That sort of business is bloody, Morath. There is always interrogation, always reprisal—you can only create a resistance movement when people don't care about their lives."

Novotny drove him back to the Europa that evening. A fine summer dusk, flights of swallows swooping and climbing in the sky above the hotels. In the lobby, the mother and daughter smiled at him, looking warmer than ever. *Who would know?* On a leather couch, a man in muttonchop whiskers and mountaineering costume was reading the *Völkischer Beobachter.* CZECH POLICE BURN SUDETEN FARMS went the headline. DOZENS INJURED. Animals confiscated. Dogs shot. Three young women missing.

Dr. Lapp, wearing a flat-brimmed straw boater at a jaunty angle, was waiting for him in the room, fanning himself with a room-service menu.

"I didn't hear you knock," Morath said.

"Actually, I did knock," Dr. Lapp said, slightly amused. "Of course, I'll be happy to apologize, if you wish."

"Don't bother."

Dr. Lapp stared out the window. The streetlamps were on, couples strolling in the mountain air. "You know, I cannot abide these people, the Czechs."

Morath hung up his jacket, then began undoing his tie. He did not want there to be a war in Europe, but he was going to take a bath.

"They have no culture," Dr. Lapp said.

"They think they do."

"What, Smetana? Perhaps you like Dvorak. Good God."

Morath took off his tie, looped it over a hanger, sat on the edge of the bed, and lit a Chesterfield.

"I should mention," Dr. Lapp said, "that I saw Count Polanyi not so long ago and that he sends his best regards. He said that you were considering, at one time, a vacation in Britain. Is it so?"

"Yes."

Dr. Lapp nodded. "Can you still go?"

Morath thought about Cara. "Maybe," he said. "Maybe not."

"I see. Well, if you can, you should."

"I'll try," Morath said.

"They're weakening, the British. This morning's London *Times* says that the Czech government ought to grant 'self-determination' to the Sudeten Germans, 'even if it should mean their secession from Czechoslovakia.' I would suppose that comes from Chamberlain's office. We know he met American correspondents at a lunch at Lady Astor's a few weeks ago and told them that Britain thought the Sudetenland ought to be turned over to Germany. In the interest of world peace, you understand. What his problem really is, is that he doesn't trust the French, he doesn't trust the Russians, and he fears, politically, the possibility that Britain might have to fight alone."

"He doesn't trust the French?"

Dr. Lapp's laugh was dry, and delicate, and very brief.

It was almost dark, they sat in silence for a long time. Finally, Dr. Lapp stood. "There is something I want you to look at," he said. "I'll send it along tomorrow, if you don't mind."

He closed the door silently behind him. Morath left the room in darkness. He went into the bathroom and turned on the water. There was a bright green mineral stain below the spout. *Good for the health*. If you believed in it, he thought. The water ran slow, just then, and Morath waited patiently and listened to the distant thunder.

He booked a call to Paris early the next morning, the hotel operator rang his room an hour later. "So much traffic, sir," she apologized. "Not usual for August."

In Paris, a very elegant voice: "Good morning, this is Cartier."

Polanyi liked to say that the great fault in poets was that they never sang of the power of money in affairs between men and women. "So for that we are left to the mercy of cynics—bartenders, novelists, or lubricious aunts." Amusing when he said it but not so amusing in real life. Morath didn't like himself for making this telephone call, but he could think of nothing else. The other possibility was flowers, and flowers weren't enough.

He found himself telling the saleswoman almost everything. "I understand," she said. She thought a moment, then added, "We have just completed a new design, a bracelet, which might be exactly right for Madame. A little exotic—emeralds set in silver and black onyx—but very personal. And not at all the usual thing. Do you think she would like that?"

"Yes."

"She would be the first in Paris to have it—it's a new style for us. Would she like *that?*"

He knew she would. The saleswoman explained that the size was easily adjusted—so the bracelet could be sent by Cartier messenger to the residence. "And finally, *monsieur*"—now there was a different note in her voice, she was, for a moment, speaking from the heart—"the card."

"Just say, 'Love, Nicky.' "

Later on, he was able to get through to an officer at the Crédit Lyonnais. A bank draft would be sent over to Cartier that afternoon.

Novotny showed up at eleven and they worked most of the day, spending much of the time in the car, driving east on the northern borders of Moravia and Bohemia. More fortifications, more barbed wire, more artillery pointed toward Germany. "What happens to all this," he asked, "if the Sudetenland is granted independence?"

Novotny laughed. "Then it all belongs to Hitler," he said. "With good, flat roads running straight to Prague. A hundred kilometers, more or less, about two hours."

By nightfall they had turned back to the west, headed for the Kreslice barracks and a regimental dinner—a farewell dinner—with the general in attendance. "There may be a speech," Novotny said.

He paused a moment, peering into the darkness to find his way. They rattled over the crest of a mountain, then Novotny rode the brakes down the steep grade on the other side. "Decin," he said—a cluster of lights in the trees. This was, Morath thought, one last demonstration: that Czech forces could move east and west without returning to the roads in the valleys. They'd improved the old village paths, used mostly for cows and goats. In the beams of the headlights he could see where holes had been filled with small stones and packed down flat.

"And then, after the speech . . ." Novotny said.

"Yes?" *Oh no, he would refuse.*

"Perhaps you would consider . . ."

Morath was blinded. An explosion of yellow light, then blackness, with the dazzling afterimage of a fiery star. He pressed his hands against his eyes but it wouldn't fade. Something had burnt the air in front of his face then gone whizzing away into the trees. Novotny yelled—apparently in Czech, Morath didn't understand. He shoved the door open, then reached for Novotny, who seemed frozen in place. As he grabbed hold of a sleeve there were two pings, metal on metal, and another tracer bullet, this one on the other side of the windshield. Morath could hear the machine gun, firing disciplined, five-round bursts. When he smelled gasoline he pulled with all his strength, dragging Novotny across the seat and out the passenger door.

Lying flat on the ground, he rubbed his eyes as the star began to fade.

"Can you see?" Novotny was now back in German.

"Not much."

From the front of the car, a loud bang as a round hit the engine block, followed by the sharp smell of steam from the radiator. "Christ," Morath said. He began to crawl away from the road, pulling Novotny with him. He fought his way into a tangle of vines and branches, a thorn raked him across the forehead. He could now see gray shapes resolving into trees and forest. He took a deep breath—a burned retina meant blindness for life and Morath knew it.

"What about you?" he said.

"Better." Novotny probed his hairline with an index finger. "The thing actually burned me," he said.

The machine gunner wouldn't leave the car alone. He stitched frosted holes in the window glass, then blew out the tires on the traverse. Morath could hear gunfire in the distance, and an orange light flickered on a cloud above the town.

"Is it the invasion?" Morath said.

Novotny snorted with contempt. "It's the oppressed Sudeten Germans," he said. "Crying out for justice and equality."

Morath got to his knees. "We'll be better off in Decin."

"I can't," Novotny said, "without the stick."

Morath crawled back to the car, opened the back door, lay flat on the seat, and retrieved the walking stick and the holstered pistol. Novotny was glad to have both. He staggered to his feet, held the butt of the pistol, unsnapped the holster with his teeth, and swept the belt over his shoulder as the pistol slid free. "Now let them come," he said, laughing at himself and the whole stupid business.

They walked through the woods, Novotny limping along and breathing hard but keeping up with Morath. As it turned out, they were fortunate he was in uniform—a sixteen-year-old militiaman with a machine pistol almost cut them down as they reached Decin.

Headed for the police station, they kept to the alleys, the walls pocked and chipped from small-arms fire. "I knew there was trouble here," Morath said. "Marching and rioting, you see it in the newsreels. But nothing like this."

From Novotny, a sour smile. "These are commando units, armed and trained by the SS. You won't see *that* in the newsreels."

The alley ended at a side street, Morath and Novotny crouched at the edge of a stucco wall. To their left, on the other side of a broad avenue, the town school was on fire, bursts of red sparks blown up into the night sky. There were two bodies lit by the firelight, their faces pressed into the angle between the street and the sidewalk. One of them had a bare foot.

"Go ahead," Morath said. There was some small nobility in this—*first across the road* was a sacred axiom under fire. The enemy gunners saw the first, shot the second.

"Thanks just the same," Novotny said. "We'll go together."

Even so, Morath took the side toward the gunfire, ran out of bravado midway across, grabbed Novotny around the waist and the two of them galloped to cover—a three-legged race—laughing like madmen as bullets sang past them.

It took them twenty minutes to reach the police station, where a shredded Czech flag hung limp above the barred windows. "Poor fucking thing," said the Decin chief of police. "These fucking people keep *shooting* it."

A strange scene at the station house. Policemen, some off duty when the attack came—one of them firing a rifle out the window with a forgotten napkin tucked in his belt—a few soldiers, local citizens. In the corner, lying flat on a desk, holding a compress to a bloody head wound, was a tall, spare man in a high collar and cutaway coat, one of the lenses in his eyeglasses was cracked in half.

"Our Latin teacher," the police chief explained. "They beat him up. Forced their way into the school, started throwing Czech schoolbooks out in the street, set them on fire, started *singing*, you know, and set the school on fire. Then they marched around the neighborhood chanting *Teach our children in German* while a little man filmed from the roof of a car.

"We did—nothing. We're under orders up here: don't let them provoke you. So we smiled and bowed, unprovoked, got the nurse over here to paste the Latin teacher back together, and everything was just perfectly lovely.

"But, of course, *they* were under orders to provoke us or else, so they went and took a shot at a policeman. He shot back, everyone ran away, and now we have this."

"You radioed the army?" Novotny said.

The policeman nodded. "They're coming. In armored cars. But they've got four or five of these things to deal with, so it might not be right away."

"You have weapons for us," Morath said. It wasn't a question.

Before the police chief could answer, Novotny spoke to him in rapid Czech. Then, later on, he explained as they moved toward the safe end of town. "I'm sorry," he said. "But they'd *kill* me if I let anything happen to you."

But the safe end of town wasn't all that safe. At the bottom of a winding street, they found the milkman's horse and cart, the milkman himself lying facedown on the cobblestones, the back of his jacket flung up over his head. The blinkered horse, standing patiently with his wagonload of milk cans, turned and stared at them as they went past.

The chief of police had directed them to a three-story brick monstrosity, perhaps the grandest house in Decin, on a broad boulevard shadowed by linden trees. The building was guarded by two policemen wearing French-style helmets and armed with rifles. They followed one of them to an overstuffed parlor on the top floor, the walls crowded with oil portraits of very fat people in very expensive clothing. As Morath and Novotny settled in, a local functionary came puffing up the stairs carrying two ledgers, a clerk and a secretary close behind him with two more. Still wheezing, he stopped dead, bowed politely, then spun on his heel and hurried off.

"His honor the mayor," said the policeman. "The Germans keep trying to burn the town hall, so he brings the tax records up here."

"Keep trying?"

The policeman nodded grimly. "Third time since March."

From the parlor window, Morath looked out over Decin. According to the policeman, the German units held several buildings—garages and small workshops on the north side of the town—and the railroad station. Morath saw them once or twice as they changed positions; shapeless forms in peaked caps and jackets, bent low, running close to the walls. Once he got a clear view of a machine gunner and his helper, caught for an instant in the glow of a streetlamp, one carrying a Maxim gun, the other its tripod and belts. Then they scurried away into the darkness, disappearing between the deserted office buildings on the other side of the boulevard.

Midnight. The crackle of small-arms fire intensified. Then the town lights went out, and, a few minutes later, a call came on the radio, and Novotny and the senior policeman returned to the station. The other policeman came upstairs, took his helmet off, and sat on a sofa. He was young, Morath saw, not much more than twenty. "The armored cars should come soon," he said.

Morath stared out into the street. It was hard to see, the warm, misty night darkened by smoke from the burning buildings. The distant firing slowed, then stopped, replaced by heavy silence. Morath looked at his watch. Two-twenty. Cara likely asleep, by now, on the avenue Bourdonnais, unless she'd gone out somewhere. The bracelet would have arrived that afternoon. Strange how far away that seemed. *Not so far.* He remembered the bars on the Mediterranean beach, the crash of the waves, people saying "half past eight in Juan-les-Pins, half past nine in Prague."

A low, distant rumble, resolving, as Morath listened, to the throb of heavy engines. The policeman leaped to his feet. He was openly relieved—Morath hadn't realized how frightened he'd been. "Now we'll see," he said, running his hand over a cowlick of wheat-colored hair. "Now we'll see."

Two of the armored cars crept up the boulevard, going no more than ten miles an hour. One of them broke off and headed for the north side of the town; the other stood in the middle of the street, its turret turning slowly as the gunner looked for a target. Somebody—somebody not very bright, Morath thought—shot at it. The response was a blast of the turret cannon, a yellow flare and a ragged boom that rolled over the empty streets.

"Idiot."

"A sniper," the policeman said. "He tries to fire into the aiming port of the turret."

They both stood at the window. As the armored car moved forward, there was a second shot.

"Did you see it?"

Morath shook his head.

"Sometimes you can." Now, quite excited, he spoke in a loud whisper. He knelt in front of the window, rested the rifle on the sill, and sighted down the barrel.

The armored car disappeared. From the other end of town, a serious engagement—cannon and machine-gun fire. Morath, leaning out the window, thought he could see flickers of light from the muzzle flashes. Something exploded, an armored car sped past, headed in the direction of the fighting. And something was on fire. Very slowly, the outlines of the buildings sharpened, touched with orange light. Downstairs, in the kitchen, an angry burst of static from the radio. The policeman swore softly, under his breath, as he ran off to answer it.

Four in the morning. The policeman was snoring away on the couch while Morath kept watch. The policeman had apologized for being so tired. "We spent two days in the street," he said. "Fighting them with batons and shields." Morath smoked to stay awake, making sure to keep well away from the window when he lit a match, cloaking the end of the cigarette with his hand. At one point, to his amazement, a freight train came through the town. He could hear it from a long way off. It didn't stop, the slow chuffing of the locomotive moved from east to west, and he listened to it until the sound faded away into the distance.

A silhouette.

Morath came wide awake, crushed the cigarette out on the floor, snatched the rifle from the corner and rested it on the windowsill.

Was it there? He didn't think so. A ghost, a phantom—*the same phantoms we saw in Galicia.* Until the dawn.

But no. Not this time.

A shape, on one knee, tight to the wall of a building across the boulevard and very still. It stood, ran a few feet, and stopped again. It held, Morath thought, something in its hand.

He touched the bolt of the rifle, making sure it was locked, then let his finger rest gently against the trigger. When he squinted over the open sight, he lost the shape until it moved again. Then he tracked it as it stood, ran, and knelt down. Stood, ran, knelt down. Stood, ran.

Tracked, squeezed.

The policeman cried out and rolled off the couch. "What happened?" he said, breathless. "Are they here?"

Morath shrugged. "I saw something."

"Where is it?" The policeman knelt by his side.

Morath looked, there was nothing there.

But it was there an hour later, in gray light, when they crossed the boulevard. "A runner!" the policeman said. "To supply the sniper."

Maybe. Not much more than a kid, he'd been knocked backward and tumbled into a cellar entry and died there, halfway down the steps, arms flung out to stop his fall, a sandwich wrapped in newspaper dropped on the sidewalk.

At daybreak they walked back to the police station but it wasn't there anymore. What remained was a burned-out shell, blackened beams, smoke rising from the charred interior. One corner of the building had been blown out—a hand grenade, Morath thought, or a homemade bomb. There was no way to know; there was nobody left to tell the story. He stayed for a while, talking to the firemen as they wandered around and looked for something to do. Then an army captain showed up and drove him back to the hotel. "It wasn't only Novotny," he said. "We lost three others. They bicycled in from an observation post when they heard a call on the radio. Then there was the police chief, several officers, militia. At the end, they let the drunks out of the cells and gave them rifles." He shook his head, angry and disgusted. "Somebody said they tried to surrender when the building caught on fire but the Germans wouldn't let them." He was silent for a time. "I don't know, that might not be true," he said. "Or maybe it doesn't matter."

Back at the Europa, there was a spray of gladioli in a silver vase on a table in the lobby. In the room, Morath slept for an hour, couldn't after that. Ordered coffee and rolls, left most of it on the tray, and called the railroad station. "Of course they're running," he was told. As he hung up the phone, there was a knock at the door. "Fresh towels, sir."

Morath opened the door and Dr. Lapp settled himself in the easy chair.

"Well, where are my towels?"

"You know, I once actually did that. Back when. In a maid's uniform, pushing the little trolley."

"There must have been—at least a smile."

"No, actually not. The man who answered the door was the color of wood ash."

Morath started to pack, folding underwear and socks into his valise.

"By the way," Dr. Lapp said. "Have you met the two women who sit in the lobby?"

"Not really."

"Oh? You didn't, ah, avail yourself?"

A sideways glance. *I told you I didn't.*

"They were arrested last night, is the reason I ask. In this very room, as it happens. Taken through the lobby in handcuffs."

Morath stopped dead, a pair of silver hairbrushes in his hands. "Who were they?"

"Sudeten Germans. Likely working for the Sicherheitsdienst, SD, the SS intelligence service. It caused quite a stir downstairs. *In Marienbad! Well!* But the women hardly cared—they were laughing and joking. All the Czechs can do is keep them overnight in the police station, and they barely dare to do that."

Morath slipped the brushes through loops in a leather case, then zipped it closed.

Dr. Lapp reached in his pocket. "As long as you're packing." He handed over a cellophane envelope, an inch square. Fitted neatly within was a photographic negative cut from a strip of film. Morath held it up to the light and saw a typed document in German.

A death sentence. He'd put his drawings of the mountain fortifications in a manila folder and slid it down the side of the valise. He could, he thought, get away with that, even if he was searched. Could say it was a property for sale or a sketch for a planned ski lodge. But not this.

"What is it?"

"A memorandum, on Oberkommando Wehrmacht stationery. From General Ludwig Beck, who has just resigned as head of the OKW, to his boss, General von Brauchitsch, the commander in chief of the German army. It says that Hitler 'must abandon the intention of solving the Czech question by force.' Actually, he said a great deal more, in person, to do with getting rid of the Gestapo and the Nazi party bosses and returning Germany to 'probity and simplicity.' Then, in protest, he quit. And his successor, General Halder, believes these things even more strongly than Beck did."

"I will be asked how I came to have it."

Dr. Lapp nodded. "The Abwehr, military intelligence, is part of the OKW. We go to the same meetings, then, at night, to the same dinner parties." He crossed his legs, tapped the heel of his shoe, and gave Morath a look that said, *of course you know where to put that.* He leaned over the table, took the Hotel Europa butter knife from the place setting, held it to the light and studied its edge, then handed it to Morath.

Morath took off his shoe and went to work on the heel. He was very tired and sick of the world and had to force himself to be patient and careful. He prized up a corner of the heel and slid the negative in. It didn't work, he could see the space easily enough and he could feel it when he walked.

Dr. Lapp shrugged. "Improvisation," he said, letting his voice trail away into a sigh.

Morath finished packing, pulled the straps tight on his valise and buckled them.

"I don't know who you'll find to talk to, Herr Morath, but the more powerful the better. We're opening as many lines of communication as we can, surely one of them will work." From his voice, he didn't believe it, sounded as though he were trying to persuade himself that two and two was five. "All we ask of the English is that they do nothing." He looked up at Morath. "Is that asking too much?"

Morath glanced at his watch, lit a cigarette, and sat down to wait until it was time to leave for the train. It was quiet in the hotel: muffled voices in the hall, the sound of a maid's vacuum cleaner.

"My poor country," Dr. Lapp said. He hunted around in the inner pocket of his jacket, took out a pair of spectacles in a leather case, then a small metal box. "Perhaps you'd better have this."

Morath opened it and found a gold swastika pin. He fastened it to his breast pocket and went to look at himself in the bathroom mirror.

"Use it when you reach the German border," Dr. Lapp said, one hand on the doorknob. "But please do remember to take it off before you cross into France."

"The two women," Morath said. "Were they after me, in particular?"

Dr. Lapp shook his head slowly and looked sad. "God knows," he said. "I don't."

17 August. Bromley-on-Ware, Sussex.

Morath stood at the end of a gravel driveway as a taxi rattled off down the lane. Francesca's friend, Simon the lawyer, came smiling toward him, walking across the saintly lawn. He wore shorts and sandals, a shirt with the cuffs folded back, a jacket thrown over his shoulders, a pipe clenched in his teeth, and a newspaper under his arm. Behind him, a brick house with many chimneys, a blue sky, a white cloud.

Simon took his bag with one hand and his arm with the other and said, "So pleased you could come, Nicholas."

As Morath followed him toward the house, Cara came out, wearing a thin summer dress that floated as she ran. "Oh you are *terrible,* Nicky," she said, angry and forgiving in the same breath, holding him tight against her. Relieved, he thought, because she knew he had been up to something he couldn't talk about, but most of all unwilling to sulk at someone's country house. "You will have to make it up to me," she said as they went up the steps.

On the terrace, women in straw hats, men with white hair, a whiskey and soda for Morath.

"How do you do, name's Bromley."

So then it is your village, and your castle, and your peasants. "Good afternoon, Mr. Bromley."

"Heh, heh, that's 'Bramble'!"

"Mr. Bramble?"

"No, no. '*Bram*-well.' Yes. Hmm."

Cara's bare behind was blue in the Sussex moonlight. "Not so loud," she hissed.

"The bed squeaks—I can't help it."

"*Méchant!* We can't make noise like that. Here, lie on your back."

The bank of the river lay on the other side of a cow pasture. "Mind the cowpats," Simon told him.

They sat on a bench by a huge willow, where the sun sparkled on the water as it left the shadow of the tree. "I have an old friend," Morath said. "When he heard I was going to England for the August vacation, he asked me to take along some papers."

"Oh?" Simon had thought *the private conversation* would be about Cara, women, that sort of thing. "Papers?"

"Confidential papers."

"Oh." Simon had a mop of brown hair that he pushed back off his forehead. "Are you a spy then, Nicholas?"

"No. Just someone who doesn't like Hitler," Morath said. "Doesn't like Hitlers." He told Simon about the Czechoslovakian mountain defense and the memorandum from General Beck. "My friend believes," he explained, "that Hitler cannot be overthrown unless he fails. If your government holds firm, he will. One way or another."

Simon took a minute to think it over. "It's difficult, you see, because there are two sides to this. Like all politics, really. On one side, the side that doesn't want to get involved, is Nevile Henderson, the ambassador to Germany. Very pro-German—pro-Nazi, it is said—and very anti-Czech. But Chamberlain *does* listen to him. Then, on the other side, there are people like Vansittart, the adviser to the foreign secretary, who'd be more in Churchill's camp. So the question is, who do we talk to? For me, you see, Vansittart is the hero and Henderson the villain." *Un homme néfaste,* Simon called him. A man who does harm.

"But then, if I find you a friend who can talk to Vansittart, eventually, aren't you simply preaching to the choir?"

Morath thought Simon was in his late twenties but it sometimes amused him to be younger, to be terribly silly. Now, however, he seemed suddenly older, much older.

Simon stared down at the slow water. "So then," he said. "What to do."

Morath didn't know. The serenity of the countryside—of the country itself—was like the airs of springtime, it made the Continent and its intrigues seem foolish and brutal and distant.

In the end, Simon got on the telephone and had a word with a friend of a friend.

Who stopped by for a drink that very evening. Left alone on the terrace with the family spaniel, they stumbled along in Morath's hesitant English and the friend of a friend's university French. Still, they managed. Morath explained the defenses and handed over the memo and passed along Dr. Lapp's message as strongly as he could. He did somewhat better the following day, when friend of a friend—very good suit and military rank—brought along a smiling gnome who spoke Hungarian, Budapest Hungarian.

"We can always use a friend in Paris," they said to him.

Morath declined with a smile.

They were never quite rude, after that. Inquisitive. How did *he* come to be involved with this? Was he simply an officer in the VK-VI, the Hungarian intelligence service? Had he met *Germans*? But it was none of their business and he didn't tell them and was rescued, in the end, by Simon's mother, who came out on the terrace and talked and laughed and flirted at them until they went away.

·

August 1938, the summer before the war. At night, the wireless crackled and the cicadas whirred. The Czechs mobilized, the British fleet mobilized, Benes offered Henlein and the Sudetenlanders everything either of them could think of—starting with complete autonomy and going on from there. But, not enough. In England, gas masks were issued and air-raid trenches dug in London parks. "But what will become of *you*, Nicholas?" Simon's mother asked him at the lunch table.

He'd thought about that. More than he wanted to. He supposed he would be called back to duty, told to report to the regimental barracks, amid the chubby stockbrokers and balding lawyers, and ordered to fight alongside the Wehrmacht.

He discovered Cara, one night, wearing the Cartier bracelet, facedown on the bedspread, weeping into the pillow. "I shall tell my father," she whispered, "that we must sell one of the *estancias,* because I am going to buy a villa in Lugano."

At drinks the next day he was, *attacked* was the only word for it, by a neighbor in an army officer's uniform, fierce, and crimson with anger. The man had a totally incomprehensible accent—his words disappeared in a thick black mustache—and Morath took a step back and had no idea what to do. It was Simon who saved him, whisking him away because he simply must meet the uncle from Perth. They were terribly, almost violently, kind to him at the house in Sussex. One rainy afternoon, when everyone but Morath and Cara played bridge, they dug deep in a chest and extracted a faded jigsaw puzzle, *The Defeat of the Spanish Armada.*

Speaking of which:

On the twenty-sixth, the radio reported Admiral Horthy's visit to the Reich, to Kiel, ostensibly as the last commander in chief of the Austro-Hungarian navy, to christen a new German battleship, the *Prinz Eugen,* and to have, the BBC said, "private consultations with Chancellor Hitler." Nobody in the room looked at Morath; all eyes found something else infinitely more interesting. What the BBC didn't say, the Count Polanyi did, three weeks later when they met in Paris. The whole business was staged so that Hitler could tell Horthy this: "If you want to join in the meal, you must help with the cooking."

•

It took two cars to get them all to the railroad station, the maids and the gardener stood by the door when they drove away. The thirty-first of August turned out to be, of course, a diabolically perfect day. The sky chalk-blue, the children's-book clouds with chiseled edges, the little train from another time. Simon shook his hand and said, "We'll hope for the best, right?" Morath nodded. Cara dabbed at her eyes with a handkerchief and held on to Francesca as the train pulled in. And Simon's mother took his hands in hers. She had cool gray eyes and gave him a good long look. "I'm so glad you could come," she said. "And we do want you to come back, Nicholas. You'll try, won't you?"

He promised he would, and held her hands.

NIGHT
TRAIN
TO
BUDAPEST

PARIS THAT SEPTEMBER WAS TENSE AND BROODING, ON THE EDGE OF war, darker than Morath had ever known it. The *retour,* the return to daily life after the August vacation, was usually a sweet moment in Parisian life, but not that autumn. They came back to the office, the dinner party, the love affair, but Hitler was screaming at them from every newspaper stand and they had no taste for any of it. At Morath's morning café the waiter said, "Let them come and drop their bombs, I'm tired of waiting."

They couldn't bear it, the idea of another war—they'd never really recovered from the last one. The man who came home from the trenches and made love to his wife on the day the war ended in 1918 now had a nineteen-year-old son, just the right age for the army. On the sixth of September, the morning papers wondered if the Sudeten issue was really worth a world war. The next day, a *Times* of London editorial supported partition.

In Germany, the annual Nazi party rally in Nuremberg began on the sixth and was to end on the twelfth, with torchlight parades, gymnastic maidens, and, the grand finale, a speech in the colossal Hall of the Fifty Thousand, where the Führer promised to reveal what he had in mind for the Czechs.

On the tenth, Parisian radio reported Roosevelt's statement that it was "one hundred percent wrong" to assume the United States would join Britain and France in a war over Czechoslovakia. On the eleventh, the proprietor of the stationery store on the rue Richelieu showed Morath his old Lebel revolver from the Great War. "Well, here is *my* answer to all this," he said. Which answer was that? Suicide? Shooting a German tourist? Sniping at the Wehrmacht?

"He has us where he wants us," Polanyi said, at lunch on the quai de la Tournelle. "Did you see the newsreel of Horthy's arrival at Kiel station?" Morath hadn't. "You get a glimpse of me, just over Count Csaky's shoulder." Then he described how Hungary had been offered a return of disputed territories if she would agree to march into Slovakia when Hitler attacked the Czechs.

"Horthy declined. On the basis that we barely have an army, and what we have barely has guns and bullets," Polanyi said, then went on to repeat Hitler's remark about the meal and the cooking.

They were eating *blanquette de veau* at a table on the terrace of a Norman restaurant. Polanyi waited while two young men hurried past. "So naturally," he said, "some units are being recalled to service. But I made sure you weren't included in *that*." He ran a forkful of fried potatoes through a dish of mayonnaise, then paused before eating and said, "I trust I did the right thing."

Morath didn't bother to answer.

"Why waste your life in a barracks?" Polanyi said. "And besides, I need you with me."

Eight-thirty in the morning on the fourteenth of September—Chamberlain had flown to Berchtesgaden to consult with Hitler—the phone rang in Morath's apartment. It was Cara, in a voice he'd never heard her use. "I hope you will come over and say good-bye to me," she said.

He started to say "What—" but she hung up on him.

Twenty minutes later he was there. The door was open, he walked in. Two men in blue smocks were packing Cara's clothing in the drawers of a large steamer trunk, its wardrobe side already crammed with dresses on little hangers. A third man, bigger than the others, stood and watched them, his arms folded across his chest. A chauffeur or a bodyguard, Morath thought, with a heavy face and a collarless jacket. When Morath came into the room he took a half step toward him and let his arms hang by his sides.

Cara was sitting on the edge of the bed, the Picasso nude in its gold frame held on her knees. "Monsieur Morath," she said, her voice dull and flat, "allow me to present my father, Señor Dionello."

A short man, sitting in the bedroom chair, got to his feet. He had a black-and-white mustache and wore a double-breasted suit with black and white stripes and a black Borsalino-style hat. He said "Sir" in Spanish, tipped his hat, and shook hands. It was clear to Morath that he was not pleased to meet his daughter's forty-four-year-old lover, Hungarian lover, Parisian lover, but he would agree not to make a scene if Morath didn't.

Morath sought Cara's eyes—*What do you want me to do?* Family was family, but he was not going to allow her to be abducted against her will.

She shook her head and closed her eyes. It was subtle, a small, fragile gesture of surrender, but she'd told him what he needed to know.

His heart sank, he'd lost her.

Señor Dionello spoke to her in rapid Spanish, his voice not unkind.

"It's the war, Nicky," Cara said. "My father expresses his regrets, but my mother and grandmother are sick with worry, he says, that I will be, hurt."

Señor Dionello smiled ruefully at Morath as Cara spoke, in his expression a plea for understanding, a plea that he not be forced to use power or money to get his way.

"My father is staying at the Meurice, I am to join him there for a few days, until the boat leaves."

Morath nodded to Señor Dionello, forcing himself to be as gracious as he could.

Señor Dionello spoke again and smiled at Morath. "My father

would be pleased if you would join us for dinner at the hotel." She hesitated, then said, "It's a lot for him, Nicky."

Morath declined. Cara translated, then said, *"Un momentito, por favor."*

As they went out into the hall, Señor Dionello made a small gesture and the bodyguard stayed where he was.

In the hall, Cara clenched his shirt in her fists and sobbed, silently, with her face pressed against him. Then she pushed him away, wiped the tears off with her hand, took two steps toward the door, looked at him one last time, and went back into the apartment.

On the twenty-first of September, Chamberlain tried again. Flew to Bad Godesberg and offered Hitler what he said he wanted. The Sudetenland, with French and British approval, would become a German possession. But the Führer didn't quite work the way Chamberlain thought he did. Once he got what he wanted, he wanted more. Now it was military occupation, by October 1.

Or else, war.

So, on the twenty-ninth, Chamberlain flew back to Germany, this time to Munich, and agreed to the occupation. The Czechoslovakian army abandoned its forts and moved back from the mountains.

18 October.

Morath stared out the train window, a tiny village slid away down the track. Was it called Szentovar? Maybe. Or that was another place, a hundred kilometers and a hundred years away from Budapest, where the peasants still rubbed garlic on barn doors to keep the vampires from milking the cows at night.

On the road, a Gypsy wagon. The driver looked up just as Morath's window went by. Prosperously fat, with three chins and clever eyes, perhaps a *primas,* a clan leader. He held the reins loosely in his hands and turned and said something to the women in the wagon behind him. Morath never saw their faces, simply the red and yellow colors of their clothing as the train clattered past.

October was a dead month, he thought. The brutal politics played out in the newspapers. The French relaxed, congratulated themselves on having done the right thing, the *smart* thing, for once in their dreamy lives. Morath smoked too much and stared out the window when he woke up in the morning.

He was surprised at his broken heart. He had always told himself that the love affair with Cara was a passing thing that stayed. But now she was gone, he missed what he'd taken for granted, and he ached for what she'd lost. "When I lived in Paris," she would say to her friends in Buenos Aires.

Count Polanyi didn't care for this mood and let Morath know it. "We've all been thrown off the horse," he said. "The thing to do is get back in the saddle." When that didn't work, he tried harder. "This is no time to feel sorry for yourself. Need something to do? Go back to Budapest and save your mother's life."

Keleti Palyuadvar. The east railroad station where, this being Hungary, all important trains arrived from the west. There were cabs in the street but Morath decided to walk—in the late afternoon of an autumn day, what else. *It is your nose that tells you you're home,* he thought. Burnt coffee and coal dust, Turkish tobacco and rotten fruit, lilac water from the barbershops, drains and damp stone, grilled chicken, God only knew what it really was. A deep breath, another—Morath inhaled his childhood, his country, the exile returned.

He walked for a long time, taking the cobbled alleys, heading more or less across the city, toward a villa in the hills of the Third District, on the Buda side of the Danube. He dawdled, stopped to look in shop windows. As always, this time of day, a melancholy, speculative idleness settled over the city and Morath slowed down to meet its rhythm. At five-thirty, when the sun hit the windows of a tenement on Kazinczy Avenue and turned them flaming gold, Morath took the number-seven tram across the Chain Bridge and went home.

They didn't really talk until the next morning. In the living room, the rugs were still up for the summer, so when his mother spoke there was a faint echo. She sat, perfectly composed, on a spindly chair in front of the French doors, a silhouette in garden light. She was, as always, slim and lovely, with ice-colored hair set in steel and pale skin that showed in the vee of her silk dress.

"And do you see Lillian Frei?" she asked.

"Now and then. She always asks for you."

"I miss her. Does she still wear the suits from De Pinna?"

"Where?"

"A store on Fifth Avenue, in New York."

Morath shrugged politely, he had no idea.

"In any event, you'll kiss her for me."

Morath drank a sip of coffee.

"Would you care for a pastry, Nicholas? I can send Malya to Gundel's."

"No, thank you."

"Bread and butter, then."

"Really, just coffee."

"Oh Nicholas, what a *Parisian* you are. You're sure?"

Morath smiled. He'd never in his life been able to eat anything before noon. "How long has it been, *anyuci,* since you've seen Paris?" This was *mother,* very much her preference. She had never been *mama.*

His mother sighed. "Oh a long time," she said. "Your father was alive, the war just over. 1919—could that be right?"

"Yes."

"Has it changed? People say it has."

"There are more automobiles. Electric signs. Cheap restaurants on the boulevards. Some people say it's not as nice as it was."

"Here it is the same."

"*Anyuci?*"

"Yes?"

"Janos Polanyi feels that, with the situation in Germany, you, and perhaps Teresa, should consider, should find a place . . ."

When she smiled, his mother was still incredibly beautiful. "You haven't come all the way here for *that,* I hope. Ferenc Molnar has moved to New York. He is living at the Plaza and is said to be utterly miserable."

A long look, mother and son.

NIGHT TRAIN TO BUDAPEST · 127

"I won't leave my house, Nicholas." *And how can you not have known it?*

They went to the movies in the afternoon. A British comedy, dubbed in Hungarian, from the 1920s. It had a cruise ship, nightclubs with shiny floors, a hound called Randy, a hero with patent-leather hair called Tony, a blonde with kiss curls that they fought over, called Veronica, which sounded very strange in Hungarian.

Morath's mother loved it—he glanced over and saw her eyes shining like a child's. She laughed at every joke and ate caramels from a little bag. During a song-and-dance sequence at the nightclub, she hummed along with the music:

> Akor mikor, Lambeth utodon
> Bar melyek este, bar melyek napon,
> Ugy találnád hogy mi mind is
> Sétalják a Lambeth Walk. Oi!

> Minden kis Lambeth leany
> Az ö kis, Lambeth parjával
> Ugy találnád hogy ök
> Sétalják a Lambeth Walk. Oi!

Afterward, they went to the tearoom of the Hotel Gellert and had acacia honey and whipped cream on toasted cake.

3:30 in the morning. In the rambling, iron-gated gardens of the villa district, some people kept nightingales. Other than that, he could hear wind in the autumn leaves, a creak in a shutter, a neighbor's fountain, a distant rumble of thunder—north, he thought, in the mountains.

Still, it was hard to sleep. Morath lay in his old bed and read Freya Stark—this was the third time he'd started it, a travel narrative, adventures in the wild mountain valleys of Persia.

He'd always stayed up late in this house, his father's very own son. He used to hear him, sometimes, pacing around the living room. Often he played records on the Victrola while he worked in his office—sliding stamps into glassine envelopes with a silver tweezers.

They weren't rich, but his father never worked for money. He had been one of the great philatelists of Hungary, very strong in both nineteenth-century Europe and colonials. Morath supposed his father had traded in the international markets, perhaps he'd made some money that way. Then, too, before the war, nobody really had to work. At least, nobody they knew.

But, after Trianon, everything changed. Families lost the income they'd had from land in the countryside. Even so, most of them managed, they simply had to learn to improvise. It became fashionable to say things like "If only I could afford to live the way I live."

Then, on a June day in 1919, the communists killed his father.

In the spasms of political chaos that followed the loss of the war, there came a Soviet Republic of Hungary—a government born of a national desperation so deluded it persuaded itself that Lenin and the Red Army would save them from their enemies, the Serbs and the Roumanians.

The Soviet was led by a Hungarian journalist named Bela Kun who, while serving in the Austro-Hungarian army, had deserted to the Russians during the war. Kun, his henchman Szamuelly, and forty-five commissars began a rule of one hundred and thirty-three days, and shot and burned and hanged their way from one end of Hungary to the other. They were then chased out of the country—across the border and, eventually, into the Lubianka—by a Roumanian army, which occupied Budapest, wandered aimlessly about the countryside, and spent its days in desultory looting until it was shooed back across the border by a Hungarian army, led by Miklos Horthy. The counterrevolution then gave birth to the White Terror, which shot and burned and hanged its way from one end of Hungary to the other, paying particular attention to the Jews, since Jews were Bolsheviks (or bankers), and Kun and a number of his comrades were Jewish.

It was one of Kun's wandering bands that murdered Morath's father. He had gone, one weekend, to the country house in the Carpathian foothills. The communist militia rode into the yard at dusk, demanded jewelry for the oppressed masses, then bloodied the farm manager's nose, threw Morath's father into a horse trough, took three stamp albums—1910 commemoratives from Luxembourg—all the cash they could find, several shirts, and a lamp. They chased the servant girls into the woods but couldn't catch them and, in one corner of the kitchen, set a fire, which burned a hole in the pantry wall and went out.

Morath's father dried himself off, calmed the servant girls, put a cold spoon on old Tibor's neck to stop the bleeding, then poured a small glass of plum brandy and sat down in his favorite chair, where, with his glasses folded up and held gently in one hand, he died.

Morath went to his sister's house for dinner. A new villa, also in the Third District but up in the newly elegant quarter known as Rose Hill. His sister, in a low-cut dress and red felt boots with tiny mirrors on them—oh, Cara—gave him a sexy hug and a warm kiss on the lips. "I'm so happy to see you, Nicholas. I am." She didn't let him go until a maid came into the room.

This was not new. She was three years older than Morath. When he was nine and she was twelve, she liked to comb his hair, would slip into his bed during a scary thunderstorm, would always know when he was melancholy and be tender to him.

"Teresa," he said. "My only love." They both laughed.

Morath looked around. There was too much furniture in the Duchazy house, much too expensive and much too new. How his sister could have married that idiot Duchazy was beyond him. They had three children, including a ten-year-old Nicholas—the absolute image of that idiot Duchazy.

Still, Teresa had married him, and her days of worrying about money were long over. The Duchazy family owned flour mills—thirty years earlier there'd been more mills in Budapest than in any other city in the world. Morath's mother, who disliked Duchazy even more than he did, would refer to him in private as "the miller."

Not the typical miller. He strode toward Morath and embraced him. He was a sinewy man with uncomfortably stiff posture, a pencil mustache, and strange, pale-green eyes. Well then, how was Paris? Still in the advertising business? Still a bachelor? What a life! The children were brought out, shown off, and put away. Duchazy poured brandies and had the fire lit.

The conversation wandered here and there. The Duchazy family was not exactly *nyilas* but close enough. Teresa warned him with a glance, more than once, when he was headed into a sensitive area. By the end of the second brandy, Duchazy had thrown a second log on the fire, which blazed merrily in a newly installed surround of yellow tile.

"Janos Polanyi thinks Mother ought to leave Budapest," Morath said.

"Why is that?" Duchazy was annoyed.

"War," Morath said.

Teresa shrugged. "She won't go."

"Maybe if you two considered it, she might."

"But we won't," Duchazy said. "We're patriots. Besides, I think it's going to go on this way for a long time." He meant diplomacy, marches, street fighting—the sort of thing they'd seen in the Sudetenland. "Hitler means to dominate the Balkans," he continued. "Someone's going to, it might as well be him. And he wants it quiet in Hungary and south of here—that's the granary, and the oil fields. I don't think the British dare to fight him, but, if it comes to that, he'll need the wheat and the oil. Anyhow, if we're smart, we'll stay in his good graces, because the borders are going to start moving."

"They already are," Teresa said.

That was true. Hungary, having supported the occupation of the Sudetenland, was to be rewarded with the return of some of its northern territory, especially in lower Slovakia, where the population was eighty-five percent Magyar.

"Laszlo's brother is fighting up in Ruthenia," Teresa said.

Morath found this puzzling. Duchazy gave his wife the look that meant *you've been indiscreet.*

"Really?" Morath said.

Duchazy shrugged. "Nothing's secret around here." He meant, Morath thought, the house, Budapest, the nation itself.

"In Ruthenia?"

"Near Uzhorod. We're in it with the Poles. They have irregulars, in the north, and we have the Rongyos Garda." The Ragged Guard.

"What's *that?*"

"Arrow Cross men, the street-corner boys and what have you, led by a few army officers in civilian clothing. They're fighting the Sich, the Ukrainian militia. The next thing is, local Hungarians demand an end to the instability, and we send in the regular army. This used to be Hungary, after all, why should it belong to the Czechs?"

Jackals, Morath thought. Now that the prey was down they'd tear off a piece for themselves.

"The world's changing," Duchazy said. His eyes sparkled. "And about time."

Dinner was exceptional. Deviled carp with onions, cabbage stuffed with ground pork, and a Médoc from the Duchazy estates near Eger.

After dinner, Teresa left the men to themselves, and Morath and Duchazy sat by the fire. Cigars were lit, and for a time they smoked in companionable silence. "One thing I did want to ask you," Duchazy said.

"Yes?"

"A few of us have gotten together to support Szalassy. Can I put you down for a contribution?" Szalassy was one of the leaders of the Arrow Cross.

"Thank you for asking, but not right now," Morath said.

"Mmm. Oh well, I promised some people I'd ask."

"I don't mind."

"Do you ever see Colonel Sombor, at the legation?"

"I'm hardly ever there."

"Oh. He asked for you. I thought maybe you were friends."

Tuesday. In the late afternoon, Morath took a trolley to the Kobanya district, where factory walls rose high above the track on both sides of the street. There was a smoky haze, as evening came on, and a light rain dappled the surface of the river. A young woman sat across from him, she had the liquid radiance of some Hungarian girls and long hair that blew across her face as the trolley went around a curve. She swept it back with one hand and glanced at Morath. The trolley stopped in front of a brewery, and the girl got off in a crowd of workmen. Some of them knew her, called her by name, and one of them gave her a hand down from the high step.

The slaughterhouse was at the next stop, where a metal sign bolted to the brickwork said GERSOVICZY. When Morath got off the trolley, the air was like ammonia and made his eyes water. It was a long way to the entrance that led to the office, past loading docks with open doors where he could see red carcasses hung on hooks and butchers in leather aprons. One of them rested a sledgehammer in the sawdust, the iron head beaten flat at both ends, while he took a minute to smoke a cigarette.

"The office?"

"Upstairs. Just keep going till you see the river."

In the Gersoviczy brothers' office there was a desk with a telephone and an adding machine, an ancient safe in one corner, a clothes tree behind the door. The brothers were waiting for him. They wore black homburgs and heavy suits and silver ties, and they had the long sidelocks and beards of Orthodox Jews. On the wall was a Hebrew calendar with a picture of a rabbi blowing a ram's horn. Across the top it said, in Hungarian, *Gersoviczy Brothers Wish You a Happy and Prosperous New Year.*

A soot-blackened window looked out over the Danube, lights twinkling on a hill above the far bank. The brothers, both smoking oval cigarettes, peered at Morath through the gloom of the unlit office.

"You are Morath *Uhr*?" He used the traditional form of address, Morath Sir.

"Yes. Count Polanyi's nephew."

"Please do sit down. I'm sorry we cannot offer you anything."

Morath and the older brother, his beard streaked with silver, took the two wooden swivel chairs, as the younger brother leaned on the edge of the desk. "I am Szimon Gersoviczy," he said. "And this is Herschel." The older brother gave him a stiff nod.

Szimon spoke heavily accented Hungarian. "We're Polish," he explained. "From Tarnopol, twenty years ago. Then we came down here. Half of Galicia came here, a hundred years ago. We came for the same reason, to get away from the pogroms, to get a little opportunity. And it worked out like that. So, we stayed, and we Magyarized the name. It used to be just Gersovicz."

The older brother finished his cigarette and stubbed it out in a tin ashtray. "Your uncle came to us for help, that was in September. I don't know if he told you."

"Not then, no."

"Well, he did. Through our brother-in-law, in Paris. He asked if we would help, help the country. He saw the handwriting on the wall, as they say."

He paused a moment. Outside, the drumming of a tugboat engine, hauling a line of barges north on the river.

"We don't *ask* for anything," he went on, "but now Polanyi knows, and you know, so . . ."

Szimon went over to the safe and began to work the combination. Then he pulled the handles to the up position and swung the doors open. Herschel leaned close to Morath. He smelled strong, of sweat and onions, cigarettes.

"It's in pengo," he said. "Maybe if the community was more involved, we could make it in something else. But the Count wanted it kept close, so it's just a few people. Szimon and me, our family, you know, one or two others, but mostly us."

Szimon began stacking piles of pengo on the desk, each fifty notes pinned at the corner. He flipped the ends of the stacks, wet his thumb, then counted in Yiddish as he shuffled through the bills. Herschel laughed. "For some reason," he said, "it's hard to do that in Hungarian."

Morath shook his head. "Nobody ever thought it would come to this," he said.

"Forgive me, sir, but it always comes to this."

"*Zvei hundrit toizend,*" Szimon said.

"What will you call it?"

"I don't know. The Free Hungary Committee—something like that."

"In Paris?"

"Or London. If the country is occupied, the best place is the closest place. Closest safe place."

"So, do you like New York?"

"God forbid."

Szimon finished counting, then squared the stacks off by tapping the edges on the desk. "Four hundred thousand pengo," he said. "About the same in French francs. Or, just in case God doesn't forbid, eighty thousand dollars."

"Tell me one thing," Herschel said. "Do you think the country will be occupied? Some people say sell and get out."

"And lose everything," Szimon said. He slid the money across the desk—thousand-pengo notes, wider than French currency, with black and red engravings of Saint Istvan on one side and a castle on the other. Morath opened a briefcase, placed the stacks on the bottom, put Freya Stark on top.

"Don't we have rubber bands?" Herschel said.

Morath pulled the straps tight and buckled them. Then he shook hands, very formally, with each of the brothers. "Go with God," Herschel said.

That night, he met Wolfi Szubl at the Arizona, a *nachtlokal* in Szint Josef Alley on Margaret Island. Szubl wore a pale-blue suit and a flowery tie and smelled of heliotrope. "You never know," he said to Morath. "It gets very late at night here."

"Wolfi," Morath said, shaking his head.

"There's someone for everyone," Szubl said.

Szubl led him to a table on a platform by the wall, then pressed a button which raised them ten feet. "Here it's good." They shouted down to a waiter for drinks, Polish vodkas, that came up on a mechanical tray.

The orchestra was dressed in white tuxedos and played Cole Porter songs to a packed dance floor, which sometimes disappeared into the basement to a chorus of shrieks and laughter from the dancers.

A naked girl floated past in a harness, dark hair streaming out behind her. Her pose was artistic, lofty, an insouciant hand resting against the wire that hung from the ceiling.

"Ahh," Szubl said.

"You like her?"

Szubl grinned—who wouldn't?

"Why 'Arizona'?" Morath asked.

"The couple who own it got an unexpected inheritance, a fortune, from an uncle in Vienna. Decided to build a nightclub on Margaret Island. When they got the telegram they were in Arizona, so . . ."

"No. Really?"

Szubl nodded. "Yes," he said. "Tucson."

The drinks came. The girl went by again, headed the other way. "You see? She ignores us," Szubl said.

"She just happened to fly past, naked on a wire. Don't make assumptions."

Szubl raised his glass. "To the Free Hungary Committee."

"May it never exist."

Morath liked Polish vodka, potato vodka. It had a ghost of a taste he could never quite understand. "So, how did you do?"

"Not bad. From the Salon Kitty, on Szinyei Street, two hundred and fifty thousand pengo. Most of it from Madame Kitty, but she wanted us to know that three of the girls contributed. Then, from the nephew of the late, lamented minister of finance, another one hundred and fifty."

"That's all? His uncle would steal the wool from a sheep."

"Too late, Nicholas. The casino got most of it—he's a candidate for the boat."

The citizens of Budapest were partial to suicide, so the municipal authority maintained a boat tied up below the Ferenc Josef Bridge. A riverman waited in the bow with a long pole, ready to haul in the night's jumpers before they drowned.

"What about you?" Szubl said.

"Four hundred thousand from the Gersoviczy brothers. I go out to Kolozsvár tomorrow."

"Shooting animals?"

"Christ, I hadn't thought of that."

"I'm to see Voyschinkowsky."

" 'The Lion of the Bourse.' He lives in Paris, what's he doing here?"

"Nostalgia."

"Waiter!"

"Sir?"

"Two more, please."

A big redhead came gliding by. She blew a kiss, put her hands beneath her breasts and wobbled them, then raised an eyebrow.

"Let me buy her for you, Wolfi. All night, my treat."

They drank their vodkas, ordered doubles. The dance floor reappeared. The leader of the orchestra had shiny black hair and a little mustache and smiled like a saint as he waved his baton.

"When you begin-n-n, the beguine." Szubl took a deep breath and sighed. "You know," he said, "what I really like is to look at naked women."

"You do?"

"No, Nicholas, don't make fun of me, I'm serious. I mean, I really don't like anything else. If I could have begun this at fourteen, as my life's work, as the only thing I did, day and night, there never would have been a reason for me to disturb the world in any other way.

"But, of course, they wouldn't let me do that. So, now I crowd into trains, make telephones ring, throw orange peels into trash cans, make women buy girdles, ask for change, it doesn't stop. And, worst of all, on a lovely day, when you're happy and calm you go out in the street—and there I am! Really, there's no end to it. And it won't stop until I take up the space in the graveyard you wanted for your mother."

The orchestra played the "Tango du Chat." Morath remembered the song from the bar on the beach in Juan-les-Pins. "Tell you what," he said to Szubl. "We'll go over to Szinyei Street, to Kitty's. Order a parade around the parlor, every girl in the house. Or, a game of tag. No, wait, hide-and-seek!"

"Nicholas. You know, you're a romantic."

Later, Morath went to the WC, met an old friend, gossiped for a few minutes. When he came back, the redhead was sitting on Szubl's lap, playing with his tie and laughing. Wolfi's voice floated down from the platform. "Good night, Nicholas. Good night."

At Kolozsvar railroad station, a bright, cold morning.

There were two other Hungarians who left the train with him. Hunters, with shotguns under their arms. The conductor on the platform wished him good morning, in Hungarian, as he got off the train. And the two women mopping the floor in the station waiting room bantered in Hungarian and, in fact, laughed in Hungarian. A pleasant Magyar world—it just happened to be in Roumania. Once Kolozsvar, now Cluj. *Nem, nem, soha.*

A journey to the estate of Prince Hrubal turned out to be infernally complicated to arrange. It had required, in the end, several medieval phone calls, three telegrams—one of which went, inexplicably, to Wales, a verbal message taken to the castle by a gamekeeper's daughter, and a personal intervention by the village mayor. But, in the end, it worked.

In the street outside the station, Prince Hrubal's head groom was waiting for him, mounted on a bay gelding and holding the reins of a dock-tailed chocolate mare. This was, Morath knew, much the best way. You could try the road by automobile, but you spent more time digging than driving, and the trip by horse and carriage would hammer your teeth flat. That left walking and riding, and riding was faster.

He swung up into the saddle and tucked his briefcase under his arm. He'd made sure, in Budapest, to wear boots for the journey.

"Your excellency, I kiss your hands," said the steward.

"Good morning to you," Morath said, and they were off.

The good road in Cluj led to the bad road outside Cluj, then onto a road paved long ago, by some nameless dreamer/bureaucrat, and soon forgotten. This was northern Transylvania, mountainous and lost, where for generations Hungarian nobles ruled the lives of Roumanian serfs. There were, now and then, savage *jacqueries*, peasant risings, and the looting and burning would go on until the army arrived, coils of rope hung on their saddles. The trees were already there. Now, for the moment at least, it was quiet. Very quiet. Out in the countryside, a ruined castle broke the line of a mountain crest, then there was only forest, sometimes a field.

It took Morath back to the war. They'd been no different than any of the armies who came down these roads on mornings in the fall. He remembered wisps of autumn mist caught on the barbed wire, the sound of wind in the stubble of the rye fields, the creak of harness, crows wheeling in the sky and laughing at them. Sometimes they saw geese flying south; sometimes, when it rained at dawn, they only heard them. A thousand horses' hooves rang on the paved roads— their coming was no secret, and the riflemen waited for them. Once there was a sergeant, a Croat, adjusting a stirrup in the shade of an oak tree. The air cracked, an officer shouted. The sergeant put a hand over his eye, like a man reading an eye chart. The horse reared, galloped down the road a little way, and began to graze.

Prince Hrubal owned forests and mountains.

A servant answered Morath's knock and led him to the great hall— stag heads on the wall and tennis racquets in the corner. The prince showed up a moment later. "Welcome to my house," he said. He had merciless eyes; black, depthless, and cruel, a shaven head, a drooping Turkish mustache, the nickname "Jacky," acquired during his two years at Cornell, a taste for Italian fashion models, and a near manic passion for charity. His bookkeeper could barely keep track of it— broom factories for the blind, orphanages, homes for elderly nuns, and, lately, roof repairs on ancient monasteries. "This may do it for me, Nicholas," he said, a heavy arm draped around Morath's shoulders. "I've had to sell my sugar contracts in Chicago. But, still, the contemplative life must be lived, right? If not by you and me, by *somebody*, right? We can't have wet monks."

The baroness Frei once told Morath that the prince's life was the story of an aristocrat of the blood seeking to become an aristocrat of the heart. "Hrubal's a little mad," she said. "And it remains to be seen if his wealth can accommodate his madness. But whatever happens, these are thrilling races to watch, don't you agree? Poor man. Thirty generations of ancestors, brutal and bloody as the day is long, roasting rebels on iron thrones and God knows what, and only one lifetime for redemption."

The prince led Morath outside. "We've been moving boxwood," he said. He wore high boots, corduroy field pants, and a peasant blouse, a pair of cowhide gloves in his back pocket. At the end of the lawn, two peasants waited for him, leaning on their shovels.

"And Janos Polanyi," Hrubal said. "He's in good form?"

"Always up to something."

Hrubal laughed. "The King of Swords—that's his tarot card. A leader, powerful, but dark and secretive. His subjects prosper but regret they ever knew him." The prince laughed again, fondly, and patted Morath's shoulder. "Hasn't killed you yet, I see. But have no fear, Nicky, he will, he will."

Dinner for twelve. Venison from Hrubal's forest, trout from his stream, sauce from his red currants and sauce from his figs, a traditional salad—lettuce dressed with lard and paprika—and burgundy, Bull's Blood, from the Hrubal vineyards.

They ate in the small dining room, where the walls were lined with red satin, sagging, here and there, in melancholy folds and well spotted with champagne, wax, and blood. "But it proves the room," Hrubal said. "Last burned in 1810. A long time, in this part of the world." Dinner was eaten by the light of two hundred candles, Morath felt the sweat running down his sides.

He sat close to the head of the table, between Annalisa, the prince's friend from Rome—pale as a ghost, with long white hands, last seen in the April *Vogue*—and the fiancée of the Reuters correspondent in Bucharest, Miss Bonington.

"It is miserable now," she said to Morath. "Hitler is bad enough, but the local spawn are worse."

"The Iron Guard."

"They are everywhere. With little bags of earth around their necks. Sacred earth, you see."

"Come to Rome," Annalisa said. "And see them strut, our *fascisti.* Chubby little men, they think it's their *time.*"

"What are we supposed to do?" Miss Bonington said, her voice shrill. "Vote?"

Annalisa flipped a hand in the air. "Be worse than they are, I suppose, that's the tragedy. They have created a cheap, soiled, empty world, and now we are to have the pleasure of living in it."

"Well, personally, I never imagined—"

"*Basta,*" Annalisa said softly. "Hrubal is looking at us. To talk politics with food is against the rules."

Miss Bonington laughed. "What then?"

"Love. Poetry. Venice."

"Dear man."

The three of them turned their eyes to the head of the table.

"I loved the life there," Hrubal said. "On Saturday afternoon, the big game. That's what they called it—the big game! As for me, well, I was their saber champion, what else, and only our girlfriends came to the matches. But we all went to see the football. I had a giant horn, for cheering."

"A giant horn?"

"Damn. Somebody . . ."

"A megaphone, I think," said the Reuters man.

"That's it! Thank you, for years I've wanted to remember that."

A servant approached the table and whispered to Hrubal. "Yes, very well," he said.

The string quartet had arrived. They were shown into the dining room and the servants went for chairs. The four men smiled and nodded, wiping the rain from their hair and drying their instrument cases with their handkerchiefs.

When everyone had gone to their rooms, Morath followed Hrubal to an office high in a crumbling turret, where the prince opened an iron box and counted out packets of faded Austrian schillings. "These are very old," he said. "I never know quite what to do with them." Morath converted schilling to pengo as the money went into the briefcase. Six hundred thousand, more or less. "Tell Count Janos," Hrubal said, "that there's more if he needs it. Or, you know, Nicholas, whatever it might be."

Later that night, Morath heard a soft tapping and opened his door. *After venison from Prince Hrubal's forest and trout from his stream, a servant girl from his kitchen.* They never spoke a word. She stared at him with grave, dark eyes and, when he'd closed the door, lit the candle by his bedside and pulled her shift over her head. She had a faint mustache, a lush body, and wore knitted, red-wool stockings that came to midthigh.

A sweet morning, Morath thought, riding through the orange leaves on the floor of the forest. Delicately, the mare walked across a wide stream—a few inches of fast silver water—then down a series of rocky ledges. Morath kept the reins loose, let her find her own way. It was an old Magyar cavalryman who'd taught him that a horse can go anywhere a man can go without using his hands.

Morath kept his weight balanced, steadied the briefcase on the saddle, tugged a gentle reproach when the mare saw something she wanted for breakfast. "Manners," he whispered. Did she speak Hungarian? A Transylvanian horse, she must.

Up ahead, Hrubal's head groom rode his bay gelding. Morath pulled up for a moment and whistled softly, the groom half turned in the saddle to look back at him. He thought he'd heard other horses, not far away, but, when he listened, they weren't there. He rode up even with the groom and asked him about it.

"No, your excellency," the groom said. "I believe we are alone."

"Hunters, perhaps."

The groom listened, then shook his head.

They rode on. Morath watched a bank of mist as it drifted over the side of a mountain. He looked at his watch—a little after noon. The groom carried a picnic hamper of sandwiches and beer. Morath was hungry, but decided to ride for another hour.

In the forest, somewhere above him on the gentle slope, a horse whickered, then stopped, abruptly, as though someone had put a hand over its muzzle.

Morath rode even with the groom. "Surely you heard that."

"No, your excellency. I did not."

Morath stared at him. He had a sharp face, with gray hair and beard cut short, and there was something in his voice, subtle but there, that suggested defiance: *I chose not to hear it.*

"Are you armed?"

The groom reached under his shirt, held up a large revolver, then put it away. Morath wanted it.

"Are you able to use it?" he asked.

"Yes, your excellency."

"May I see it for a moment?"

"Forgive me, your excellency, but I must decline."

Morath felt the heat in his face. He was going to be murdered for this money and he was very angry. He threw the reins over hard and dug his heels in the horse's side. She sped off, dead leaves whispering beneath her hooves as she galloped down the slope. Morath looked back and saw that the groom was following him, his horse easily keeping pace. But there was no revolver to be seen, and Morath let the mare slow to a walk.

"You'd better go back now," he called out to the groom. "I'll go on by myself." He was breathing hard, after the gallop.

"I cannot, your excellency."

Why don't you shoot me and get it over with? Morath let the mare walk downhill. Something made him look back once more, and he saw, through the bare trees, a horse and rider, then another, some way up the slope. When they realized he'd seen them they walked their horses into cover, but seemed to be in no great hurry. Morath thought of tossing the briefcase away, but by then he knew it wouldn't matter.

He called up to the groom, "Who are your friends?," his voice almost mocking, but the man wouldn't answer.

A few minutes later he came to the road. It had been built in Roman times, the stone blocks hollowed and cracked by centuries of horse and wagon traffic. Morath turned toward Kolozsvar. When he looked up into the forest, he caught an occasional glimpse of the other riders, keeping pace with him. Directly behind him was the groom, on the bay gelding.

When he heard the automobile, sputtering and tapping, he stopped, and stroked the mare on her heaving side. A gentle animal, she'd done her best, he hoped they wouldn't shoot her. It was an old Citroën that appeared from a grove of birch trees by the side of the road. There was mud spattered on the doors and the wheel guards, a brown sweep across the windshield where the driver had tried to clear the dust with the single wiper.

The Citroën stopped with a loud squeak from the brakes and two men climbed out, both of them heavy and short. They wore straw hats, dark suits, and soiled white shirts buttoned at the throat. *Siguranza,* he thought. Roumanian secret police. Obviously they'd been waiting for him.

"Get down from there," the driver said. It was Hungarian, badly spoken. Morath took a little longer to dismount than they liked. The man on the passenger side of the car opened his jacket, showing Morath the handgrip of an automatic pistol in a shoulder holster. "If you need to be shot, we'll be happy to oblige you," he said. "Maybe it's a matter of honor, or something."

"Don't bother," Morath said. He got off the horse and held her by the bridle. The driver approached and took the briefcase. Something about him made the mare nervous, she tossed her head and stamped her feet on the stone block. The driver unbuckled the briefcase and had a look inside, then he called out to the groom, "You can go home now, Vilmos. Take his horse."

"Yes, excellency," the groom said. He was very frightened.

"And keep your mouth shut."

Morath watched as he rode back up into the forest, leading the mare by the reins.

The Siguranza men tied his wrists with a length of cord and shoved him into the backseat of the car, then made jokes as the starter engine whined and faded until the engine caught. They talked for a moment more—Morath didn't understand Roumanian but caught the word *Bistrita,* a small town north of Kolozsvar. As the car bounced along the road, the passenger opened the briefcase and divided up Morath's underwear and shaving kit. The two men argued briefly over Morath's spare shirt but the driver gave in almost immediately. The passenger then turned in his seat and stared at Morath. He hadn't shaved for several days, the stubble on his face black and gray.

He leaned over the back of the seat and slapped Morath in the face. Then did it again, harder. The driver laughed. The passenger stretched sideways until he could see himself in the rearview mirror and adjusted the brim of his hat.

Morath did not feel pain where he'd been slapped, he felt it in his wrists, where he'd tried to break the cord as the Siguranza man hit him. Later on, when he managed to twist around and get a look, he saw that he was bleeding.

Bistrita had been part of the Ottoman Empire until 1878, and not that much had changed. Dusty streets and lime trees, stucco buildings painted yellow and pale green, with fishscale roofing on the better houses. The Catholic crosses were mounted on the domes of the former mosques, the women on the street kept their eyes lowered, and so did the men.

The Citroën pulled up in front of the police station, and the two men hauled Morath out by the elbow and kicked him through the door. He made a point of not falling down. Then they beat him down the stairs, along a hallway, and to the door of a cell. When they cut the cord on his wrists, the knife sliced through the back of his jacket. One of them made a joke, the other one snickered. Then they cleaned out his pockets, took his shoes and socks, jacket and tie, threw him in the cell, slammed the iron door, shot the bolt.

Black dark in the cell, no window, and the walls breathed cold air. There was a straw mattress, a bucket, and a pair of rusted, ancient brackets in the wall. Used for chains—in 1540, or last night. They brought him a salt herring, which he knew better than to eat—he would suffer terribly from thirst—a lump of bread, and a small cup of water. He could hear, in the room directly above him, somebody pacing back and forth.

Heidelberg. Half-timbered houses, the bridge over the Neckar. When he was at Eötvös they'd gone up there for Schollwagen's lectures on Aristophanes. And—it was late February—just to be somewhere else. In a *weinstube,* Frieda. Curly hair, broad hips, a wonderful laugh. He could hear it.

A two-day love affair, and long ago, but every minute of it stayed in his memory and, now and then, he liked to go back over it. Because she liked to make love in every possible way and shivered with excitement. He was nineteen, he thought that women did such things as favors, maybe, when they loved you, on your birthday, or you paid whores a special rate.

There was a thump above him. *A sack of flour thrown on the floor.* Cara had no particular interest in *choses affreuses.* She would have done them—would have done anything, to be sophisticated and chic, that's what excited Cara. Did she do it with Francesca? She liked to tease him that she did, because she knew it interested him. *Another sack of flour.* This one cried out when it hit the floor.

Fuck you, he told them.

He'd thought about seeing Eva Zameny in Budapest, his former fiancée, who'd left her husband. Jesus, she'd been so beautiful. No other country made women who looked like that. Not much of a film of Eva—passionate kisses in the vestibule of her house. Once he had unbuttoned her blouse. She had wanted, she told him, to become a nun. Went to Mass twice a day because it gave her peace, she said, and nothing else did.

Married to Eva, two children, three, four. To work as a lawyer, spend his days with wills and contracts. Friday-night dinner at his mother's house, Sunday lunch at hers. Make love on Saturday night under a feather quilt in the Hungarian winter. Summer cabin on Lake Balaton. He'd have a coffeehouse, a gentlemen's club, a tailor. Why had he not lived his life in this way?

Really, why?

He wouldn't be in a Roumanian dungeon if he had. Who'd sold

him, he wondered. And would he—God grant!—have a chance to square that account? Was it somebody at Hrubal's house? Duchazy? *Stop it.* Here is Frieda: curly hair, broad hips, sweet laugh.

"Bad luck, Monsieur Morath. For you and for us. God only knows how we are going to get this straightened out. What, in the name of heaven, were you thinking of?"

This one was also from the Siguranza, Morath thought, but much higher up. Well shaven, well pomaded, and well spoken, in French.

The man rested his elbows on the desk and steepled his fingers. Told Morath he was guilty of technical crimes, no question, but who really cared. He didn't. Still, what the hell was he doing with all that *money*? Playing Hungarian—minority—politics? In Roumania? "Couldn't you have murdered somebody? Robbed a bank? Burned down a church? No. You had to make my life complicated, on Saturday morning, when I'm supposed to play golf with my father-in-law." Yes, it was Roumania, *douce décadence, Byzance après Byzance,* it was all too true. Still, they had laws.

Morath nodded, he knew. But what law, exactly, had he broken?

Overwhelmed, the Siguranza officer barely knew what to say—too many, too few, old ones, new ones, some we're just now making up. "Let's talk about Paris. I've told them to bring you coffee and a brioche." He looked at his watch. "They've gone to the café across the square."

Now here he really envied Morath, he might as well admit it. A man of his class and connection, taking the pleasures of this delightful city. One would know, don't bother denying it, the most stimulating people. French generals, Russian émigrés, diplomats. Had he met Monsieur X, Herr Y, Señor Z? What about, Colonel Something at the British embassy. Don't know him? Well, really you ought to meet him. He is, one hears, an amusing fellow.

No, Morath told him.

No? Well, why not? Morath was certainly the sort of gentleman who could meet anybody he liked. What could be—oh, was it money? Not to be indelicate, but the bills did pile up. Annoying people sent annoying letters. Being in debt could be a full-time occupation.

A lifelong hobby. But Morath didn't say it.

Life didn't have to be so hard, the officer told him. He himself had, for example, friends in Paris, businessmen, who were always seeking the advice and counsel of somebody like Morath. "And for them, believe me, money is no problem."

A policeman brought in a tray with two cups, a zinc coffeepot, and a large brioche. Morath tore a strip off the fluted brioche, yellow and sweet. "I'll bet you have this every morning, at home," the officer said.

Morath smiled. "I am traveling, as you know, on a Hungarian diplomatic passport."

The officer nodded, brushing a crumb off his lapel.

"They will want to know what's become of me."

"No doubt. They will send us a note. So we will send them one. Then they will send us one. And so on. A deliberate sort of process, diplomacy. Quite drawn out."

Morath thought it over. "Still, my friends will worry. They'll want to help."

The officer stared at him, made it clear he had a bad, violent temper. Morath had offered him a bribe, and he didn't like it. "We have been very good to you, you know." *So far.*

"Thank you for the coffee," Morath said.

The officer was again his affable self. "My pleasure," he said. "We're not in a hurry to lock you up. Twenty years in a Roumanian prison won't do you any good. And it doesn't help us. Much better, put you over the border at Oradea. Good-bye, good luck, good riddance. But, it's up to you."

Morath indicated he understood. "Perhaps I need to think it over."

"You must do what's best for you," the officer said. "I'll be back tomorrow."

In the room above him, the pacing never stopped. Outside, a storm. He heard the thunder and the drumming of the rain. A slow seep of water covered the floor, rose an inch, then stopped. Morath lay on the straw mattress and stared at the ceiling. *They didn't kill me and take the money.* For the Siguranza thugs who'd arrested him it was a fortune, a life on the French Riviera. But this was Roumania, "kiss the hand you cannot bite," and they had done what they'd been told to do.

He slept, sometimes. The cold woke him, and bad dreams. Even when he woke up, bad dreams.

In the morning, they took him to a small room on the top floor, likely the office, he thought, of the chief of the Bistrita police. There was a calendar on the wall, scenic views of Constanta on the Black Sea coast. A framed photograph on the desk, a smiling woman with dark hair and dark eyes. And an official photograph of King Carol, in white army uniform with sash and medals, hung on the wall.

Out the window, Morath could see life in the square. At the stalls of the marketplace, women were buying bread, carrying string bags of vegetables. In front of the fountain there was a Hungarian street singer. A rather comic fat man who sang like an opera tenor, arms thrown wide. An old song of the Budapest *nachtlokals:*

> Wait for me, please wait for me,
> even when the nights are long,
> my sweet, my only dove,
> oh please, wait for me.

When somebody dropped a coin in the battered hat on the ground in front of him, he smiled and nodded gracefully and somehow never missed a beat.

It was Colonel Sombor who entered the office, pulling the door shut behind him. Sombor, with glossy black hair like a hat and slanted eyebrows, in a sharp green suit and a tie with a gold crown on it. Very tight-lipped and serious, he greeted Morath and shook his head— *Now look what you've done.* He took the swivel chair at the police chief's desk, Morath sat across from him. "I flew right over when I heard about it," Sombor said. "Are you, all right?"

Morath was filthy, unshaven, and barefoot. "As you see."

"But they haven't *done* anything."

"No."

Sombor took a pack of Chesterfields from his pocket, laid it on the desk, put a box of matches on top. Morath tore the foil open, extracted a cigarette, and lit it, blowing out a long, grateful stream of smoke.

"Tell me what happened."

"I was in Budapest. I came over to Roumania to see a friend, and they arrested me."

"The police?"

"Siguranza."

Sombor looked grim. "Well, I'll have you out in a day or two, don't worry about that."

"I would certainly appreciate it."

Sombor smiled. "Can't have this sort of thing happening to our friends. Any idea what they're after?"

"Not really."

Sombor looked around the office for a moment, then he stood, walked to the window, and stared out at the street. "I've been wanting to talk to you," he said.

Morath waited.

"This job I have," Sombor said, "seems to grow bigger every day." He turned back toward Morath. "Europe is changing. It's a new world, we're part of it, whether we want to be or not, and we can win or lose, depending how we play our cards. The Czechs, for instance, have lost. They trusted the wrong people. You'll agree to that, I think."

"Yes."

"Now look, Morath, I have to be frank with you. I understand who you are and what you think—Kossuth, civil liberty, democracy, all that Shadow Front idealism. Perhaps I don't agree, but who cares. You know the old saying, 'Let the horse worry about politics, his head is bigger.' Right?"

"Right."

"I have to see the world in a practical way, I don't have time to be a philosopher. Now I have the greatest respect for Count Polanyi, he too is a realist, perhaps more than you know. He does what he needs to do, and you've helped him do it. You're not a virgin, is what I mean."

Sombor waited for a response. "And so?" Morath said it quietly.

"Just as I've come to help you, I would like you to help me. Help your country. That, I trust, would not be against your principles."

"Not at all."

"You will have to get your hands dirty, my friend. If not today, tomorrow, whether you like the idea or don't like it. Believe me, the time has come."

"And if I say no?"

Sombor shrugged. "We will have to accept your decision."

It didn't end there.

Morath lay on the wet straw and stared into the darkness. Outside, a truck rumbled past, driving slowly around the square. A few minutes later it returned, paused briefly in front of the station, then drove off.

Sombor had gone on at length—whatever light there'd been in his eyes had blown out like a candle but his voice never changed. *Getting you out may not be so easy. But don't you worry. Do our best. The prison at Iasi. The prison at Sinaia. Forced to stand with his nose touching the wall for seventy-two hours.*

For supper, they'd brought him another salt herring. He broke off a tiny piece, just to see what it tasted like. Ate the bread, drank the cold tea. They'd taken his cigarettes and matches when they put him back in the cell.

I flew right over when I heard about it. Said casually enough. The legation in Paris had two Fiesler Storch airplanes, sold to Hungary by the Germans after endless, agonizing negotiation and God only knew what favors. *I'm more important than you think,* Sombor meant. I command the use of the legation airplane.

When Sombor got up to leave, Morath said, "You'll let Count Polanyi know what's happened."

"Naturally."

Polanyi would never know. *Nacht und Nebel,* Adolf Hitler's phrase, night and fog. A man left his home in the morning and was never heard of again. Morath worked hard, *think only of the next hour,* but despair rose in his heart and he could not make it go away. Petofi, Hungary's national poet, said that dogs were always well looked after and wolves starved, but only wolves were free. So here, in this cell or those to come, was freedom.

They came for him at dawn.

The door opened and two guards took him under the arms, ran

him down the hall, and hauled him up the staircase. It was barely daylight, but even the soft gloom hurt his eyes. They gave him back his shoes, then shackled him at the wrists and ankles, and he shuffled out the front door to a waiting truck. There were two other prisoners in there, one a Gypsy, the other perhaps a Russian, tall, with sheared white hair and blue tears tattooed at the corners of his eyes.

Only the women who swept the street saw him leave. They paused for a bare moment, their brooms, made of bundles of reeds, resting on the ground. *Poor boys. God help you.* Morath never forgot it.

The truck bounced on the cobbles. The Gypsy caught Morath's eye and sniffed the air—they'd driven past a bakery. It wasn't a long ride, maybe fifteen minutes. Then they were at the railroad station where trains, Morath understood perfectly, left for towns like Iasi, or Sinaia.

Three men in chains and six policemen. That was something worth looking at when your train stopped in Bistrita. Passengers lowered the tops of their windows to see the show. A commercial traveler, from the look of him, peeling an orange and throwing the rind on the station platform. A woman in a pillbox hat, the dark veil hiding her eyes, white hands resting atop the window. Other faces, pale in the early light. A man made a joke, his friend laughed. A child, who watched Morath with wide eyes, knowing she was allowed to stare. A man in an overcoat with a velvet collar, stern, elegant, who nodded to Morath as though he knew him.

Then, chaos. Who were they? For slow-motion moments the question raced through Morath's mind. They came from nowhere. Moving too fast to count, shouting in—was it Russian? Polish? The policeman at Morath's side was hit. Morath heard the impact, then a yelp, then he staggered off somewhere, groping at his holster. A man in a soft hat stepped from a cloud of steam vented by the locomotive. A cool, frosty morning, he'd wrapped a muffler around his throat, tucked the ends inside his jacket, and turned up the collar. He studied Morath carefully, for what seemed like a long time, then swung his shotgun a little to one side and fired both barrels. Several passengers gasped, the sound, to Morath, was clear as a bell.

The Russian prisoner knew. *Maybe too much,* Morath thought later. He stretched out full length on the platform and covered his head with his shackled hands. A lifelong convict, perhaps, who knew that this business was, sadly, not for him, his gods weren't that powerful. The Gypsy cried out to a man with a handkerchief tied over his face and extended his wrists. Free me! But the man pushed him aside. He almost fell, then tried to run away, taking tiny steps, his ankle chain scraping along the concrete.

In the killing, they almost forgot Morath. He stood alone at the center of it. A detective, at least a man in a suit holding a revolver, ran past, then turned toward Morath, his face anxious, uncertain, the right thing must be done. He hesitated, started to raise his pistol, closed his eyes, bit his lip, and sat down. Now he knew what to do but it was too late. The pistol moved only a few inches, a red gash opened in his forehead, and, very slowly, he collapsed. A few yards away, the train conductor was lying back against a wheel of the coal car. In his eyes, a look Morath knew. He was dying.

Now a black car came driving, very slowly, along the platform. Driven by a young boy, no more than thirteen, hands white on the wheel, face knotted with concentration. He stopped the car while the man in the soft hat dragged another man by the back of his jacket, sliding him up to the rear door of the car. He opened the door and threw him in the backseat. In the middle of it all, screams and shots, Morath could hardly believe that anybody could be that strong.

"Move, dumb ox!" The words in German, the Slavic accent so thick it took Morath a moment to understand. The man gripped his arm like a steel claw. A hook nose, dark face, an unlit cigarette in his lips. "To the *truck*, yes?" he said. "*Yes?*"

Morath walked as fast as he could. Behind him, from the train, a cry in Hungarian. A woman, cursing, enraged, screaming, telling them all, brutes, devils, to cease this fouling of the world and go and burn in hell. The man at Morath's side lost all patience—the rise and fall of distant sirens coming nearer—and dragged Morath toward the truck. The driver reached over and helped him and he sprawled across the passenger seat, then fought his way upright.

The driver was an old man with a beard and a scar that cut across his lips. He pressed the gas pedal, gingerly, the engine raced, then died back. "Very good," he said.

"Hungarian?"

The man shook his head. "I learn in war."

He pressed the clutch pedal to the floor as the man in the soft hat ran toward the truck and violently waved his shotgun. *Go. Move.* "Yes, yes," the driver said, this time in Russian. He shoved the gear lever forward, and, after a moment, it engaged. He gave Morath an inquisitive look. Morath nodded.

They drove away slowly, into the street behind the station. A police car was idling at the corner, both doors open. Morath could hear the train moving out of the station—the engineer at last come to his senses. A black sedan came flying past and, tires squealing, cut in front of them, then slowed down. A hand came out of the driver's window and beckoned them forward. The sedan accelerated and, at the next street, turned sharply and sped away.

They were quickly out of Bistrita, the road narrowed, turned to dirt, wound past a few dilapidated farms and villages, then climbed into the Transylvanian forest. At sunset, despite the cold iron on his wrists and ankles, Morath slept. Then woke in darkness. Out the window, a field painted in frost and moonlight. The old man was bent over the wheel, squinting to see the road.

"Where are we?" Morath said.

From the old man, an eloquent shrug. He took a scrap of brown paper from atop the dashboard and handed it to Morath. A crosshatch of lines, drawn in blunt pencil, with notes in Cyrillic script scrawled along the margin. "So, where we are?"

Morath had to laugh.

The old man joined him. Maybe they would find their way, maybe not, so life went.

The truck worked its way up a long hill, the wheels slipping in the frozen ruts, the old man restlessly shifting gears. "Like tractor," he said. In the distance, Morath saw a dull glow that appeared and disappeared through the trees. This turned out to be, a few minutes later, a low stone building at the junction of two ancient roads, its windows lit by oil lamps. An inn, a wooden sign hung on chains above the door.

The old man smiled in triumph, let the truck roll to a stop in the cobblestone yard, and honked the horn. This produced two barking mastiffs, galloping back and forth in the headlights, and an innkeeper wearing a leather apron, a blazing pitch-pine torch held high in one hand. "You are welcome in this house," he said, in formal Hungarian.

A deliberate man, round and genial. He took Morath to the stable, set the torch in a bracket, and, with hammer and chisel, broke the shackles and took them off. As he worked, his face grew sorrowful. "So my grandfather," he explained, repositioning the chain atop an anvil. "And his."

When he was done he led Morath to the kitchen, sat him in front of the fire, and served him a large glass of beer and a thick slice of fried cornmeal. When Morath had eaten, he was shown to a room off the kitchen, where he fell dead asleep.

When he woke, the truck was gone. The innkeeper gave him an old jacket and a peaked cap, and, later that morning, he sat next to a farmer on a wagon and entered Hungarian territory by crossing a hayfield.

Morath had always liked the Novembers of Paris. It rained, but the bistros were warm, the Seine dark, the lamps gold, the season's love affairs new and exciting. The 1938 November began well enough, *tout Paris* ecstatic that it wouldn't have to go to war. But then, Kristallnacht, on the night of 9 November, and in the shimmering tons of shattered Jewish glass could be read, more clearly than anybody liked, what was coming. Still, it wasn't coming *here*. Let Hitler and Stalin rip each other's throats out, went that week's thinking, we'll go up to Normandy for the weekend.

Morath arranged to meet his uncle at some *cuisine grand-mère* hole-in-the-wall out in Clichy. He'd spent ten days in Budapest, collecting money, listening to poor Szubl's misadventures with the redheaded chorus girl he'd met at the nightclub. Then the two of them had hidden the cash in a cello and taken the night express back to Paris. For the moment, Morath was a man with well over two million pengo in his closet.

It was obvious to Morath that Count Polanyi had gotten an early start on lunch. Trying to sit down, he lurched into the neighboring table, very nearly causing a soup accident and drawing a sharp glance from the *grand-mère*. "It seems the gods are after me today," he said, in a gust of cognac fumes.

It wasn't the gods. The pouches beneath his eyes had grown alarmingly and darkened.

Polanyi peered at the chalked menu on the blackboard. *"Andouillette,"* he said.

"I hear you've been away," Morath said.

"Yes, once again I'm a man with a house in the country, what's left of it." On 2 November, the Vienna Commission—Hitler—had awarded Hungary, in return for supporting Germany during the Sudeten crisis, the Magyar districts of southern Czechoslovakia. Twelve thousand square miles, a million people, the new border running from Pozsony/Bratislava all the way east to Ruthenia.

The waiter arrived with a carafe of wine and a plate of snails.

"Uncle Janos?"

"Yes?"

"How much do you know about what happened to me in Roumania?"

From Polanyi's expression it was clear he didn't want to talk about it. "You had difficulties. It was seen to."

"And that's that."

"Nicholas, don't be cross with me. Basically, you were lucky. Had I left the country two weeks earlier you might have been gone for good."

"But, somehow, you heard about it."

Polanyi shrugged.

"Did you hear that Sombor appeared? At the Bistrita police station?"

His uncle raised an eyebrow, speared a snail on the third try and ate it, dripping garlic butter on the table. "Mmm? What'd he want?"

"Me."

"Did he get you?"

"No."

"So where's the problem?"

"Perhaps Sombor is a problem."

"Sombor is Sombor."

"He acted like he owned the world."

"He does."

"Was he responsible for what happened to me?"

"Now that's an interesting idea. What would you do if he was?"

"What would you suggest?"

"Kill him."

"Are you serious?"

"Kill him, Nicholas, or don't ruin my lunch. Choose one."

Morath poured himself a glass of wine and lit a Chesterfield. "And the people who rescued me?"

"*Très cher*, Nicholas."

"Who shall I thank for it?"

"Somebody owed me a favor. Now I owe him one."

"Russian? German?"

"Eskimo! My dear nephew, if you're going to be inquisitive and difficult about this . . ."

"Forgive me. Of course I'm grateful."

"Can I have the last snail? That grateful?"

"At least that."

Polanyi jammed the tiny fork into the snail and frowned as he worked it free of its shell. Then, for a moment, he looked very sad. "I'm just an old, fat Hungarian man, Nicholas. I can't save the world. I'd like to, but I can't."

The last days of November, Morath pulled his overcoat tight and hurried through the streets of the Marais to the Café Madine. It was, Morath thought, frozen in time. Empty, as before, in the cold morning light, a cat asleep on the counter, the *patron* with his spectacles down on his nose.

The *patron*, Morath suspected, remembered him. Morath ordered a café au lait and, when it came, warmed his hands on the bowl. "I was here, once before," he said to the *patron*. "Last March, I think it was."

The *patron* gave him a look. *Really?*

"I met an old man. I can't recall his name, I don't think he mentioned it. At the time, a friend of mine had difficulties with a passport."

The owner nodded. Yes, that sort of thing did happen, now and then. "It's possible. Somebody like that used to come here, once in a while."

"But not anymore."

"Deported," the owner said. "In the summer. He had a little problem with the police. But for him, the little problem became a big problem, and they sent him back to Vienna. After that, I can't say."

"I'm sorry to hear it," Morath said.

"He is also sorry, no doubt."

Morath looked down, felt the height of the wall between him and the *patron,* and understood there was nothing more to be said. "He had a friend. A man with a Vandyke beard. Quite educated, I thought. We met at the Louvre."

"The Louvre."

"Yes."

The *patron* began drying a glass with a cloth, held it up to the light, and put it back on the shelf. "Cold, today," he said.

"Perhaps a little snow."

"You think so?"

"You can feel it in the air."

"Maybe you're right." He began wiping the bar with the cloth, lifting Morath's bowl, scooping up the cat and setting it gently on the floor. "You must let me clean, Sascha," he said.

Morath waited, drinking his coffee. A woman with a baby in a blanket went past in the street.

"It's quiet here," Morath said. "Very pleasant."

"You should come more often, then." The *patron* gave him a tart smile.

"I will. Perhaps tomorrow."

"We'll be here. God willing."

It took a half hour, the following morning. Then a woman—the woman who had picked up the money and, Morath remembered, kissed him on the steps of the Louvre, appeared at the café. "He'll see you," she told Morath. "Try at four-fifteen tomorrow, in the Jussieu Métro station. If he can't get there, try the next day, at three-fifteen. If that doesn't work, you'll have to find another way."

He wasn't there on the first try. The station was crowded, late in the day, and if somebody was taking a look at him, making sure there were no detectives around, Morath never saw it. On the second day, he waited forty-five minutes, then gave up. As he climbed the stairs to the street, the man fell in step with him.

Not as portly as Morath remembered him, he still wore the Vandyke beard and the tweed suit, and something about him suggested affinity with the world of commercial culture. *The art dealer.* He was accompanied, as before, by a man with a white, bony face who wore a hat set square on a shaven head.

"Let's take a taxi," the art dealer said. "It's too cold to walk."

The three of them got in the back of a taxi that was idling at the curb. "Take us to the Ritz, driver," said the art dealer.

The driver laughed. He drove slowly down the rue Jussieu and turned into the rue Cuvier.

"So," the art dealer said. "Your friends still have problems with their papers."

"Not this time," Morath said.

"Oh? Then what?"

"I would like to meet somebody in the diamond business."

"You're selling?"

"Buying."

"A little something for the sweetheart."

"Absolutely. In a velvet box."

The driver turned up the hill on the rue Monge. From the low sky, a few drops of rain, people on the street opened their umbrellas. "A substantial purchase," Morath said. "Best would be somebody in the business a long time."

"And discreet."

"Very. But please understand, there's no crime, nothing like that. We just want to be quiet."

The art dealer nodded. "Not the neighborhood jeweler."

"No."

"Has to be in Paris?"

Morath thought it over. "Western Europe."

"Then it's easy. Now, for us, it's a taxi ride and, maybe tomorrow, a train ride. So, we'll say, five thousand francs?"

Morath reached into his inside pocket, counted out the money in hundred-franc notes, and put the rest away.

"One thing I should tell you. The market in refugee diamonds is not good. If you bought in Amsterdam a year ago and went to sell in Costa Rica tomorrow, you'd be badly disappointed. If you think a thousand carats of value is a thousand carats of value, like currency in a normal country somewhere, and all you'll have to do is carve up the heel in your shoe, you're wrong. People think it's like that but it isn't. Since Hitler, the gem market is a good place to lose your shirt. *F'shtai?*"

"Understood," Morath said.

"Say, want to buy a Vermeer?"

Morath started to laugh.

"No? A Hals then, a little one. Fits in a suitcase. *Good,* too. I'll vouch for it. You don't know who I am, and I'd rather you never did, but I know what I'm talking about."

"You need somebody rich."

"Not this week, I don't."

Morath smiled regret.

The chalk-white man took off his hat and ran his hand over his head. Then said, in German, "Stop. He's moral."

"Is that it?" the art dealer said. "You don't want to take advantage of a man who's a fugitive?"

The driver laughed.

"Well, if you ever, God forbid, have to run for your life, then you'll understand. It's beyond *value,* by then. What you'll be saying is 'take the picture, give the money, thank you, good-bye.' Once you only plan to live till the afternoon, you'll understand."

For a time, there was silence in the cab. The art dealer patted Morath on the knee. "Forgive me. What you need today is a name. That's going to be Shabet. It's a Hasidic family, in Antwerp, in the diamond district. There's brothers, sons, all sorts, but do business with one and you're doing business with all of them."

"They can be trusted?"

"With your life. I trusted them with mine, and here I am." The art dealer spelled the name, then said, "Of course I need to certify you to them. What should I call you?"

"André."

"So be it. Give me ten days, because I have to send somebody up there. This is not business for the telephone. And, just in case, you and I need a confirmation signal. Go to the Madine, ten days from now. If you see the woman, it's all settled."

Morath thanked him. They shook hands. The chalk-white man tipped his hat. "Good luck to you, sir," he said in German. The driver pulled over to the curb, in front of a charcuterie with a life-size tin statue of a pig by its doorway, inviting customers inside with a sweep of his trotter. *"Voilà le Ritz!"* the driver called out.

Emile Courtmain sat back in his swivel chair, clasped his hands behind his head, and stared out at the avenue Matignon. "When you first think about it, it should be easy. But then you start to work, and it turns out to be very difficult."

There were forty wash drawings set out around the office—pinned to the walls, propped up on chairs. *French life.* Peasant couples in the fields, or in the doorways of farmhouses, or sitting on wagons. Like Millet, perhaps, a benign, optimistic sort of Millet. Then there were Parisian *papas* and *mamans* out for a Sunday stroll, by a carousel, at the Arc de Triomphe. A pair of lovers on a bridge over the Seine, holding hands, she with bouquet, he in courting suit—*facing the future.* A soldier, home from the front, seated at the kitchen table, his good wife setting a tureen in front of him. This one wasn't so bad, Morath thought.

"Too gentle," Courtmain said. "The ministry will want something with a little more clenched fist in it."

"Any text?"

"A word or two—Mary's going to join us in a minute. Something like, 'In a dangerous world, France remains strong.' It's meant to dispel defeatism, especially after what happened at Munich."

"Exhibited where?"

"The usual places. Métro, street kiosk, post office."

"Hard to dispel defeatism in a French post office."

Morath sat down in a chair across from Courtmain. Mary Day knocked lightly on the frame of the open door. "Hello, Nicholas," she said. She pulled up a chair, lit a Gitane, and handed Courtmain a sheet of paper.

" 'France will win,' " he read. Then, to Morath, "That's not poor Mary's line." From Courtmain, an affectionate grin. Mary Day had the smart person's horror of the fatuous phrase.

"It's the little man at the interior ministry," she explained. "He, *had an idea.*"

"I hope they're paying."

Courtmain made a face. *Not much.* "Advertising goes to war—you can't say no to them."

Mary Day took the paper back from Courtmain. " 'France forever.' "

"*Bon Dieu,*" Courtmain said.

" 'Our France.' "

Morath said, "Why not just 'La France'?"

"Yes," Mary Day said. "The *Vive* understood. That was my first try. They didn't care for it."

"Too subtle," Courtmain said. He looked at his watch. "I have to be at RCA at five." He stood, opened his briefcase and made sure he had what he needed, then adjusted the knot of his tie. "I'll see you tomorrow?" he said to Morath.

"About ten," Morath said.

"Good," Courtmain said. He liked having Morath around and wanted him to know it. He said good-bye to each of them and went out the door.

Which left Morath alone in the room with Mary Day.

He pretended to look at the drawings and tried to think of something clever to say. She glanced at him, read over her notes. She was the daughter of an Irish officer in the Royal Navy and the French artist Marie d'Aumonville—an extraordinary combination, if you asked Morath, or anybody. A light sprinkle of freckles across the bridge of the nose; long, loose brown hair; and pleading brown eyes. She was flat-chested, amused, impish, absentminded, awkward. "Mary's a certain type," Courtmain had once told him. When she was sixteen, he suspected, all the boys wanted to die for her, but they were afraid to ask her to go to the movies.

She sat back in the chair and said, "Well, I suppose we have to go back to work."

Morath agreed.

"And then, you'll take me for a drink." She started to gather up her papers. "Right?"

Morath stared, did she mean it? "With pleasure," he said, retreating into formality. "At seven?"

Her smile was, as always, rueful. "You don't have to, Nicholas." She was just teasing him.

"I want to," he said. "Fouquet, if you like."

"Well," she said. "That would be nice. Or the place around the corner."

"Fouquet," he announced. "Why not?"

A comic shrug—don't know why not. "Seven," she said, a little startled at what she'd done.

They hurried through the crowds, up the Champs Elysées, a few flakes of snow in the night air. She walked with big strides, shoulders hunched over, hands thrust in the pockets of what Morath thought was a very odd coat—three-quarter length, maroon wool with big buttons covered in brown fabric.

Fouquet was packed and noisy, throbbing with life, they had to wait for a table. Mary Day rubbed her hands to get warm. Morath gave a waiter ten francs and he found them a table in the corner. "What would you like?" Morath said.

She thought it over.

"*Garçon,* champagne!"

She grinned. "A vermouth, maybe. Martini *rouge.*"

Morath ordered a *gentiane,* Mary Day changed her mind and decided to have the same thing. "I like it, I just never remember to ask for it." She spent a long moment watching the people around them—Parisian theatre of the night—and from the look on her face took great pleasure in it. "I wrote something about this place, back when, a piece for the Paris *Herald.* Restaurants with private rooms—what really goes on?"

"What does?"

"Balzac. But not as much as you'd like to think. Little anniversary parties. Birthday. First Communion."

"You worked for the *Herald?*"

"Freelance. Anything and everything, as long as they'd pay for it."

"Such as . . ."

"Wine festival in Anjou! Turkish foreign minister feted at the Lumpingtons!"

"Not so easy."

"Not hard. You need stamina, mostly."

"Somebody at the office said you wrote books."

She answered in the tough-guy voice from American gangster movies. "Oh, so you found out about that, did ya?"

"Yes, you're a novelist."

"Oh, sort of, maybe. Naughty books, but they pay the rent. I got tired of wine festivals in Anjou, believe it or not, and somebody introduced me to an English publisher—he's got a little office up in the place Vendôme. The kindest man in the world. A Jew, I think, from Birmingham. He was in the textile business, came to France to fight in the war, discovered Paree, and just couldn't bear to go home. So he started to publish books. Some of them famous, in a certain set, but most of them come in plain brown wrappers, if you know what I mean. A friend of mine calls them 'books one reads with one hand.' "

Morath laughed.

"Not so bad, the best of them. There's one called *Tropic of Cancer*."

"Actually, I think the woman I used to live with read it."

"Pretty salty."

"That was her."

"Then maybe she read *Suzette*. Or the sequel, *Suzette Goes Boating*."

"Are those yours?"

"D. E. Cameron, is what the jacket says."

"What are they like?"

" 'She slipped the straps from her white shoulders and let the shift fall to her waist. The handsome lieutenant . . .' "

"Yes? What did he do?"

Mary Day laughed and shook her hair back. "Not much. Mostly it's about underwear."

The *gentianes* arrived, with a dish of salted almonds.

•

They had two more. And two more after that. She touched his hand with the tips of her fingers.

An hour later, they'd had all of Fouquet they wanted and went off to find dinner. They tried Lucas Carton but it was *complet* and they didn't have a reservation. Then they wandered along the rue Marbeuf, found a little place that smelled good, and ate soup and omelettes and Saint Marcellin.

They gossiped about the office. "I have to travel, now and then," Morath said, "but I like the time I spend in the office, I like what we do—the clients, what they're trying to sell."

"It can take over your life."

"That's not so bad."

She tore a piece of bread in half and put some crumbly Saint Marcellin on it. "I don't mean to pry, but you said 'the woman I used to live with.' Is she no more?"

"She left, had to leave. Her father came all the way from Buenos Aires and took her away. He thought we'd be at war by now."

She ate the bread and cheese. "Do you miss her?"

It took Morath a moment to answer. "Of course I do, we had a good time together."

"Sometimes that's the most important thing."

Morath agreed.

"I lost my friend a year ago. Maybe Courtmain told you."

"He didn't, it's mostly all business with us."

"It was very sad. We'd lived together for three years—we were never going to get married, it wasn't like that. But we were in love, most of the time. He was a musician, a guitarist, from a town near Chartres. Classically trained, but he got to playing in the jazz clubs up in Montparnasse and fell in love with the life. Drank too much, smoked opium with his friends, never went to bed until the sun rose. Then, one night, they found him dead in the street."

"From opium?"

She spread her hands, *who knows?*

"I am sorry," Morath said.

Her eyes were shining, she wiped them with a napkin.

•

They were silent in the taxi, going back to her apartment. She lived on the rue Guisarde, a quiet street in the back of the Sixth Arrondissement. He came around to her side of the cab, opened the door, and helped her out. Standing in the doorway, she raised her face for the good-night *bisou* on the cheek but it became a little more than that, then a lot, and it went on for a long time. It was very tender, her lips dry and soft, her skin warm beneath his hand. He waited in the doorway until he saw her light go on, then he went off down the street, heart pounding.

He was a long way from home but he wanted to walk. *Too good to be true*, he told himself. Because the light of day hit these things and they turned to dust. A *folie*, the French would say, an error of the heart.

He'd been very low since he came back to Paris. The days in Bistrita the cell, the railroad station—it didn't go away. He woke up at night and thought about it. So he'd sought refuge, distraction, at the Agence Courtmain. And then, an office romance. Everybody was a little in love with Mary Day, why not him?

The streets were cold and dark, the wind hit him hard as he crossed the Pont Royal. On the boulevard, an empty taxi. Morath climbed in. Go back to her apartment? "The rue Richelieu," he told the driver.

But the next morning, in the light of day, she was wearing a pale gray dress with buttons up the front and a belt that tied, a dress that showed her in a certain way and, when their eyes met for the first time, he knew.

So the letter waiting for him in his mailbox that night brought him down to earth in a hurry. Préfecture de Police, Quai du Marché Neuf, Paris 1ᵉʳ. The *Monsieur* was printed, on the form letter, the *Morath, Nicholas* written in ink. Would he please present himself at *la salle 24* of the *préfecture* on *le 8 Decembre,* between the hours of *9 et 12 du matin.*

Veuillez accepter, Monsieur, l'expression de nos sentiments distingués.

This happened, from time to time. The summons to the *préfec-ture*—a fact of life for every foreigner, a cold front in the bureaucratic weather of the city. Morath hated going there; the worn linoleum and green walls, the gloomy air of the place, the faces of the summoned, each one with its own particular combination of boredom and terror.

Room 24. That was not his usual room, good old 38, where resident foreigners with mild diplomatic connections were seen. What did *that* mean, he wondered, putting on his best blue suit.

It meant a serious inspector with a hard, square face and military bearing. Very formal, very correct, and very dangerous. He asked for Morath's papers, made notations on a form. Asked if there had been any changes in his *situation:* residence, employment, marital status. Asked if he had recently traveled to Roumania.

Morath felt the thin ice. Yes, at the end of October.

Exactly where, in Roumania.

In the district of Cluj.

And?

That was all.

And, please, for what purpose?

For a social engagement.

Not for, business.

Non, monsieur l'inspecteur.

Very well, would he be so good as to wait in the *réception?*

Morath sat there, the lawyer part of his mind churning away. Twenty minutes. Thirty. *Bastards.*

Then the inspector, Morath's papers in his hand. Thank you, monsieur, there will be no further questions. At this time. A long instant, then, *"Vos papiers, monsieur."*

Polanyi looked like he hadn't slept. Rolled his eyes when he heard the story. *Lord, why me.* They met that afternoon, in the office of an elegant shop on the rue de la Paix that sold men's accessories. Polanyi spoke to the owner, exquisitely dressed and barbered, in Hungarian. "May we have the use of your office, Kovacs *Uhr,* for a little while?" The man nodded eagerly, wrung his hands, there was fear in his eyes. Morath didn't like it.

"I don't believe they will pursue this," Polanyi said.

"Can they extradite me to Roumania?"

"They can, of course, but they won't. A trial, the newspapers, that's not what they want. Two things I would suggest to you: First of all, don't worry about it; second of all, don't go to Roumania."

Morath stubbed out a cigarette in the ashtray.

"Of course you are aware that relations between France and Roumania have always been important to both governments. French companies hold concessions in the Roumanian oil fields at Ploesti. So, you have to be careful."

Polanyi paused for a moment, then said, "Now, as long as we're here, I need to ask you a question. I have a letter from Hrubal, who wonders if I would find out from you what became of Vilmos, his chief groom, who never returned from escorting you to the Cluj railroad station."

"Obviously they killed him."

"Did they? Perhaps he simply ran away."

"It's possible. Does Hrubal know that his money vanished?"

"No. And he never will. I had to go to Voyschinkowsky who, without anything like a real explanation, agreed to make it good. So Prince Hrubal's contribution to the national committee will be made in his name."

Morath sighed. "Christ, it never ends," he said.

"It's the times we live in, Nicholas. Cold comfort, I know, but it's been worse in the past. In any event, I don't want you losing sleep over any of this. As long as I'm here to protect you, you're reasonably safe."

To follow the art dealer's instructions, Morath had to go to the Café Madine that morning, but he went first of all to the office. Which he found silent and deserted—he was too early. Then, suddenly, a swirl of activity. Mary Day with an apprentice copywriter, Mary Day with Léon, the artist, Mary Day talking to Courtmain through his open door. In a white, angelic sweater, she glanced at him as he hurried past like a man who actually had something to do. Morath retreated to his office, looked at his watch, came out, went back in. Finally, she was alone at her desk, head in hands over five words typed on a sheet of yellow paper. "Mary," he said.

She looked up. "Hello," she said. Where have you been?

"I tried to call, last night, I couldn't find your number."

"Oh that's a long story," she said. "The apartment is actually . . ." She looked around. People everywhere. "Damn, I'm out of pencils."

She rose brusquely and he followed her to the supply room, a large closet. He pulled the door closed behind them. "Here it is," she said, writing it down.

"I want to see you."

She handed him a slip of paper, then kissed him. He put his arms around her, held her for a moment, inhaled her perfume. "Tomorrow night?" she said.

Morath calculated. "By ten, I think."

"There's a café on the corner of the rue Guisarde." She pressed her hand against the side of his face, then grabbed a handful of pencils. "Can't get caught mugging in the supply room," she said, laughing.

He followed her swinging skirt down the hall until she disappeared into the bookkeeper's office, looking back over her shoulder as she closed the door.

At the Café Madine, Morath stood at the counter and had his usual coffee. Twenty minutes later—somebody, somewhere was watching, he decided—the woman showed up. She ignored Morath, sat at a table by the wall, read her copy of *Le Temps*.

So then, Antwerp. He went to see Boris Balki at the nightclub.

"Still at it?" Balki said, pouring two Polish vodkas.

"I guess I am," Morath said.

"Well, I should say thank you." Balki raised his glass in a silent toast and drank the vodka. "My friend Rashkow's out of prison. They brought him his clothes in the middle of the night, took him to the back gate, gave him a good kick in the ass, and told him not to come back."

"I'm glad I could help."

"Poor little Rashkow," Balki said.

"I need to go up to Antwerp," Morath said. "I'm hoping you'll come with me."

"Antwerp."

"We'll need a car."

•

At dawn, Morath stamped his feet to keep warm and curled into his overcoat, waiting in a white fog by the entry to the Palais Royal Métro station. A splendid car, Morath thought. It came, very slowly, up the rue Saint-Honoré, a 201 Peugeot, ten years old, painted deep forest-green and glowing with polish and affection.

They drove north, following lines of trucks, into Saint-Denis. Morath directed Balki through a maze of winding streets to a park behind a church where, working hard at the reluctant latches, they took out the backseat. "Please, Morath," Balki said. "Don't hurt anything. This is somebody's life, this car." He wore a stiff brown suit, white shirt, no tie, and a peaked cap—a bartender on his day off.

Morath opened his valise and stuffed thick packets of pengo under the wire coils in the seat. Balki was grim, shook his head as he saw all the money.

Route 2, headed north and east of Paris, went through Soissons and Laon, with signs for Cambrai and Amiens, the flat, weedy plain where they'd always fought the Germans. In the villages, smoke rose from the chimneys, women opened their shutters, glanced up at the sky, and put the pillows and blankets out to air. There were kids going to school, their dogs trotting along beside them, shop assistants raising the metal shutters of their shops, milkmen setting bottles on the doorsteps.

Just beyond the French town of Bettignies, the Belgian police at the border post were busy smoking and leaning against their shed and couldn't be bothered looking at the Peugeot as it drove past.

"Half done," Balki said, relief in his voice.

"No, that's it," Morath said as the shed disappeared in the mirror. "Once we get to Antwerp, we're tourists. Probably I should've just taken the train."

Balki shrugged. "Well, you never know."

They turned off the road, drove out into the farmland, and put the money back in the valise.

It was slow going through Brussels, they stopped for eels and *frites* in a bar on the outskirts, then drove along the Schelde River into Antwerp. They could hear a foghorn in the distance as a freighter worked its way out into the harbor. The diamond district was on Van

Eycklei Street, in a luxurious neighborhood by a triangular park. "I'll walk from here," Morath said. Balki pulled over, wincing as a tire scraped against the curb.

"Shabet? Two stalls down," they told him. He'd found the diamond exchange on Pelikaanstraat—long tables of diamond brokers, with the cutters' offices on the floor above. The Shabet he found was in his thirties, balding and worried. "I think you'd better see my uncle," he said. Morath waited by the table while a phone call was made, and ten minutes later the uncle showed up. "We'll go to my office," he said.

Which was back on Van Eycklei, on the second floor of an imposing gray stone building, and rather splendid: Persian carpets, a vast mahogany breakfront crowded with old books, an ornate desk with a green baize inset.

The elder Shabet settled himself at the desk. "So then, how can we help you?"

"An acquaintance in Paris gave me your name."

"Paris. Oh, are you Monsieur André?"

"It's the name I asked him to use."

Shabet looked him over. He was in his sixties, Morath thought, with fine features and silver hair, a white silk yarmulke on the back of his head. A comfortable man, wealthy, and confident in what he knew about the world. "The times we live in," he said, forgiving Morath a small deception. "Your friend in Paris sent someone up to see me. Your interest is, I believe, investment."

"More or less. The money is in Hungarian pengo, about two million."

"You don't interest yourself in shape or quality, that you leave to us. Simply a question of conversion."

"To diamonds."

Shabet folded his hands on the desk, his thumbs pressed together. "The stones are available, of course." He knew it wasn't that simple.

"And once we own them, we would like them sold."

"By us?"

"By your associates, perhaps family associates, in New York. And the money paid into an account in America."

"Ah."

"And if, to save the expense of shipping, the firm in New York was to use its own inventory, stones of equal value, that would not concern us."

"You have in mind a letter, I think. Us to them, and the accounting worked out within the family, is that it?"

Morath nodded and handed Shabet a sheet of cream-colored writing paper.

Shabet took a pince-nez from his breast pocket and settled it on the bridge of his nose. "United Chemical Supply," he read. "Mr. J. S. Horvath, treasurer. At the Chase National Bank, the Park Avenue branch." He laid the paper on the desk and put the pince-nez back in his pocket.

"Monsieur André? What sort of money is this?"

"Donated money."

"For espionage?"

"No."

"What then?"

"For certain funds. To be available in case of—national emergency."

"Am I doing business with the Hungarian government?"

"You are not. The money is given by private donors. It is not Fascist money, not expropriated, not extorted, not stolen. The politics of this money is the politics of what the newspapers call 'the Shadow Front.' Which is to say, liberals, legitimists, Jews, intellectuals."

Shabet wasn't pleased, he frowned, the look of a man who might want to say no but can't. "It's a great deal of money, sir."

"We ask just this single transfer."

Shabet looked out the window, a few flakes of snow drifted through the air. "Well, it's a very old method."

"Medieval."

Shabet nodded. "And you trust us to do this? There will be no receipt, nothing like that."

"You are, we believe, an established firm."

"I would say we are, Monsieur André, I would have to say we are. Since 1550."

Shabet took the sheet of paper from his desk, folded it in half, and slipped it in the desk drawer. "There was a time," he said, "when we

might have suggested you do business with somebody else. But now—"
It wasn't necessary to finish the sentence, and Shabet didn't bother.
"Very well," he said, "you have the money with you?"

It was dusk by the time they tried to find their way out of Antwerp.
They had a city map, apparently drawn by a high-spirited Belgian an-
archist, and argued with each other as the Peugeot wound through
the narrow streets, Morath stabbing his finger at the map and telling
Balki where they were, Balki looking at the street signs and telling
Morath where they weren't.

The windshield wipers squeaked as they swept wet snow back and
forth across the cloudy glass. In one street, a fire, it took forever to
back the car out. They turned into the next street behind a junk man's
horse and wagon, then tried another, which led to a statue of a king
and a dead end. Balki said, "*Merde,*" got the car going in the opposite direction, took the next left.

Which was, for some reason, vaguely familiar to Morath, he'd
been there before. Then he saw why—the shop called Homme du
Monde, Madame Golsztahn's tuxedo-rental business. But there was
no mannequin in the window. Only a hand-lettered sign saying
FERMÉ.

"What is it?" Balki said.

Morath didn't answer.

Maybe the Belgian border guards didn't care who came and went, but
the French customs inspectors did. "The watch, monsieur. Is it, ah,
new?"

"Bought in Paris," Balki told them.

It was hot in the customs shed, an iron stove glowed in one corner,
and it smelled of wet wool from the inspectors' capes. *A Russian?
And a Hungarian? With residence permits? Work permits? The Hungarian with a diplomatic passport? In a borrowed automobile?*

So then, just exactly what kind of, *business* had them crossing the
border in a snowstorm? Perhaps we'll have a look in the trunk. The
key, *monsieur,* if you please.

Morath began to calculate time. To be at the café on the rue Guisarde at ten o'clock, they should have left this hell an hour earlier. Outside, a truck driver honked his horn. The traffic began to back up as one of the inspectors tried to reach the Paris *préfecture* on the telephone. Morath could hear the operator's voice as she argued with the inspector, who held his hand over the receiver and said to his supervisor, "She says there's a line down in Lille."

"Our calls don't go through Lille, she of all people should know that!"

Morath and Balki exchanged a look. But the chief officer grew bored with them a few minutes later and sent them on their way with an imperious flip of the hand. If they insisted on being foreigners it certainly wasn't *his* fault.

Out on Route 2, snow.

The Peugeot crawled behind an old Citroën *camionnette* with the name of a Soissons grocery painted on the rear door. Balki swore under his breath and tried to pass, the wheels spun, the Peugeot began to fishtail, Balki stamped on the brake, Morath saw the white, furious face of the *camionnette*'s driver as it skidded past, the Peugeot spun in a circle, then plowed into a field, wheels bouncing on ruts beneath the snow.

They came to rest a few feet from a large plane tree, its trunk scarred by the indiscretions of past motorists. Balki and Morath stood in the falling snow and stared at the car. The right rear tire was flat.

Ten minutes to midnight, the rue Guisarde white and silent in the whispering snow, the lights of the café an amber glow at the end of the street. He saw her right away, the last customer, looking very sorrowful and abandoned, sitting hunched over a book and an empty cup of coffee.

He sat down across from her. "Forgive me," he said.

"Oh, it doesn't matter."

"A nightmare, out on the roads. We had to change a tire."

He took her hands.

"You're wet," she said.

"And cold."

"Maybe you should go home. It hasn't been a good night."

He didn't want to go home.

"Or you could come upstairs. Dry your hair, at least."

He rose. Took a few francs from his pocket and put them on the table for the coffee.

A very small apartment, a single room with a bed in an alcove and a bathroom. He took off his overcoat, she hung it by the radiator. Put his jacket in the armoire and his soaked shoes on a sheet of newspaper.

They sat on an elaborate old sofa, a Victorian horror, the sort of thing that, once it came up five flights of stairs, was never going anywhere again. "Dear old thing," she said affectionately, smoothing the brown velvet cushion with her hand. "She often plays a role in the D. E. Cameron novels."

"Field of honor."

"Yes." She laughed and said, "Actually, I was lucky to find this place. I'm not the legal tenant, that's why my name isn't in the phone book. It belongs to a woman called Moni."

"Moni?"

"Well, I think she's actually Mona but, if you're Mona, I guess the only pet name is Moni."

"Short and dark? Likes to stir up trouble?"

"That's her. She's an artist, from Montreal, lives with her girlfriend over by Bastille somewhere. Where did you meet Moni?"

"Juan-les-Pins. She was one of Cara's friends."

"Oh. Well, anyhow, she was a godsend. When Jean-Marie died, I swore I was going to stay in that apartment, but I couldn't bear it. I miss a refrigerator, in the summer, but I have a hotplate, and I can see Saint Sulpice."

"It's quiet."

"Lost in the stars."

She took a bottle of wine from the windowsill, opened it and poured him a glass, and one for herself. He lit a cigarette and she got him a Ricon ashtray.

"It's Portuguese," she said.

He took a sip. "Very good."

"Not bad, I'd say."

"Not at all."

"I like it."

"Mm."

"Garrafeira, it's called."

Christ it's a long way across this couch.

"What was it you were reading, in the café?"

"Babel."

"In French?"

"English. My father was Irish, but I had to learn it in school. My mother was French, and we lived in Paris and spoke French at home."

"So, officially, you're French."

"Irish. I've only been there twice, but on my eighteenth birthday I had to pick one or the other. Both my parents wanted me to be Irish— something my mother wanted for my father, I think that's what it was. Anyhow, who cares. Citizen of the world, right?"

"Are you?"

"No, I'm French, my heart is, I can't help it. My publisher thought I wrote in English, but I lied about it. I write in French and translate."

Morath walked over to the window, stared down at the snow float-ing past the street lamps. Mary Day followed, a moment later, and leaned against him. He took her hand.

"Did you like Ireland?" His voice was soft.

"It was very beautiful," she said.

It was a relief to get it over with, the first time, because God only knew what could go wrong. The second time was much better. She had a long, smooth body, silky and lean. Was a little shy to begin with, then not. The bed was narrow, not really meant for two, but she slept in his arms all night so it didn't matter.

Christmas Eve. A long-standing tradition, the baroness Frei's Christ-mas party. Mary Day was tense in the taxi—this was a party they hadn't quite fought over. He had to go, he didn't want to leave her home alone on Christmas Eve. "Something new for you," he'd said. "A Hungarian evening."

"Who will I talk to?"

"Mary, *ma douce,* there is no such thing as a Hungarian who speaks only Hungarian. The people at the party will speak French, perhaps English. And if, God forbid, you are presented to somebody only to discover that you cannot say a single comprehensible word to each other, well, so what? A smile of regret, and you escape to the buffet."

In the end, she went. In something black—and very faintly strange, like everything she wore—but she looked even more heartbreaking than usual. She was of course delighted at the impasse Villon, and the house. And the servant who bowed when they came to the door and whisked away their coats.

"Nicholas?" she whispered.

"Yes?"

"That was a liveried footman, Nicholas." She looked around. The candles, the silver, the hundred-year-old crèche above the fireplace, the men, the women. In a distant room, a string quartet.

The baroness Frei was pleased to see him accompanied, and obviously approved of his choice. "You must come and see me sometime, when we can talk," she said to Mary Day. Who stayed on Morath's arm for only ten minutes before a baron took her away.

Morath, glass of champagne in hand, found himself in conversation with a man introduced as Bolthos, an official at the Hungarian legation. Very refined, with gray hair at the temples, looking, Morath thought, like an oil painting of a 1910 diplomat. Bolthos wanted to talk politics. "Hitler is enraged with them," he said of the Roumanians. "Calinescu, the interior minister, made quick work of the Iron Guard. With the king's approval, naturally. They shot Codreanu and fourteen of his lieutenants. 'Shot while trying to escape,' as the saying goes."

"Perhaps we have something to learn from them."

"It was a message, I think. Keep your wretched trash out of our country, Adolf."

Morath agreed. "If we joined with Poland and Roumania, even the Serbs, and confronted him, we might actually survive this."

"Yes, the Intermarium. And I agree with you, especially if the French would help."

The French had signed a treaty of friendship with Berlin two weeks earlier—Munich reconfirmed. "Would they?" Morath said.

Bolthos had some champagne. "At the last minute, perhaps, after we've given up hope. It takes the French a long time to do the right thing."

"The Poles won't have any Munich," Morath said.

"No, they'll fight."

"And Horthy?"

"Will slither, as always. In the end, however, it may not be enough. Then into the cauldron we go."

Bolthos's stunning wife joined them, all platinum hair and diamond earrings. "I hope I haven't caught you talking politics," she said with a mock scowl. "It's *Christmas,* dearest, not the time for duels."

"Your servant, sir." Morath clicked his heels and bowed.

"There, you see?" Madame Bolthos said. "Now you'll have to get up at dawn, and serves you right."

"Quick!" said a young woman. "It's Kolovitzky!"

"Where?"

"In the ballroom."

Morath followed her as she cut through the crowd. "Do I know you?"

The woman looked over her shoulder and laughed.

In the ballroom, the eminent cellist Bela Kolovitzky stood on the raised platform and grinned at the gathering crowd. His colleagues, the remainder of the string quartet, joined them. Kolovitzky tucked a handkerchief between his neck and shoulder and settled himself around a violin. He'd been famous and successful in Budapest, then, in 1933, had gone to Hollywood.

" 'Flight of the Bumble Bee'!" somebody called out, clearly joking.

Kolovitzky played a discordant bleat, then looked between his feet. "Something else?"

Then he began to play, a slow, deep, romantic melody, vaguely familiar. "This is from *Enchanted Holiday*," he said.

The music grew sadder. "Now Hedy Lamarr looks up at the steamship."

And now, wistful. "She sees Charles Boyer at the railing. . . . He is searching for her . . . among the crowd. . . . She starts to raise her hand . . . halfway up . . . now back down . . . no, they can never be together . . . now the steamship blows its horn"—he made the sound on the violin—"Charles Boyer is frantic . . . where is she?"

"What *is* that?" a woman asked. "I almost know it."

Kolovitzky shrugged. "Something midway between Tchaikovsky and Brahms. *Brahmsky*, we call him." He began to speak English, in a comic Hungarian accent. "It muzt be zo tender, ro-*man*-tic, zenti-*ment*al. Zo lovely it makes . . . Sam Goldwyn cry . . . and makes . . . Kolovitzky . . . rich."

Morath wandered through the party, looking for Mary Day. He found her in the library, sitting by a blazing fire. She was leaning forward on a settee, a thumb keeping her place in a book, as she listened earnestly to a tiny white-haired gentleman in a leather chair, his hand resting on a stick topped with a silver ram's head. At Mary Day's feet lay one of the vizslas, supine with bliss, as Mary Day's ceaseless stroking of its velvety skin had reduced it to a state of semiconsciousness. "Then, from that hill," said the white-haired gentleman, "you can see the temple of Pallas Athena."

Morath sat on a spindly chair by a French door, eating cake from a plate balanced on his knee. The baroness Frei sat close to him, back curved in a silk evening gown, face, as always, luminous. *One could say,* Morath thought, *that she is the most beautiful woman in Europe.*

"And your mother, Nicholas, what did she say?"

"She will not leave."

"I will write to her," the baroness said firmly.

"Please," he said. "But I doubt she'll change her mind."

"Stubborn! Always her way."

"She did say, just before I left, that she could live with the Germans, if she had to, but if the country was to be occupied by the Russians, I must find a way to get her out. 'Then,' she told me, 'I will come to Paris.' "

He found Mary Day and took her out into the winter garden; dead leaves plastered to the iron chairs and table, bare rose canes climbing up through the trellis. The frozen air made the sky black and the stars white and sharp. When she started to tremble, Morath stood behind her and wrapped her in his arms. "I love you, Nicholas," she said.

INTERMARIUM

10 MARCH 1939.

Amen. The world in chaos, half the armies in Europe mobilized, diplomats in constant motion, popping up here and there like tin monkeys in shooting galleries. Very much, Morath thought, like tin monkeys in shooting galleries.

Crossing the Pont Royal on his way to lunch, late, unhurried, he stopped and leaned on the stone parapet. The river ran full and heavy, its color like shining slate, its surface roughed up by the March wind and the spring currents. In the western sky, white scud blew in from the channel ports. *The last days of Pisces,* he thought, dreams and mysteries. When it rained in the middle of the night they woke up and made love.

He looked at his watch—Polanyi would be waiting for him—was there any way to avoid this? From here the Seine flowed north, to Rouen, to Normandy, to the sea. *Escape.*

No, lunch.

Thirty minutes later, the Brasserie Heininger. A white marble staircase climbed to a room of red plush banquettes, painted cupids, gold cords on the draperies. Waiters in muttonchop whiskers ran back and forth, carrying silver trays of pink langoustes. Morath was relieved. No more Prévert, "the beauty of sinister things," the Count von Polanyi de Nemeszvar had apparently risen from the lower depths, tempted by sumptuous food and a wine list bound in leather.

Polanyi greeted him formally in Hungarian and stood to shake hands.

"I'm sorry to be late."

A bottle of Echézeaux was open on the table, a waiter scurried over and poured Morath a glass. He took a sip and stared at the mirrored panel above the banquette. Polanyi followed his eyes.

"Don't look now, but there's a bullet hole in the mirror behind you," Morath said.

"Yes. The infamous Table Fourteen, this place has a history."

"Really?"

"Two years ago, I think. The headwaiter was assassinated while sitting on the toilet in the ladies' bathroom."

"Well he won't do *that* again."

"With a machine gun, it's said. Something to do with Bulgarian politics."

"Oh. And in his memory . . ."

"Yes. Also, the story goes, some kind of British spymistress used to hold court here."

"At this very table."

The waiter returned, Polanyi ordered mussels and a *choucroute royale*.

"What's '*royale*'?" Morath asked.

"They cook the sauerkraut in champagne instead of beer."

"You can taste the champagne? In sauerkraut?"

"An illusion. But one likes the idea of it."

Morath ordered *suprêmes de volaille,* chicken breast in cream, the simplest dish he could find.

"Have you heard what's happened at the French air ministry?" Polanyi said.

"Now what."

"Well first of all, they let a contract for building fighter planes to a furniture manufacturer."

"Somebody's brother-in-law."

"Probably. And then, they decided to store their secret papers at a testing facility just outside Paris. Stored them in a disused wind tunnel. Only they forgot to tell the technicians, who turned the thing on and blew the papers all over the neighborhood."

Morath shook his head; there was a time when it would have been funny. "They'll have Adolf in the Elysée Palace, if they don't watch out."

"Not in our lifetime," Polanyi said, finishing off his wine and refilling the glass. "We think Adolf is about to make a mistake."

"Which is?"

"Poland. Lately he's been screaming about Danzig—'is German, has always been German, will always be German.' His radio station tells Germans in the city to 'keep a list of your enemies, soon the German army will help you to punish them.' So what must happen now is a pact, between the Poles, the Roumanians, and us—the Yugoslavs can join if they like. The Intermarium, so-called, the lands between the seas, the Baltic and the Adriatic. Together, we're strong. Poland has the largest land army in Europe, and we can deny Hitler Roumanian wheat and oil. If we can make him back down, call his bluff, that will be the end of him."

Polanyi saw that Morath was skeptical. "I know, I know," he said. "Ancient hatreds and territorial disputes and all the rest of it. But, if we don't do something, we'll all go the way of the Czechs."

The lunch arrived, the waiter announcing each dish as he set it down.

"And what does Horthy think about all this?"

"Supports it. Perhaps you know the background of political events in February, perhaps you don't. Officially, Imredy resigned and Count Teleki became the prime minister. In fact, Horthy was told that a Budapest newspaper was about to publish proof, obtained in Czechoslovakia, that Dr. Bela Imredy, the rabid anti-Semite, was Jewish. Had, at least, a Jewish great-grandfather. So Imredy didn't jump, he was pushed. And, when he resigned, Horthy chose to replace him with Teleki, an internationally prominent geographer and a liberal. Which means Horthy supports at least some resistance to German objectives as the best means of keeping Hungary out of another war."

"With Great Britain and France. And, sooner or later, America. We'll surely win that one."

"You forgot Russia," Polanyi said. "How's your chicken?"

"Very good."

Polanyi took a moment, using a knife to pile a small mound of sauerkraut atop a bite of frankfurter on his fork, then added a dab of mustard. "You don't mind the Poles, do you, Nicholas?"

"Not at all."

"Lovely countryside. And the mountains, the Tatra, sublime. Especially this time of year."

"So it's said."

"Nicholas!"

"Yes?"

"Can it be possible that you've never been there? To the majestic Tatra?"

A memorandum on his desk at the Agence Courtmain requested that he have a look at the file on Betravix, a nerve tonic made of beets. And there he found a postcard of a wild-eyed Zeus, beard blown sideways by a thundercloud above his head, about to ravish an extraordinarily pink and naked Hera he'd got hold of by the foot. On the back of the card, a drawing, in red crayon, of a heart pierced by an exclamation point.

He sat through a meeting with Courtmain, then, back in his office, found a second message, this one scrawled on a slip of paper: *Your friend Ilya called. M.*

He walked down the hall to her office, a glassed-in cubicle by a window. "I liked your card," he said. "Is this the sort of thing that goes on when you take Betravix?"

"I wouldn't, if I were you." The late afternoon sun slanted in on her hair. "Did you get your telephone message?"

"I did. Who's Ilya?"

"A friend, he said. He wants you to meet him." She thumbed

through a stack of notes on her desk. "For a drink. At the café on rue Maubeuge, across from the Gare du Nord. At six-fifteen."

Ilya? "You're sure it was for me?"

She nodded. "He said, 'Can you tell Nicholas.' "

"Is there another Nicholas?"

She thought about it. "Not in this office. He sounded nice enough, very calm. With a Russian accent."

"Well, who knows."

"You'll go?"

He hesitated. Unknown Russians, meetings at station cafés. "Why did he call *you?*"

"I don't know, my love." She looked past him, to her doorway. "Is that it?"

He turned to see Léon with a sketch of a woman in a fur stole. "I can come back later, if you're busy," Léon said.

"No, we're done," Morath said.

For the rest of the day he thought about it. Couldn't stop. Almost called Polanyi, then didn't. Decided, finally, to stay away. He left the office at five-thirty, stood for a moment on the avenue Matignon, then waved at a taxi, intending to go back to his apartment.

"Monsieur?" the driver said.

"The Gare du Nord." *Je m'en fous,* the hell with it.

He sat in the café, an unread newspaper beside his coffee, staring at people as they came through the door. Was it something to do with the diamond dealer in Antwerp? Somebody Balki knew? Or a friend of a friend—*Call Morath when you get to Paris.* Somebody who wanted to sell him insurance, maybe, or a stockbroker, or an émigré who needed a job. A Russian client? Who wanted to advertise his . . . shoe store?

Anything, really, but what he knew it was.

Morath waited until seven, then took a taxi to Mary Day's apartment. They drank a glass of wine, made love, went out for *steak-frites,* walked home, curled up together under the blankets. But he woke up at three-thirty, and again at five.

And, when the phone rang in his office on Monday morning, waited three rings before he picked it up.

"My apology, Monsieur Morath. I hope you will forgive." A soft voice, heavily accented.

"Who are you?"

"Just Ilya. I'll be, tomorrow morning, at the open market at Maubert."

"And this concerns—?"

"Thank you," he said. In the background, somebody called out *"Un café allongé."* There was a radio playing, a chair scraped a tile floor, then the phone was hung up.

A big market, at the place Maubert, on Tuesdays and Saturdays. Cod and red snapper on chipped ice. Cabbages, potatoes, turnips, leeks, onions. Dried rosemary and lavender. Walnuts and hazelnuts. A pair of bloody pork kidneys wrapped in a sheet of newspaper.

Morath saw him, waiting in a doorway. *A spectre.* Stared for a moment, got a nod in return.

They walked among the stalls, breaths steaming in the cold air.

"Do I know you?" Morath asked.

"No," Ilya said. "But I know you."

There was something subtly mismade about him, Morath thought, perhaps a trunk too long for the legs, or arms too short. A receding hairline, with hair sheared so close he seemed at first to have a high forehead. A placid face, waxy and pale, which made a thick black mustache even blacker. And in his bearing there was a hint of the doctor or the lawyer, the man who trained himself, for professional reasons, not to show emotion. He wore a sad old overcoat, olive green, perhaps a remnant of somebody's army, somewhere, so soiled and frayed that its identity had long ago faded away.

"Did we meet, somewhere?" Morath asked him.

"Not quite. I know you from your dossier, in Moscow. The sort of record kept by the special services. It is, perhaps, more complete than you would expect. Who you know, what you earn. Political views, family—just the usual things. I had a choice of hundreds of people, in Paris. Various nationalities, circumstances. Eventually, I chose you."

They walked in silence, for a time. "I am in flight, of course. I was due to be shot, in the purge of the Foreign Directorate. My friends had been arrested, had vanished, as is the normal course of things there. At the time, I was in—I can say, Europe. And when I was recalled to Moscow—to receive a medal, they said—I knew precisely what medal that was, nine grams, and I knew precisely what was in store for me before they got around to using the bullet. So, I ran away, and came to Paris to hide. For seven months I lived in a room. I believe I left the room three times in that period."

"How did you live?"

Ilya shrugged. "The way one does. Using the little money I had, I bought a pot, a spirit stove, and a large sack of oats. With water, available down the hall from my room, I could boil the oats and make kasha. Add a little lard and you can live on that. I did."

"And me? What do you want of me?"

"Help."

A policeman walked past, his cape drawn around him for warmth. Morath avoided his glance.

"There are things that should be known," Ilya said. "Perhaps you can help me to do this."

"They are looking for you, of course."

"High and low. And they will find me."

"Should you be out on the street?"

"No."

They passed a *boulangerie*. "A moment," Morath said, entered the shop and emerged with a *bâtard*. He tore a piece off the end and handed the rest to Ilya.

Morath chewed on the bread for a long time. His mouth was very dry and it was hard to swallow.

"I've put you in danger, I know," Ilya said. "And your woman friend. For that I must apologize."

"You knew to call me through her, where she works?"

"I followed you, monsieur. It isn't so very hard to do."

"No, I suppose it isn't."

"You can walk away, of course. I would not bother you again."

"Yes. I know."

"But you do not."

Morath didn't answer.

Ilya smiled. "So," he said.

Morath reached in his pocket and handed Ilya whatever money he had.

"For your kindness, I thank you," Ilya said. "And, for anything more, if God wills, please keep in mind that I don't have very much time."

Morath took Mary Day to the movies that night, a gangster film, as luck would have it, detectives chasing a handsome bank robber down alleys in the rain. A noble savage, his dark soul redeemed by love in the previous reel, but the *flics* didn't know that. The little scarf in his hand when he died in a puddle under a streetlamp—that belonged to dear, good, stunning, tight-sweatered Dany. No justice, in this world. A covert sniffle from Mary Day, that was all he got. When the newsreel came on—coal mine cave-in at Lille, Hitler shrieking in Regensburg—they left.

Back on the rue Guisarde, they lay in bed in the darkness. "Did you find your Russian?" she said.

"This morning. Over in the Maubert market."

"And?"

"A fugitive."

"Oh?"

She felt light in his arms, fragile.

"What did he want?" she said.

"Some kind of help."

"Will you help him?"

For a moment he was silent, then said, "I might."

He didn't want to talk about it, slid his hand down her stomach to change the subject. "See what happens when I take my Betravix?"

She snickered. "Now that is something I *did* see. A week after I was hired, I think it was. You were off someplace—wherever it is you go— and this strange little man showed up with his tonic. 'For the nerves,' he said. 'And to increase the vigor.' Courtmain was anxious to take it on. We sat in his office, this green bottle on his desk, somewhere he'd found a spoon. I took the cap off and smelled it. Courtmain looked inquisitive, but I didn't say anything—I'd only been there a few days and I was afraid to make a mistake. Well, nothing scares Courtmain, he poured himself a spoonful and slugged it down. Then he turned pale and went running down the hall."

"Betravix—keeps you running."

"The look on his face." She snorted at the memory.

The Ides of March. On the fifteenth, German motorized infantry, motorcycles, half-tracks, and armored cars entered Prague in a heavy blizzard. The Czech army did not resist, the air force stayed on the ground. All day long, the Wehrmacht columns wound through the city, headed for the Slovakian border. The following morning, Hitler addressed a crowd of *Volksdeutsch* from the balcony of Hradcany Castle. Over the next few days, there were five thousand arrests in Czechoslovakia and hundreds of suicides.

Two weeks earlier, Hungary had joined the Anti-Comintern Pact—Germany, Italy, and Japan—while simultaneously initiating a severe repression of Fascist elements throughout the country. *We will oppose the Bolsheviks,* the action seemed to say, *and we can sign any paper we like, but we will not be ruled by Nazi surrogates.* In a certain light, a dark, tormented kind of light, it made sense. Even more sense when, on 14 March, the Honved, the Royal Hungarian army, marched across the border and occupied Ruthenia. Slowly, painfully, the old territories were coming back.

In Paris, the driving snow in Prague fell as rain. The news was alive on the streets. Under black, shining umbrellas, crowds gathered at the kiosks where the headlines were posted. BETRAYAL. Morath could feel it in the air. As though the beast, safely locked in the basement at the time of Munich, had kicked the door down and started smashing the china.

The receptionist at the agency answered the phone while dabbing at her eyes with a handkerchief. A subdued Courtmain showed Morath a list of younger men in the office who would likely be mobilized—how to get along without them? In the hallways, conversations in urgent whispers.

But, when Morath left the office at midday, nobody was whispering. In the streets, at the café and the bank and everywhere else, it was *merde* and *merde* again. And *merdeux, un beau merdier, merdique, emmerdé,* and *emmerdeur.* The Parisians had a lot of ways to say it and they used them all. Morath's newspaper, violently pessimistic about the future, reminded its readers what Churchill had said in response to Chamberlain's peace-with-honor speeches at the time of Munich: "You were given the choice between war and dishonor. You chose dishonor, and you will have war."

On 28 March, Madrid fell to Franco's armies, and the Spanish republic surrendered. Mary Day sat on the edge of the bed in her flannel nightshirt, listening to the voice on the radio. "You know I once had a friend," she said, close to tears. "An Englishman. Tall and silly, blind as a bat—Edwin Pennington. Edwin Pennington, who wrote *Annabelle Surprised,* and *Miss Lovett's School.* And then one day he went off and died in Andalusia."

For Morath, at work that morning, a *petit bleu,* a telegram delivered via the pneumatic-tube system used by the Parisian post offices. A simple message: NOTRE DAME DE LORETTE. 1:30.

The church of Notre Dame de Lorette was out in the scruffy Ninth Arrondissement—the whores in the neighborhood known as *Lorettes.* In the streets around the church, Ilya would not seem especially noticeable. Morath's best instincts told him not to go. He sat back in his chair, stared at the telegram, smoked a cigarette, and left the office at one.

It was dark and busy in the church, mostly older women, that time of day. *War widows,* he thought, dressed in black, early for the two o'clock Mass. He found the deepest shadow, toward the back, away from the stained-glass windows. Ilya appeared almost immediately. He was tense, the small bravado of the Maubert market was no more. He sat down, then took a deep breath and let it out, as though he'd been running. "Good," he said, speaking softly. "You are here.

"You see what happens in Prague," he said, "and next is Poland. You don't need me to tell you that. But what is not known is that the directive is *written,* the war plan is made. It has a name, *Fall Weiss,* Case White, and it has a date, any time after the first of September."

Morath repeated the name and the date.

"I can prove," Ilya said, excited, losing his French. "With papers." He paused a moment, then said, "This is good Chekist work, but it must go—up high. Otherwise, war. No way to stop it. Can you help?"

"I can try."

Ilya stared into his eyes to see if he was telling the truth. "That is what I hope." He had enormous presence, Morath thought. Power. Even battered and hungry and frightened, he had it.

"There's somebody I can go to," Morath said.

Ilya's expression said *If that's what I can get, I'll take it.* "The Poles are in the middle of this thing," he said. "And they are difficult, impossible. In the five-man junta that runs the country, only Beck and Rydz-Smigly matter—Beck for foreign policy, Rydz-Smigly for the army—but they are all Pilsudski's children. When he died, in 1935, they inherited the country, and they have the same experience. They fought for independence in 1914, and got it. Then they beat the Russians, in 1920, before the gates of Warsaw, and now they want nothing to do with them. Too many wars, the last hundred years. Too much blood spilled. There's a point where, between nations, it's too late. That's Russia and Poland.

"Now, they think they can beat Germany. Jozef Beck's background is in clandestine service—he was expelled from France in 1923 when he served as Polish military attaché, suspected of spying for Germany. So what he knows of Russia and Germany he knows from the shadows, where the truth is usually to be found.

"What the Poles want is alliance with France and Britain. Logical, on the surface. But how can Britain help them? With ships? Like Gallipoli? It's a joke. The only nation that can help Poland, today, is Russia—look at a map. And Stalin wants the same thing the Poles want, alliance with Britain, for the same reason, to keep Hitler's wolves away from the door. But we are despised by the British, feared, hated, Godless communists and murderers. That's true, but what is also true, even more true, is that we are the only nation that can form, with Poland, an eastern front against the Wehrmacht.

"Chamberlain and Halifax don't like this idea, and there is more than a little evidence that what they do like is the idea of Hitler fighting Stalin. Do they think Stalin doesn't know it? Do they? So here is the truth: If Stalin can't make a pact with the British, he will make one with Germany. He will have no choice."

Morath didn't answer, trying to take it all in. The two o'clock Mass had begun, a young priest serving in the afternoon. Morath thought he would hear about bloody crimes: famines, purges. Ilya wasn't the only defector from the Russian secret service—there was a GRU general, called Krivitsky, who'd written a bestseller in America. Ilya, he assumed, wanted protection, refuge, in return for evidence that Stalin meant to rule the world.

"You believe?" Ilya said.

"Yes." More or less, from a certain angle.

"Your friend, can approach the British?"

"I would think he could. And the papers?"

"When he agrees, he'll have them."

"What are they?"

"From the Kremlin, notes of meetings. NKVD reports, copies of German memoranda."

"Can I contact you?"

Ilya smiled and, slowly, shook his head. "How much time do you need?"

"A week, perhaps."

"So be it." Ilya stood. "I will go first, you can leave in a few minutes. Is safer, that way."

Ilya headed for the door. Morath stayed where he was. He glanced at his watch, followed along with the priest's Latin phrases. He'd grown up with it, then, when he came home from the war, stopped going.

Finally, he rose and walked slowly to the back of the church.

Ilya was standing just inside the door, staring out into the rain. Morath stood beside him. "You're staying here?"

He nodded toward the street. "A car."

In front of the church, a Renault with a man in the passenger seat.

"For me, maybe," Ilya said.

"We'll go together."

"No."

"Out the side door, then."

Ilya looked at him. They're waiting at only one door? He almost laughed. "Trapped," he said.

"Go back where we were, I'll come and get you. Just stay where people are."

Ilya hesitated, then walked away.

Morath was furious. *To die in the rain on Tuesday afternoon!* Out in the street, he hunted for a taxi. Hurried along the rue Peletier, then rue Drouot. At the corner, an empty taxi pulled up in front of a small hotel. As Morath ran for it, he saw a portly gentleman with a woman on his arm come out of the lobby. Morath and the portly gentleman opened the rear doors at the same moment and stared at each other across the backseat. "Forgive me, my friend," the man said, "but I telephoned for this taxi." He offered the woman his hand and she climbed in.

Morath stood there, water running down his face.

"Monsieur!" the woman said, pointing across the street. "What luck!"

An empty taxi had stopped in traffic, Morath thanked the woman and waved at it. He got in and told the driver where to go. "I have a friend waiting," he said.

At the church, Morath found Ilya and hurried him to the door. The taxi was idling at the foot of the steps, the Renault had disappeared. "Quickly," Morath said.

Ilya hesitated.

"Let's go," Morath said, his voice urgent. Ilya didn't move, he seemed frozen, hypnotized. "They're not going to kill you here."

"Oh yes."

Morath looked at him. Realized it was something Ilya knew, had seen. Had, perhaps, done. From the taxi, an impatient bleat of the horn.

He took Ilya by the arm and said, *"Now."* Fought the instinct to stay low and sprint, and they trotted down the steps together.

In the taxi, Ilya gave the driver an address and, as they drove away, turned around and stared out the back window.

"Was it somebody you recognized?" Morath said.

"Not this time. Once before, maybe. And once, certainly."

For long minutes, the taxi crawled behind a bus, the rear platform crowded with passengers. Suddenly, Ilya called out, "Driver, stop here!" He leapt from the taxi and ran down the entry of a Métro station. Chaussée d'Antin, Morath saw, a busy *correspondence* where riders could transfer from one line to another.

The driver watched him go, then twisted an index finger against his temple, which meant *crazy* in taxi sign language. He turned and gave Morath a sour look. "And now?" he said.

"Avenue Matignon. Just off the boulevard."

That was a long way from Chaussée d'Antin, especially in the rain. Taking people from one place to another was fundamentally an imposition—clearly that was the driver's view. He sighed, rammed the gearshift home, and spun his tires as he took off. "What goes on with your friend?" he said.

"His wife is chasing him."

"Woof!" Better him than me.

A few minutes later he said, "Seen the papers?"

"Not today."

"Even old *J'aime Berlin* is giving it to Hitler now." He used the Parisian pun on Chamberlain's name with great relish.

"What's happened?"

"A speech. 'Maybe Adolf wants to rule the world.' "

"Maybe he does."

The driver turned to look at Morath. "Just let him take his army up into *Poland,* and that'll be the end of that."

"I forbid you to see him again," Polanyi said. They were at a café near the legation. "Anyhow, there's a part of me wants to tell you that."

Morath was amused. "You sound like a father in a play."

"Yes, I suppose. Do you buy it, Nicholas?"

"Yes and no."

"I have to admit that everything he says is true. But what troubles me is the possibility that someone on Dzerzhinsky Street sent him here. After all, anybody can buy an overcoat."

"Does it matter?"

Polanyi acknowledged that it might not. If diplomats couldn't persuade the British, maybe *a defector* could. "These games," he said. " 'Hungarian diplomats in contact with a Soviet operative.' "

"He said he had papers to prove it."

"Papers, yes. Like overcoats. Any way to get back in touch with him?"

"No."

"No, of course not." He thought for a moment. "All right, I'll mention it to somebody. But if this blows up, in some way we can't see from here, don't blame me."

"Why would I?"

"Next time he calls, if he calls, I'll see him. For God's sake don't tell *him* that, just accept the meeting and leave the rest to me."

Polanyi leaned forward and lowered his voice. "You see, whatever else happens now, we must not do anything that will compromise the prime minister. Teleki's our only way out of this mess—that little man's a *knight,* Nicholas, a hero. Don't go telling anyone this, but last week he paid some boys in Budapest to rub garlic on the doors of the foreign office, with a note that said 'German vampires keep out.' "

"Amen," Morath said. "How could contact with a defector damage Teleki?"

"I won't know until it's too late, Nicholas—that's the way things are done now. Sad, but true."

Sad, but true for Morath was, on the last day of March, another letter from the *préfecture.* Once again, Room 24, and six days until the appointment to worry about it. The Roumanians, he guessed, would not go away, but it wasn't a good guess.

They kept him waiting, outside the inspector's office, for forty-five minutes. *Calculated,* he thought, but he felt it working on him anyhow. The inspector hadn't changed: sitting at attention, square-faced and predatory, cold as ice. "You'll forgive us for troubling you again," he said. "A few things we're trying to clarify."

Morath waited patiently.

The inspector had all the time in the world. Slowly, he read over a page in the dossier. "Monsieur Morath. Have you, by chance, ever heard of a man called Andreas Panea?"

The name on the passport he'd obtained for Pavlo. He took a moment to steady himself. "Panea?"

"Yes, that's right. A Roumanian name."

Why this? Why now? "I don't believe I know him," he said.

The inspector made a note in the margin. "Please be certain, monsieur. Think it over, if you like."

"Sorry," he said. Graciously.

The inspector read further. Whatever was in there, it was substantial. "And Dr. Otto Adler? Is that name known to you?"

Able this time to tell the truth, Morath was relieved. "Once again," he said, "someone I don't know."

The inspector noted his response. "Dr. Otto Adler was the editor of a political journal—a socialist journal. An émigré from Germany, he came to France in the spring of 1938 and set up an editorial office in his home, in Saint Germain-en-Laye. Then, in June, he was murdered. Shot to death in the Jardin du Luxembourg. A political assassination, no doubt, and these are always difficult to solve, but we pride ourselves on keeping at it. Murder is murder, Monsieur Morath, even in times of—political turmoil."

The inspector saw it hit home—Morath thought he did. "Once again," Morath said, regret in his voice, "I don't believe I can help you."

The inspector seemed to accept what he'd said. He closed the dossier. "Perhaps you'll try to remember, monsieur. At your leisure. Something may come back to you."

Something had.

"If that should be the case," the inspector went on, "you can always get in touch with me here."

He called Polanyi. He called Polanyi from the café just across the Seine—the first public telephone you came to when you left the *préfecture*. They made a living from their neighbor, Morath thought, pushing a *jeton* into the slot. The refugees were easy to spot—a couple celebrating with wine they couldn't afford, a bearded man with his head in his hands.

"The count Polanyi is not available this afternoon," said a voice at the legation. Morath hung up the phone, a woman was waiting to use it. Polanyi would never decline to talk to him, would he?

He went to the Agence Courtmain, but he couldn't stay there. Saw Mary Day, for a moment. "Everything all right?" she said. He went to the WC and looked in the mirror—what had she seen? He was perhaps a little pale, nothing more. But the difference between Cara at twenty-six and Mary Day at forty, he thought, was that Mary Day understood what the world did to people. Sensed, apparently, that it had done something to Morath.

She didn't mention it, that evening, but she was immensely good to him. He couldn't say exactly how. Touched him more than usual, maybe that was it. He was sick at heart, she knew it, but didn't ask him why. They went to bed, he fell asleep, eventually, woke long before dawn, slid out of bed as quietly as he could and stood at the window, watching the night go by. *Nothing you can do, now.*

He didn't get to his apartment until noon of the following day, and the letter was waiting for him there. Hand-delivered, there was no stamp.

A clipping, from the 9 March edition of the newspaper that served the German community in Sofia. He supposed it was in the Bulgarian papers as well, some version of it, but the anonymous sender knew he could read German.

A certain Stefan Gujac, the story went, a Croat, had apparently hanged himself in his cell in a Sofia jail. This Gujac, using the false passport of a deceased Roumanian named Andreas Panea, was suspected by the security agencies of several Balkan countries of having taken part in more than a dozen political assassinations. Born in Zagreb, Gujac had joined the Fascist Ustachi organization and had been arrested several times in Croatia—for agitation and assault—and had served time in jail, three months, for robbing a bank in Trieste.

At the time of his arrest in Sofia, he had been sought for questioning by authorities in Salonika after a café bombing that killed seven people, including E. X. Patridas, an official in the interior ministry, and injured twenty others. In addition, police in Paris had wanted to question Gujac with regard to the killing of a German émigré, editor of a political journal.

Gujac's arrest in Sofia resulted from the attempted murder, thwarted by an alert police sergeant, of a Turkish diplomat in residence at the Grand Hotel Bulgarie. He had been questioned by Bulgarian police, who suspected the plot against the diplomat had been organized by Zveno, the terrorist gang based in Macedonia.

Gujac, twenty-eight years old, had hanged himself by fashioning a noose from his underwear. Sofia authorities said the suicide remained under investigation.

Polanyi agreed to see him later that afternoon, in the café near the Hungarian legation. Polanyi read his face when he walked in and said,

"Nicholas?" Morath wasted no time. Recounted his interrogation at the *préfecture,* then slid the newspaper clipping across the table.

"I didn't know," Polanyi said.

From Morath, a bitter smile.

"At the time it happened, I didn't know. Whatever you want to believe, that's the truth. I found out later, but by then the thing was done, and there was no point in telling you. Why? What good would it have done?"

"Not your fault, is that it?"

"Yes. That's it. This was Von Schleben's business. You don't understand what goes on in Germany now—the way power works. They trade, Nicholas, trade in lives and money and favors. The honorable men are gone. Retired mostly, if not murdered or chased out of the country. Von Schleben abides, that's his nature. He abides, and I deal with him. I must deal with somebody, so I deal with him. Then it's my turn to trade."

"A reciprocal arrangement." Morath's voice was cold.

"Yes. I assume an obligation, then I pay it off. I'm a banker, Nicholas, and if, at times, a sorrowful banker, so what?"

"So, reluctantly, but owing favors, you organized this killing."

"No. Von Schleben did that. Maybe it was a favor, a debt he had to pay, I don't know. Perhaps all *he* agreed to do was bring this, this *thing,* to Paris. I can't say who gave him his instructions once he got here, I don't know who paid him. Someone in the SS, start there, you'll find the culprit. Though I suspect you know that long before you find him he'll find you."

Polanyi paused a moment, then said, "You see, some days Von Schleben is a king, some days a pawn. Like me, Nicholas. Like you."

"And what I did in Czechoslovakia? Whose idea was that?"

"Again Von Schleben. On the other side, this time."

A waiter brought them coffee, the two cups sat untouched. "I'm sorry, Nicholas, and more concerned with this *préfecture* business than who did what to who last year, but what's done is done."

"Done for the last time."

"Then farewell and Godspeed. I would wish it for myself, Nicholas, but I can't resign from my country, and that's what this is all about. We can't pick up the nation and paste it on Norway. We are where we are, and everything follows from that."

"Who set the *préfecture* on me?"

"The same person who sent the clipping. Sombor, both times."

"You know?"

"You never know. You assume."

"To gain what?"

"You. And to damage me, who he sees as a rival. That's true—he's in the hands of the Arrow Cross, I most decidedly am not. What's at play here is Hungarian politics."

"Why send the clipping?"

"*It's not too late,* he means. So far, the *préfecture* knows only this much. Do you want me to tell them the rest? That's what he's asking you."

"I have to do something," Morath said. "Go away, perhaps."

"It may come to that. For the moment, you will leave it to me."

"Why?"

"I owe you at least that much."

"Why not have Von Schleben deal with it?"

"I could. But are you prepared to do what he asks in return?"

"You know he would?"

"Absolutely. After all, you are already in debt to him."

"I am? How?"

"Lest you forget, when the Siguranza had you in Roumania, he saved your life." Polanyi reached across the table and took his hand. "Forgive me, Nicholas. Forgive, forgive. Try and forgive the world for being what it is. Maybe next week Hitler drops dead and we all go out to dinner."

"And you'll pay."

"And I'll pay."

In April, the *grisaille,* the grayness, settled down on Paris as it always did. Gray buildings, gray skies, rain and mist in the long evenings. The artist Shublin had told him, one night in Juan-les-Pins, that in the spring of the year the art-supply stores could not keep the color called Payne's Gray in stock.

The city didn't mind its gray—found all that bright and sunny business in late winter a little too cheerful for its comfort. For Morath, life settled into a kind of brooding peace, his fantasy of *the ordinary life* not so sweet a reality as he liked to imagine. Mary Day embarked on a new novel, *Suzette* and *Suzette Goes Boating* now to be followed by *Suzette at Sea*. A luxury liner, its compass sabotaged by an evil competitor, wandering lost in the tropics. There was to be a licentious captain, a handsome sailor named Jack, an American millionaire, and the oily leader of the ship's orchestra, all of them scheming, one way or another, for a glimpse of Suzette's succulent breasts and rosy bottom.

Mary Day wrote for an hour or two every night, on a clackety typewriter, wearing a vast, woolly sweater with its sleeves pushed up her slim wrists. Morath would look up from his book to see her face in odd contortions, lips pressed together in concentration, and schemed for his own glimpse, which was easy to come by when writing was done for the night.

The world on the radio drifted idly toward blood and fire. Britain and France announced they would defend Poland if she was attacked. Churchill stated that "there is no means of maintaining an eastern front against Nazi aggression without the active aid of Russia." A speaker in the House of Commons said, "If we are going in without the help of Russia, we are walking into a trap." Morath watched as people read their newspapers in the cafés. They shrugged and turned the page, and so did he. It all seemed to happen in a faraway land, distant and unreal, where ministers arrived at railroad stations and monsters walked by night. Somewhere in the city, he knew, Ilya hid in a tiny room, or, perhaps, he had already been beaten to death in the Lubianka.

The chestnut trees bloomed, white blossoms stuck to the wet streets, the captain peeked through Suzette's keyhole as she brushed her long blond hair. Léon, the artist from the Agence Courtmain, went to Rome to see his fiancée and returned to Paris with a bruised face and a broken hand. Lucinda, the baroness Frei's sweetest vizsla, gave birth to a litter of puppies and Morath and Mary Day went to the rue Villon to eat Sacher torte and observe the new arrivals in a wicker basket decorated with silver passementerie. Adolf Hitler celebrated his fiftieth birthday. Under German pressure, Hungary resigned from the League of Nations. Morath went to a shop on the rue de la Paix and bought Mary Day a silk scarf, golden loops and swirls on a background of Venetian red. Wolfi Szubl called, clearly in great distress, and Morath left work and journeyed out to a dark little apartment in the depths of the 14th Arrondissement, on a street where Lenin had once lived in exile.

The apartment smelled like boiled flour and was everywhere corsets. Violet and lime green, pale pink and rose, white and black. A large sample case lay open on the unmade bed.

"Forgive the mess," Szubl said. "I'm taking inventory."

"Is Mitten here?"

"Mitten! Mitten's rich. He's on location in Strasbourg."

"Good for him."

"Not bad. *The Sins of Doktor Braunschweig.*"

"Which were—"

"Murders. Herbert is stabbed to death in the first ten minutes, so it's not a big part. With a knitting needle. Still, the money's good."

Szubl picked up a typed sheet of yellow paper and ran his finger down the page. "Nicholas, there's a bustier on the radiator, can you see the name?"

"This?" It was silver, with buttons up the back and garter snaps on the bottom. As Morath looked for the label he thought he smelled lavender bath powder. "Marie Louise," he said.

Szubl made a check mark on the list.

"Women try these on? The samples?"

"Now and then. Private fittings." He began to count through a small mound of girdles on the edge of the bed. "I just heard they want to promote me," he said.

"Congratulations."

"Disaster."

"Why?"

"The company is in Frankfurt, I'd have to live in Germany."

"So turn it down."

"It's the son—the old man got old and the son took over. 'A new day,' he says. 'New blood in the home office.' Anyhow, him I can deal with. This is why I called."

He took a folded paper from his pocket and handed it to Morath. A letter from the *préfecture*, summoning *Szubl, Wolfgang* to Room 24.

"Why this?" Szubl said.

"An investigation—but they don't know anything. However, they *will* try to scare you."

"They don't have to try. What should I say?"

"Don't know, wasn't there, never met him. You aren't going to make them like you, and don't start talking to fill up the silence. Sit."

Szubl frowned, a pink girdle in his hand. "I knew this would happen."

"Courage, Wolfi."

"I don't want to break rocks."

"You won't. You'll have to keep the appointment, this time, because they sent you the letter, it's official. But it won't go on. All right?"

Szubl nodded, unhappy and scared.

Morath called Polanyi and told him about it.

Count Janos Polanyi sat in his office in the Hungarian legation. It was quiet—sometimes a telephone, sometimes a typewriter, but the room had its own particular silence, the drapes drawn over the tall windows keeping the weather and the city outside. Polanyi stared down at a stack of cables on his desk, then pushed them aside. Nothing new, or, at least, nothing good.

He poured some apricot brandy in a little glass and drank it down. Closed his eyes for a moment and reminded himself who he was, where he came from. *Riders in the high grass, campfires on the plain.* Idle dreams, he thought, romantic nonsense, but it was still there, somewhere, rattling around inside him. At least he liked to think it was. In his mind? No, in his heart. *Bad science, but good metaphysics.* And that, he thought, was pretty much who he'd always been.

Count Janos Polanyi had two personal telephone books, bound in green leather. A big one, which stayed in his office, and a small one, which went wherever he did. It was the small one he opened now, and placed a telephone call to a woman he knew who lived, in very grand style, in an apartment in the Palais Royal. *White and fine,* was the way he thought of her, *like snow.*

As the phone rang he looked at his watch. 4:25. She answered, as she always did, after many rings—condescended to answer, from the tone of her voice. There followed an intricate conversation. Oblique, and pleasantly devious. It concerned certain friends she had, women, some a little younger, others more experienced. Some quite outgoing, others shy. Some ate well, while others were slim. So varied, people nowadays. Fair. And dark. From foreign lands, or the 16th Arrondissement. And each with her own definition of pleasure. Miraculous, this world of ours! One was stern, prone to temper. Another was playful, didn't care what as long as there was a laugh in it.

Eventually, they came to an agreement. A time. And a price. *Business before pleasure.* A vile saying. He sighed, stared up at the huge portraits on his wall, Arpad kings and their noble hounds, and had a little more brandy, then a little more. *The Magyar chieftan prepares for battle.* He mocked himself, an old habit, but then they all did that, an instinct of the national consciousness—irony, paradox, seeing the world inside out, amused by that which was not supposed to be amusing. Likely that was why the Germans didn't much care for them, Polanyi had always believed. It was the Austrian archduke Franz Ferdinand who said of the Hungarians, "It was an act of bad taste on the part of these gentlemen ever to have come to Europe." Well, here they were, whether the neighbors liked it or not.

Polanyi once again looked at his watch. For a few minutes yet he could postpone the inevitable. His evening pleasure was not to arrive until 6:00, he'd put it back an hour later than usual. *And speaking of pleasure, business before it.* He took a moment and swore merrily, various Hungarian anathemas. Really, *why* did he have to do this? *Why* did this Sombor creature have to come swooping down onto his life? But, here he was. Poor Nicholas, he didn't deserve it. All he wanted was his artists and actors and poets, had thought, in 1918, that he'd done his fighting. And done it well, Polanyi knew, it was there in the regimental history. A hero, his nephew, and a good officer, a miser with the lives of his men.

He put the brandy bottle away in the bottom drawer. Stood, straightened his tie, and left the office, closing the door carefully behind him. He walked along the corridor, past a vase of fresh flowers on a hall table with a mirror behind it. Greeted Bolthos, who hurried past with a courier envelope under his arm, and climbed up a flight on the marble staircase.

The floor above was busier, noisier. The commercial attaché in the first office, then the economic man, then Sombor. Polanyi rapped twice and opened the door. Sombor looked up when he entered and said, "Your excellency." He was busy writing—transferring jotted notes to a sheet of paper that would be retyped as a report.

"Colonel Sombor," Polanyi said. "A word with you."

"Yes, your excellency. In a moment."

This was pure rudeness, and they both knew it. It was Sombor's place to rise to his feet, offer a polite greeting, and attempt to satisfy the wishes of a superior. But, he as much as said, the business of state security took precedence. Now and forever. Polanyi could stand there and wait.

Which, for a time, he did.

Sombor's gold fountain pen scratched across the paper. *Like a field mouse in the granary.* He made eternal notes, this man with his leather hair and sharp ears. Scratch, scratch. *Now where did I put that pitchfork?* But he did not have a pitchfork.

Sombor felt it. "I'm sure it must be important, your excellency. I mean to give it my full attention."

"Please, sir," Polanyi said, his voice barely under control. "I must tell you that certain confidential information, pertaining to my office, has been made available to the Paris *préfecture.*"

"Has it. You're certain?"

"I am. It may have been done directly, or through the services of an informant."

"Regrettable. My office will definitely take an interest in this, your excellency. Just as soon as we can."

Polanyi lowered his voice. "Stop it," he said.

"Well, I must certainly try to do that. I wonder if you would be prepared to address a report to me, on this matter."

"A report."

"Indeed."

Polanyi stepped close to the edge of the desk. Sombor glanced up at him, then went back to writing. Polanyi took a small silver pistol out of his belt and shot him in the middle of the head.

Sombor sprang to his feet, furious, eyes hot with indignation, unaware that a big drop of blood had left his hairline and was trickling down his forehead. "Cur!" he shouted. Leapt into the air, clapped his hands to his head, spun around in a circle, and went crashing backward over his chair. Screamed, turned blue, and died.

Polanyi took the white handkerchief from his breast pocket, wiped off the grip of the pistol, and tossed it on the floor. In the hall, running footsteps.

The police arrived almost immediately, the detectives followed a half hour later. The senior detective questioned Polanyi in his office. Over fifty, Polanyi thought, short and thick, with a small mustache and dark eyes.

He sat across the desk from Polanyi and took notes on a pad. "Monsieur Sombor was, to your knowledge, despondent?"

"Not at all. But I saw him only on official business, and then only rarely."

"Can you describe, monsieur, exactly what happened?"

"I came to his office to discuss legation business, nothing terribly urgent, in fact I was on my way to see the commercial attaché, and I decided to stop in. We spoke for a minute or two. Then, when I had turned to go, I heard a shot. I rushed to his assistance, but he was gone almost immediately."

"Monsieur," the detective said. Clearly he'd missed something. "The last words he spoke, would you happen to recall them?"

"He said good-bye. Before that, he'd asked for a written report on the matter we'd discussed."

"Which was?"

"Pertained to, to an internal security matter."

"I see. So, he spoke normally to you, you turned to leave the office, at which time the deceased extended his arm to its fullest length—I'm guessing here, pending a report from the coroner, but the nature of the wound implies, um, a certain *distance*. Extended his arm to its fullest length, as I said, and shot himself in the top of the head?"

He was on the verge of bursting into laughter, as was Polanyi.

"Apparently," Polanyi said. He absolutely could not meet the detective's eyes.

The detective cleared his throat. After a moment he said, "Why would he do that?" It wasn't precisely a police question.

"God only knows."

"Do you not consider it," he searched for a word, "bizarre?"

"Bizarre," Polanyi said. "Without a doubt."

There were more questions, all according to form, back over the ground, and back again, but the remainder of the interview was desultory, with the truth in the air, but not articulated.

So then, take me to jail.

No, not for us to be involved in these kinds of politics. Très Balkan, as we say.

And the hell with it.

The inspector closed his notebook, put his pen away, walked to the door, and adjusted the brim of his hat. Standing in the open doorway he said, "He was, of course, the secret police."

"He was."

"Bad?"

"Bad enough."

"My condolences," the inspector said.

Polanyi arranged for Morath to know about it right away. A telephone call from the legation. "The colonel Sombor has tragically chosen to end his life. Would you care to donate to the fund for floral arrangements?"

The end of April. Late in the evening on the rue Guisarde, the lissome Suzette winding down for the night. Plans to stage a King Neptune ball had inspired the passengers, getting a little grumpy after days of being lost at sea. Even more inspired was Jack the handsome sailor, who'd been kind enough to steady the ladder while Suzette climbed to the top to tack up decorations in the ballroom.

"No underpants?" Morath said.

"She forgot."

A knock at the door produced Moni. Looking very sorrowful and asking if she could spend the night on the couch.

Mary Day brought out the Portuguese wine and Moni cried a little. "All my fault," she said. "I stomped out, in the middle of an argument, and Marlene locked the door and wouldn't let me back in."

"Well, you're welcome to stay," Mary Day said.

"Just for the night. Tomorrow, all will be forgiven." She drank some wine and lit a Gauloise. "Jealousy," she said. "Why do I do these things?"

They sent Morath out for more wine and when he returned Moni was on the telephone. "She offered to go to a hotel," Mary Day told him quietly. "But I asked her to stay."

"I don't mind. But maybe she'd prefer it."

"Money, Nicholas," Mary Day said. "None of us has any. Really, most people don't."

Moni hung up the telephone. "Well, it's the couch for me."

The conversation drifted here and there—poor Cara in Buenos Aires, Montrouchet's difficulties at the Théâtre des Catacombes, Juan-les-Pins—then settled on the war. "What will you do, Nicholas, if it happens?"

Morath shrugged. "I would have to go back to Hungary, I suppose. To the army."

"What about Mary?"

"Camp follower," Mary Day said. "He would fight, and I would cook, the stew."

Moni smiled, but Mary Day met Morath's eyes. "No, really," Moni said. "Would you two run away?"

"I don't know," Morath said. "Paris would be bombed. Blown to pieces."

"That's what everybody says. We're all going to Tangiers—that's the plan. Otherwise, doom. Back to Montreal."

Mary Day laughed. "Nicholas in a djellaba."

They drank both bottles Morath had brought back and, long after midnight, Moni and Mary Day fell dead asleep lying across the bed and it was Morath who wound up on the couch. He lay there for a long time, in the smoky darkness, wondering what would happen to them. Could they run away somewhere? Where? Budapest, maybe, or New York. Lugano? No. Dead calm by a cold lake, a month and it was over. *A Paris love affair, it won't transplant.* They couldn't live anywhere else, not together they couldn't. *Stay in Paris, then.* Another week, another month, whatever it turned out to be, and die in the war.

He had an awful headache the next morning. When he left the apartment, taking the rue Mabillon toward the river, Ilya emerged from a doorway and fell in step with him. He'd changed the green overcoat for a corduroy jacket, in more or less the same shape as the coat.

"Will your friend see me?" he said, his voice urgent.

"He will."

"Everything has changed, tell him that. Litvinov is finished—it's a signal to Hitler that Stalin wants to do business." Litvinov was the Soviet foreign minister. "Do you understand it?" He didn't wait for an answer. "Litvinov is a Jewish intellectual—an old-line Bolshevik. Now, for this negotiation, Stalin provides the Nazis with a more palatable partner. Which is perhaps Molotov."

"If you want to see my friend, you'll have to say where and when."

"Tomorrow night. Ten-thirty. At the Parmentier Métro stop."

A deserted station, out in the 11th Arrondissement. "What if he can't come?" Morath meant *won't* and he sensed Ilya knew it.

"Then he can't. And I either contact you or I don't."

Moving quickly, he turned, walked away, disappeared.

For a time, Morath considered letting it die right there. Suddenly, Ilya *knew things*. How? This wasn't hiding in a room with a sack of oats. Could he have been caught? Then made a deal with the NKVD? But Polanyi had said *leave it to me*. He was no fool, would not go unprotected to a meeting like this. You have to let him decide, Morath thought. Because if the information was real, it meant Hitler didn't have to worry about three hundred Russian divisions, and that meant war in Poland. This time, the British and the French would have to fight, and that meant war in Europe.

When Morath reached the Agence Courtmain, he called the legation.

"A fraud," Polanyi said. "We are being used—I don't exactly understand why, but we are."

They sat in the backseat of a shiny black Grosser Mercedes, Bolthos in front with the driver. On the sixth day of May, benign and bright under a windswept sky. They drove along the Seine, out of the city at the Porte de Bercy, headed south for the village of Thiais.

"You went alone?" Morath said.

Polanyi laughed. "A strange evening at the Parmentier Métro—heavyset men reading Hungarian newspapers."

"And the documents?"

"Tonight. Then *adieu* to comrade Ilya."

"Maybe it doesn't matter now." Litvinov had resigned two days earlier.

"No, we must do something. Wake the British up—it's not too late for the diplomats. I would say that Poland is an autumn project, after the harvest, before the rains."

The car moved slowly through the village of Alfortville, where a row of dance halls stood side by side on the quai facing the river. Parisians came here on summer nights, to drink and dance until dawn. "Poor soul," Polanyi said. "Perhaps he drank in these places."

"Not many places he didn't," Bolthos said.

They were on their way to the funeral of the novelist Josef Roth, dead of delirium tremens at the age of forty-four. Sharing the backseat with Polanyi and Morath, a large, elaborate wreath, cream-colored roses and a black silk ribbon, from the Hungarian legation.

"So then," Morath said, "this fugitive business is just a ruse."

"Likely it is. Allows the people who sent him to deny his existence, maybe that's it. Or perhaps just an exercise in the Soviet style—deceit hides deception and who knows what. One thing that does occur to me is that he is being operated by a faction in Moscow, people like Litvinov, who don't want to do business with Hitler."

"You will take care, when you see him again."

"Oh yes. You can be sure that the Nazi secret service will want to keep any word of a Hitler/Stalin negotiation a secret from the British. They would not like us to be passing documents to English friends in Paris." He paused, then said, "I'll be glad when this is over, whichever way it goes."

He seemed tired of it all, Morath thought. Sombor, the Russians, God only knew what else. Sitting close together, the scent of bay rum and brandy was strong in the air, suggesting power and rich, easy life. Polanyi looked at his watch. "It's at two o'clock," he said to the driver.

"We'll be on time, your excellency." To be polite, he sped up a little.

"Do you read the novels, Nicholas?"

"*Radetzky March*, more than once. *Hotel Savoy. Flight Without End.*"

"There, that says it. An epitaph." Roth had fled from Germany in 1933, writing to a friend that "one must run from a burning house."

"A Catholic burial?" Morath said.

"Yes. He was born in a Galician shtetl but he got tired of being a Jew. Loved the monarchy, Franz Josef, Austria-Hungary." Polanyi shook his head. "Sad, sad, Nicholas. He hated the émigré life, drank himself to death when he saw the war coming."

They arrived at Thiais twenty minutes later, and the driver parked on the street in front of the church. A small crowd, mostly émigrés, ragged and worn but brushed up as best they could. Just before the Mass began, two men wearing dark suits and decorations carried a wreath into the church. "Ah, the Legitimists," Polanyi said. Across the wreath, a black-and-yellow sash, the colors of the Dual Monarchy, and the single word *Otto*—the head of the House of Habsburg and heir to a vanished empire. It occurred to Morath that he was witness to the final moment in the life of Austria-Hungary.

In the graveyard by the church, the priest spoke briefly, mentioned Roth's wife, Friedl, in a mental institution in Vienna, his military service in Galicia during the war, his novels and journalism, and his love of the church and the monarchy. *We all overestimated the world,* Morath thought. The phrase, written to a friend after Roth fled to Paris, was from an obituary in the morning paper.

After the coffin was lowered into the grave, Morath took a handful of dirt and sprinkled it on top of the pinewood lid. "Rest in peace," he said. The mourners stood silent while the gravediggers began to shovel earth into the grave. Some of the émigrés wept. The afternoon sun lit the tombstone, a square of white marble with an inscription:

Josef Roth
Austrian Poet
Died in Paris in Exile

On the morning of 9 May, Morath was at the Agence Courtmain when he was handed a telephone message. *Please call Major Fekaj at the Hungarian legation.* His heart sank a little—Polanyi had told him, on the way back from Thiais, that Fekaj now sat in Sombor's office, his own replacement due from Budapest within the week.

Morath put the message in his pocket and went off to a meeting in

Courtmain's office. Another poster campaign—a parade, a pageant, the ministries preparing to celebrate, in July, the hundred and fiftieth anniversary of the revolution of 1789. After the meeting, Courtmain and Morath treated a crowd from the agency to a raucous lunch in an upstairs room at Lapérouse, their own particular answer to the latest valley in the national morale.

By the time he got back to the avenue Matignon, Morath knew he had to call—either that or think about it for the rest of the day.

Fekaj's voice was flat and cold. He was a colorless man, precise, formal, and reserved. "I called to inform you, sir, that we have serious concerns about the well-being of his excellency, Count Polanyi."

"Yes?" Now what.

"He has not been seen at the legation for two days and does not answer his telephone at home. We want to know if you, by any chance, have been in contact with him."

"No, not since the sixth."

"Did he, to your knowledge, have plans to go abroad?"

"I don't think he did. Perhaps he's ill."

"We have called the city hospitals. There is no record of admission."

"Have you gone to the apartment?"

"This morning, the concierge let us in. Everything was in order, no indication of . . . anything wrong. The maid stated that his bed had not been slept in for two nights." Fekaj cleared his throat. "Would you care to tell us, sir, if he sometimes spends the night elsewhere? With a woman?"

"If he does he doesn't tell me about it, he keeps the details of his personal life to himself. Have you informed the police?"

"We have."

Morath had to sit down at his desk. He lit a cigarette and said, "Major Fekaj, I don't know how to help you."

"We accept," Fekaj hesitated, then continued. "We understand that certain aspects of Count Polanyi's work had to remain—out of view. For reasons of state. But, should he make contact with you, we trust that you will at least let us know that he is, safe."

Alive, you mean. "I will," Morath said.

"Thank you. Of course you'll be notified if we hear anything further."

Morath held the receiver in his hand, oblivious to the silence on the line after Fekaj hung up.

Gone.

He called Bolthos at his office, but Bolthos didn't want to speak on the legation telephone and met him, just after dark, in a busy café.

"I spoke to Fekaj," Morath said. "But I had nothing to tell him."

Bolthos looked haggard. "It's been difficult," he said. "Impossible. Because of our atrocious politics, we're cursed with separate investigations. Officially, the *nyilas* are responsible, but any real work must be done by Polanyi's friends. Fekaj and his allies won't involve themselves."

"Where do you think he is?"

A polite shrug. "Abducted."

"Murdered?"

"In time."

After a moment Bolthos said, "He wouldn't jump off a bridge, would he?"

"Not him, no."

"Nicholas," Bolthos said. "You're going to have to tell me what he was doing."

Morath paused, but he had no choice. "On Tuesday, the sixth, he was supposed to meet a man who said he had defected from the Soviet special services, which Polanyi did not believe. He didn't run, according to Polanyi, he was sent. But, even so, he came bearing information that Polanyi thought was important—Litvinov's dismissal, a negotiation between Stalin and Hitler. So Polanyi met him and agreed to a second, a final meeting. Documents to be exchanged for money, I suspect.

"But, if you're looking for enemies you can't stop there—you have to consider Sombor's colleagues, certainly suspicious of what went on at the legation, and capable of anything. And you can't ignore the fact that Polanyi was in touch with the Germans—diplomats, spies, Wehrmacht staff officers. And he also had some kind of business with the Poles; maybe Roumanians and Serbs as well, a potential united front against Hitler."

From Bolthos, a sour smile. "But no scorned mistress, you're sure of that."

They sat in silence while the café life swirled around them. A woman at the next table was reading with a lorgnette, her dachshund asleep under a chair.

"That was, of course, his work," Bolthos said.

"Yes. It was." Morath heard himself use the past tense. "You think he's dead."

"I hope he isn't, but better that than some dungeon in Moscow or Berlin." Bolthos took a small notebook from his pocket. "This meeting, will you tell me where it was supposed to take place?"

"I don't know. The first meeting was at the Parmentier Métro station. But in my dealings with this man he was careful to change time and location. So, in a way, the second meeting would have been anywhere *but* there."

"Unless Polanyi insisted." Bolthos flipped back through the notebook. "I've been working with my own sources in the Paris police. On Tuesday, the sixth, a man was shot somewhere near the Parmentier Métro station. This was buried among all the robberies and domestic disturbances, but there was something about it that caught my attention. The victim was a French citizen, born in Slovakia. Served in the Foreign Legion, then discharged for political activity. He crawled into a doorway and died on the rue Saint-Maur, a minute or so away from the Métro."

"A phantom," Morath said. "Polanyi's bodyguard—is that what you think? Or maybe his assassin. Or both, why not. Or, more likely, nobody, caught up in somebody's politics on the wrong night, or killed for a ten-franc piece."

Bolthos closed the notebook. "We have to try," he said. He meant he'd done the best he could.

"Yes. I know," Morath said.

Temetni Tudunk, a Magyar sentiment, complex and ironic: *How to bury people, that is one thing we know.* It was Wolfi Szubl who said the words, at a Hungarian nightclub in the cellar of a strange little hotel out in the 17th Arrondissement. Szubl and Mitten, the baroness

Frei escorted by a French film producer, Bolthos and his wife and her cousin, Voyschinkowsky and Lady Angela Hope, the artist Szabo, the lovely Madame Kareny, various other strays and aristocrats who had floated through Janos Polanyi's complicated life.

It wasn't a funeral—there was no burial, thus Szubl's ironic twist on the phrase, not even a memorial, only an evening to remember a friend. "A difficult friend"—Voyschinkowsky said that, an index finger wiping the corner of his eye. There was candlelight, a small Gypsy orchestra, platters of chicken with paprika and cream, wine and fruit brandy, and, yes, it was said more than once as the evening wore on, Polanyi would have liked to be there. During one of the particularly heartbreaking songs, a pale, willowy woman, supremely, utterly *Parisienne* and rumored to be a procuress who lived in the Palais Royal, stood in front of the orchestra and danced with a shawl. Morath sat beside Mary Day and translated, now and then, what was said in Hungarian.

They drank to Polanyi, *wherever he is tonight,* meaning heaven or hell. "Or maybe Palm Beach," Herbert Mitten said. "I guess there's nothing wrong in thinking that if you care to."

The bill came to Morath at two in the morning, on a silver tray, with a grand bow from the *patron*. Voyschinkowsky, thwarted in his attempt to pay for the evening, insisted on taking Morath and Mary Day home in his chauffeur-driven Hispano-Suiza automobile.

We have to try, Bolthos had said it for both of them. Which meant, for Morath, one obvious but difficult strand, really the only one he knew, in what must have been a vast tangle of shadowy connections.

He went up to the Balalaika the following afternoon and drank vodka with Boris Balki.

"A shame," Balki said, and drank "to his memory."

"Looking back, maybe inevitable."

"Yes, sooner or later. This type of man lives on borrowed time."

"The people responsible," Morath said, "are perhaps in Moscow."

A certain delicacy prevented Balki from saying what he felt about that, but the reaction—Balki looked around to see who might be listening—was clear to Morath.

"I wouldn't even try to talk to them, if I were you," Balki said.

"Well, if I thought it would help."

"Once they do it, it's done," Balki said. "Fated is fated, Slavs know all about that."

"I was wondering," Morath said. "What's become of Silvana?"

"Living high." Balki was clearly relieved to be off the subject of Moscow. "That's what I hear."

"I want to talk to Von Schleben."

"Well . . ."

"Can you do it?"

"Silvana, yes. The rest is up to you."

Then, the last week in May, Morath received a letter, on thick, creamy paper, from one Auguste Thien, summoning him to the Thien law offices in Geneva "to settle matters pertaining to the estate of Count Janos von Polanyi de Nemeszvar."

Morath took the train down from Paris, staring out at the green and gold Burgundian countryside, staying at a silent Geneva hotel that night, and arriving at the office, which looked out over Lac Leman, the following morning.

The lawyer Thien, when Morath was ushered into his office by a junior member of the staff, turned out to be an ancient bag of bones held upright only by means of a stiff, iron-colored suit. He had a full head of wavy silver hair, parted in the middle, and skin like parchment. "Your excellency," the lawyer said, offering his hand. "Will you take a coffee? Something stronger?"

Morath took the coffee, which produced the junior member carrying a Sèvres service, countless pieces of it, on an immense tray. Thien himself served the coffee, his breathing audible as he worked.

"There," he said, when Morath at last had the cup in his hands.

On the desk, a metal box of the kind used in safe-deposit vaults. "These papers comprise a significant proportion of the Polanyi de Nemeszvar estate," Thien said, "which, according to my instructions, now, in substance, pass to you. There are provisions made for Count Polanyi's surviving family, very generous provisions, but the greatest part of the estate is, as of this date, yours. Including, of course, the title, which descends to the eldest surviving member of the male line— in this case the son of Count Polanyi's sister, your mother. So, before we proceed to more technical matters, it is my privilege to greet you, even in a sad hour, as Nicholas, Count Morath."

Slowly, he stood and came around the desk to shake Morath's hand.

"Perhaps I'm ignorant of the law," Morath said, when he'd sat back down, "but there is, to my knowledge, no death certificate."

"No, there is not." A cloud crossed Thien's face. "But our instructions preclude the necessity for certification. You should be aware that certain individuals, in their determination of a final distribution of assets, may presuppose, well, any condition they choose. It is, at least in Switzerland, entirely at their discretion. We are in receipt of a letter from the Paris *préfecture*, an *attestation*, which certifies, to our satisfaction, that the legator has been officially declared a missing person. This unhappy eventuality was, in fact, foreseen. And this office, I will say, is known for the most scrupulous adherence to a client's direction—no matter what it might entail. You have perhaps heard of Loulou the circus elephant? No? Well, she now lives in splendid retirement, on a farm near Coimbra, in compliance with the wishes of the late Senhor Alvares, former owner of the Circus Alvares. In his last will and testament, he did not forget this good-natured beast. And she will, one might say, never forget Senhor Alvares. And this law firm, Count Morath, will never forget Loulou."

The lawyer Thien smiled with satisfaction, took from his drawer a substantial key, opened the metal box, and began to hand Morath various deeds and certificates.

He was, he learned, very rich. He'd known about it, in a general way—the Canadian railroad bonds, the estates in Slovakia, but here it was in reality. "In addition," Thien said, "there are certain specified accounts held in banks in this city that will now come into your possession—my associate will guide you in completing the forms. You may elect to have these funds administered by any institution you choose, or they can remain where they are, in your name, with payment instructions according to your wishes.

"This is, Count Morath, a lot to absorb in a single meeting. Are there, at present, any points you would care to have clarified?"

"I don't believe so."

"Then, with your permission, I will add this."

He took from his drawer a sheet of stationery and read aloud. " 'A man's departure from his familiar world may be inevitable, but his spirit lives on, in the deeds and actions of those who remain, in the memories of those left behind, his friends and family, whose lives may reflect the lessons they have learned from him, and that shall become his truest legacy.' "

After a pause, Thien said, "I believe you should find comfort in those words, your excellency."

"Certainly I do," Morath said.

Bastard. You're alive.

On his return to Paris there was, of course, an ascension-to-the-title party, attended, as it happened, solely by the count and the countess presumptive. The latter provided, from the patisserie on the corner, a handsome cake, on top of which, in consultation with the baker's wife and aided by a dictionary, a congratulatory phrase in Hungarian was rendered in blue icing. This turned out to be, when Morath read it, something like *Good Feelings Mister Count,* but, given the difficulty of the language, close enough. In addition—shades of Suzette!—Mary Day had pinned paper streamers to the wall of the apartment, though, unlike Jack the handsome sailor, Morath had not been there to steady the ladder. Still, he saw far more than Jack was ever going to and got to lick frosting off the countess's nipples in the bargain.

There followed a night of adventure. At three, they stood at the window and saw the moon in a mist. Across the rue Guisarde, a man in an undershirt leaned on his windowsill and smoked a pipe. A spring wind, an hour later, and the scent of fields in the countryside. They decided they would go to the Closerie de Lilas at dawn and drink champagne, then she fell asleep, hair plastered to her forehead, mouth open, sleeping so peacefully he didn't have the heart to wake her.

They went to the movies that night, at one of the fancy Gaumont theatres over by the Grand Hotel. *The loveliest fluff,* Morath thought. A French obsession—how passion played itself out into romantic intrigue, with everybody pretty and well dressed. His beloved Mary Day, hardheaded as could be in so many ways, caved in completely.

He could feel it, sitting next to her, how her heart beat for a stolen embrace.

But in the lobby on the way out, all chandeliers and cherubs, he heard a young man say to his girlfriend, "*Tout Paris* can fuck itself blue in the face, it won't stop Hitler for a minute."

Thus the Parisian mood that June. Edgy but resilient, it fought to recover from the cataclysms—Austria, Munich, Prague—and tried to work its way back to normalcy. But the Nazis wouldn't leave it alone. Now there was Danzig, with the Poles giving as good as they got. Every morning it lay waiting in the newspapers: customs officers shot, post offices burned, flags pulled down and stomped into the dirt.

And not all that much better in Hungary. Quieter, maybe. The parliament had passed new anti-Semitic laws in May, and when Morath was solicited by Voyschinkowsky for a subscription to a fund for Jews leaving the country, he wrote out a check that startled even "the Lion of the Bourse." Voyschinkowsky raised his eyebrows when he saw the number. "Well, this is *terribly* generous of you, Nicholas. Are you sure you want to do all that much?"

He was. He'd had a letter from his sister. Life in Budapest, Teresa said, was "spoiled, ruined." All the talk of war, suicides, an incident during a performance of *Der Rosenkavalier*. "Nicholas, even at the *opera*." Duchazy was up to "God only knows what." Plots, conspiracies. "Last Tuesday, the phone rang twice after midnight."

He took Mary Day to afternoon tea at the baroness Frei's house, the official celebration of summer's arrival in the garden. The stars of the show were two roses that spread across the brick walls that enclosed the terrace: Madame Alfred Carrière, white flowers touched with pale pink—"a perfect noisette," the baroness told Mary Day, "planted by the baron with his own hands in 1911"—and Gloire de Dijon, soft yellow with tones of apricot.

The baroness held court in an ironwork garden chair, scolding the vizslas as they agitated for forbidden morsels from the guests and beckoning her friends to her side. Seated next to her was an American woman called Blanche. She was the wife of the cellist Kolovitzky, a vivid blonde with black eyebrows, tanned skin from a life spent by Hollywood pools, and an imposing bosom on a body that should have been Rubenesque but was forced to live on grapefruit and toast.

"Darling Nicholas," the baroness called out to him. "Come and talk to us."

As he headed toward her, he saw Bolthos in the crowd and acknowledged his glance with a friendly nod. He was, for a moment, tempted to say something of his suspicions but immediately thought better of it. *Silence,* he told himself.

Morath kissed Lillian Frei on both cheeks. "Nicholas, have you met Blanche? Bela's wife?"

"That's Kolovitzky, not Lugosi," the woman said with a laugh.

Morath laughed politely along with her as he took her hand. Why was this funny?

"At the Christmas party," Morath said. "Is good to see you again."

"She was at the Crillon," Baroness Frei said. "But I made her come and stay with me."

Kolovitzky's wife started to talk to Morath in English, while Morath tried to follow along as best he could. The baroness saw that he was lost and began to translate into Hungarian, holding Blanche's right hand tightly in her left and moving both hands up and down for emphasis as the conversation continued.

This was, Morath saw right away, a bad, potentially fatal, case of money madness. On the death of an aunt in Johannesburg, the cellist who scored Hollywood films had inherited two apartment houses in Vienna. "Nothing fancy, you know, but solid. Respectable."

Kolovitzky's friends, his lawyer, and his wife had all laughed at the absurdity of Kolovitzky going back to Austria to claim the inheritance. Kolovitzky laughed right along with them, then flew to Paris and took a train to Vienna.

"He was poor as a child," Blanche said. "So money is never enough for him. He goes around the house and turns off the lights."

She paused, found a handkerchief in her purse, and dabbed at her eyes. "Excuse me," she said. "He went to Vienna three weeks ago, he's still there. They won't let him out."

"Did someone encourage him to come?"

"See? He knows," Blanche said to the baroness. "A scoundrel, a lawyer in Vienna. 'Don't worry about a thing,' he said in his letter. 'You're an American, it won't be a problem.' "

"He's a citizen?"

"He's got papers as a resident alien. I had a letter from him, at the Crillon, and the story was that once he gave them the buildings—that lawyer's in cahoots with the Nazis, *that's* what's going on—he thought they'd let him go home. But maybe it isn't so simple."

The baroness stopped dead on *cahoots,* and Blanche said, "I mean, they're all in it together."

"Did he go to the American embassy?"

"He tried. But they don't interest themselves in Jews. Come back in July, they told him."

"Where is he, in Vienna."

She opened her purse and brought out a much-folded letter on thin paper. "He says here," she hunted for her glasses and put them on, "says here, the Schoenhof. Why I don't know—he was at the Graben, which he always liked." She read further and said, "Here. He says, 'I have put the buildings, for tax purposes, in Herr Kreml's name.' That's the lawyer. 'But they tell me that further payments may be required.' Then he says, 'I can only hope it will be acceptable, but please speak with Mr. R. L. Stevenson at the bank and see what can be done.' That too is odd, because there is no Mr. Stevenson, not that I know about."

"They won't let him out," the baroness said.

"May I have the letter?" Morath said.

Blanche handed it to him, and he put it in his pocket.

"Should I send money?"

Morath thought it over. "Write and ask him how much he needs and when he'll be coming home. Then say that you're annoyed, or show it, with how he's always getting into trouble. Why can't he learn to respect the rules? The point is, you'll bribe, but the bribe has to work, and you'll say later that it was all his fault. They're sensitive about America, the Nazis, they don't want stories in the newspapers."

"Nicholas," the baroness said. "Can anything be done?"

Morath nodded. "Maybe. Let me think it over."

The baroness Frei looked up at him, eyes blue as the autumn sky.

Blanche started to thank him, and had already said too much and was about to mention money when the baroness intervened.

"He knows, darling, he knows," she said gently. "He has a good heart, Count Nicholas."

·

Seen from a private box in the grandstand, the lawns of Longchamps racetrack glowed like green velvet. The jockeys' silks were bright in the sunshine, scarlet and gold and royal blue. Silvana tapped the end of a pencil against a racing form. "Coup de Tonnerre?" she said. Thunderbolt. "Was that the gray one with the long tail? Horst? Do you remember?"

"I think it was," Von Schleben said, peering at the program. "Pierre Lavard is riding, and they let him win once a day." He read further. "Or maybe Bal Masqué. Who do you like, Morath?"

Silvana looked at him expectantly. She wore a print silk dress and pearls, her hair now expensively styled.

"Coup de Tonnerre," Morath said. "He took a third place, the last time he ran. And the odds are attractive."

Von Schleben handed Silvana a few hundred francs. "Take care of it for us, will you?" Morath also gave her money. "Let's try Count Morath's hunch."

When she'd gone off to the betting windows, Von Schleben said, "Too bad about your uncle. We had good times together, but that's life."

"You didn't hear anything, did you? After it happened?"

"No, no," Von Schleben said. "Into thin air."

As the horses were walked to the starting line, there were the usual difficulties, a starter's assistant leaping out of the way to avoid being kicked.

"There's a lawyer in Vienna I'd like to get in touch with," Morath said. "Gerhard Kreml."

"Kreml," Von Schleben said. "I don't think I know him. What is it that interests you?"

"Who he is. What kind of business he does. I think he has connections with the Austrian party."

"I'll see what I can do for you," Von Schleben said. He handed Morath a card. "Call me, first part of next week, if you haven't heard anything. Use the second number, there, on the bottom."

The race began, the horses galloping in a tight pack. Von Schleben raised a pair of mother-of-pearl opera glasses to his eyes and followed the race. "Take the rail, idiot," he said. The horses' hooves drummed on the grass. At the halfway point, the jockeys began to use their whips. "*Ach scheiss!*" Von Schleben said, lowering the glasses.

"This Kreml," Morath said. "He has a client in Vienna, a friend of a friend, who seems to be having tax problems. There's a question of being allowed to leave the country."

"A Jew?"

"Yes. A Hungarian musician, who lives in California."

"If he pays the taxes there should be no problem. Of course, there are special situations. And if there are, irregularities, well, the Austrian tax authority can be infernally slow."

"Shall I tell you who it is?"

"No, don't bother. Let me find out first who you're dealing with. Everything in Vienna is—a little more complicated."

The winners of the race were announced. "Too bad," Von Schleben said. "Maybe better luck next time."

"I would hope."

"By the way, there's a man called Bolthos, at the legation. Friend of yours?"

"Yes. An acquaintance, anyhow."

"I've been trying to get in touch with him, but he's hard to get hold of. Very occupied, I suppose."

"Why don't I have him call you?"

"Could you?"

"I'll ask him."

"I'd certainly appreciate it. We have interests in common, here and there."

Silvana returned. Morath could see she'd freshened her lipstick. "I'll be on my way," he said.

"Expect to hear from me," Von Schleben said. "And again, I'm sorry about your uncle. We must hope for the best."

Shoes off, sleeves rolled back, a cigarette in one hand and a glass of wine by his side, Morath stretched out on the brown velvet sofa and read and reread Kolovitzky's letter.

Mary Day, wrapped in one towel with another around her head, came fresh from her bath, still warm, and sat by his side.

"Who is R. L. Stevenson?" Morath said.

"I give up, who is he?"

"It's in this letter. From Kolovitzky, who played the violin at the baroness's Christmas party. He managed to get himself trapped in Vienna, and they allowed him to write to his wife—just once, I think, there won't be another, to see if they can get anything more out of him before they throw him in a canal."

"Nicholas!"

"I'm sorry, but that's how it is."

"The name is in the letter?"

"Code. Trying to tell his wife something."

"Oh, well, then it's the writer."

"What writer?"

"Robert Louis Stevenson."

"Who's that?"

"He wrote adventure novels. Terrifically popular—my father had all the books, read them when he was growing up."

"Such as?"

"*Treasure Island.*" She unwound the towel from her head and began drying her hair. "You've never heard of it?"

"No."

"Long John Silver the pirate, with a peg leg and a parrot on his shoulder. Avast there, maties! It's about a cabin boy, and buried treasure."

"I don't know," he mused. "What else?"

"*The Master of Ballentrae?*"

"What happens there?"

She shrugged. "Never read it. Oh, also *Kidnapped.*"

"That's it."

"He's telling her he's been kidnapped?"

"Held for ransom."

8:30 P.M. The Balalaika was packed, smoky and loud, the Gypsy violins moaning, the customers laughing, and shouting in Russian, the man down the bar from Morath weeping silently as he drank. Balki glanced at him and shook his head. "*Kabatskaya melankholia,*" he said, mouth tight with disapproval.

"What's that?"

"A Russian expression—tavern melancholy."

Morath watched while Balki made up a diabolo, a generous por-tion of grenadine, then the glass filled with lemonade. Balki looked at his watch. "My relief should be here."

A few minutes later, the man showed up, and Balki and Morath headed for a bar up in the place Clichy. Earlier, during a lull in business, Morath had laid out the details of Kolovitzky's letter, and the two of them had discussed strategy, coming up with the plan that couldn't go wrong and what to do once it did.

In the bar, Balki greeted the owner in Russian and asked him if they could use the telephone.

"Maybe we should go to the railroad station," Morath said.

"Save yourself the trip. Half the White Russians in Paris use this phone. Mercenaries, bomb throwers, guys trying to put the czar back on the throne, they all come here."

"The czar is dead, Boris."

Balki laughed. "Sure he is. So?"

Morath asked for the international operator and got the call through to Vienna almost immediately. The phone rang for a long time, then a man said, "Hotel Schoenhof."

"Good evening. Herr Kolovitzky, please."

The line hissed for a moment, then the man said, "Hold on."

Morath waited, then a different voice, sharp and suspicious, said, "Yes? What do you want with Kolovitzky?"

"I just want to talk to him for a minute."

"He's busy right now, can't come to the phone. Who's calling?"

"Mr. Stevenson. I'm in Paris at the moment, but I might come over to Vienna next week."

"I'll tell him you called," the man said, and hung up.

He called Von Schleben from the Agence Courtmain. A secretary said he wasn't available, but, a few minutes later, he called back. "I have the information you wanted," he said. "Gerhard Kreml is a small-time lawyer, basically crooked. Barely made a living until the Anschluss, but he's done very well since then."

"Where is he located?"

"He has a one-room office in the Singerstrasse. But he's not your problem, your problem is an Austrian SS, Sturmbannführer Zimmer.

He and Kreml have a swindle going where they arrest Jews who still have something left to steal. I suspect your friend was lured back to Vienna, and I should also tell you that his chances of getting out are not good."

"Is there anything you can do?"

"I don't think they'll give him up—maybe if it was Germany I could help. Do you want me to try? There would have to be a quid pro quo, of course, and even then there's no guarantee."

"What if we pay?"

"That's what I would do. You have to understand, in dealing with Zimmer you're dealing with a warlord. He isn't going to let somebody come into his territory and just take away what belongs to him."

Morath thanked him and hung up.

"Liebchen."

Wolfi Szubl said it tenderly, gratefully. Frau Trudi turned at the wall, gave him a luscious smile, and walked across the room, her immense behind and heavy thighs wobbled as she swung her hips. When she reached the end of the room, she turned again, leaned toward him, shook her shoulders, and said, "So, what do you see?"

"Paradise," Wolfi said.

"And my discount?"

"*Big* discount, *liebchen*."

"Yes?" Now her face beamed with pleasure. *Even her hair is fat,* he thought. A curly auburn mop, she'd brushed it out after wriggling into the corset, and it bounced up and down, with all the glorious rest of her, as she walked for him.

"I take all you have, Wolfi. The *Madame Pompadour.* My ladies will swoon."

"Not just your ladies. What is that I see? Did you drop something, over there?"

"Did I? Oh dear." Hands on hips, she walked like a model on the runway, a shoulder thrust forward with every step, chin high, mouth set in a stylish pout. "Two dozen? Sixty percent off?"

"You read my mind."

At the wall, she bent over and held the pose. "I don't *see* anything."

Szubl rose from his chair, came up behind her and began to unsnap the tiny buttons. When he was done, she ran to the bed with baby steps and lay on her stomach with her chin propped on her hands.

Szubl began to undo his tie.

"Wolfi," she said softly. "Not a day goes by I don't think about you."

Szubl took off his underpants and twirled them around his finger.

The apartment was above her shop, also *Frau Trudi,* on the Prinzstrasse, next to a bakery, and the smell of cookies in the oven drifted up through the open window. A warmish day in Vienna, the beastly *Föhn* not blowing for a change, Frau Trudi's canary twittering in its cage, everything peaceful and at rest. By now it was twilight, and they could hear the bell on the door of the shop below them as the customers went in and out.

Frau Trudi, damp and pink after lovemaking, nestled against him. "You like it here, Wolfi? With me?"

"Who wouldn't?"

"You could stay for a while, if you liked."

Wolfi sighed. If only he could. "I wonder," he said, "if you know anybody who needs to make a little money. Maybe one of your ladies has a husband who's out of work."

"What would he have to do?"

"Not much. Lend his passport to a friend of mine for a week or so."

She propped herself on her elbow and looked down at him. "Wolfi, are you in trouble?"

"Not me. The friend pays five hundred American dollars for the loan. So I thought, well, maybe Trudi knows somebody."

He watched her. Fancied he could hear the ring of a cash-register drawer as she converted the dollars into schilling. "Maybe," she said. "A woman I know, her husband could use it."

"How old?"

"The husband?" She shrugged. "Forty-five, maybe. Always problems—she comes to me for a loan, sometimes."

"Is it possible tonight?"

"I suppose."

"I'll give you the money now, *Liebchen*, and I'll stop by tomorrow night for the passport."

28 June. A fine day with bright sunshine, but not a ray of it reached the hunting lodge. Three stories, thirty rooms, a grand hall, all sunk in dark, musty gloom. Morath and Balki had hired a car in Bratislava and driven up into the wooded hills north of the Danube. They were in historical Slovakia—Hungarian territory since 1938—and only a few miles from the Austrian border.

Balki looked around him in a kind of dispirited awe—trophy heads on every wall, their glass eyes glittering in the forest light. Tentatively, he settled himself on the leather cushion of a huge wooden chair with hunting scenes carved into the high back.

"Where giants sat," he said.

"That's the idea."

The old empire lived on, Morath thought. One of the baroness's pet aristocrats had agreed to loan him the hunting lodge. "So very *private*," he'd said with a wink. It was that. In the Little Carpathians, thick with pines, by a rushing brook that wound past the window and a picturesque waterfall that foamed white over a dark outcropping.

Balki wandered about, gazing up at the terrible paintings. Sicilian maidens caught as they filled amphorae from little streams, Gypsy girls with tambourines, a dyspeptic Napoleon with his hand on a cannon. At the far end of the room, between the stuffed heads of a bear and a tusky wild boar, he stood before a gun cabinet and tapped his fingers on the oiled stock of a rifle. "We're not going to play with these, are we?"

"We are not."

"No cowboys and Indians?"

Emphatically, Morath shook his head.

There was even a telephone. Of a sort—easy to imagine Archduke Franz Ferdinand calling his taxidermist: a wooden box on the kitchen wall, with the earpiece on a cord and a black horn in the center into which one could speak. *Or shout, more likely.* Morath lifted the earpiece from the cradle, heard static, put it back, looked at his watch.

Balki took off his workman's cap and hung it on an antler. "I'll come along if you like, Morath."

That was pure bravery—a Russian going into Austria. "Guard the castle," Morath said. "Enough that you took vacation days for this, you don't have to get arrested in the bargain."

Once again, Morath looked at his watch. "Well, let's try it," he said. He lit a cigarette, put the telephone receiver to his ear and tapped the cradle. From the static, an operator speaking Hungarian.

"I'd like to book a call to Austria," Morath said.

"I can get through right away, sir."

"In Vienna, 4025."

Morath heard the phone, a two-ring signal. Then: "Herr Kreml's office."

"Is Herr Kreml in?"

"May I say who's calling?"

"Mr. Stevenson."

"Hold the line, please."

Kreml was on right away. A smooth, confident, oily voice. Saying that it was good of him to call. Morath asked after Kolovitzky's health.

"In excellent spirits!" Well, perhaps a little, how to say, *oppressed,* what with his various tax difficulties, but that could soon be put right.

"I'm in contact with Madame Kolovitzky, here in Paris," Morath said. "If the paperwork can be resolved, a bank draft will be sent immediately."

Kreml went on a little, lawyer's talk, then mentioned a figure. "In terms of your American currency, Herr Stevenson, I think it would be in the neighborhood of ten thousand dollars."

"The Kolovitzkys are prepared to meet that obligation, Herr Kreml."

"I'm so pleased," Kreml said. "And then, in a month or so, once the draft has been processed by our banks, Herr Kolovitzky will be able to leave Austria with a clear conscience."

"A month, Herr Kreml?"

"Oh, at least that, the way things are here." The only way to expedite matters, Kreml said, would be to use a rather obscure provision of the tax code, for payments in cash. "That would clear things up immediately, you see."

Morath saw. "Perhaps the best way," he said.

Well, that was up to the Kolovitzkys, wasn't it. "Herr Stevenson, I do want to compliment you on your excellent German. For an American . . ."

"Actually, Herr Kreml, I was born in Budapest, as Istvanagy. So, after I emigrated to California, I changed it to Stevenson."

Ah! Of course!

"I will speak with Madame Kolovitzky, Herr Kreml, but please be assured that a cash payment will reach you within the week."

Kreml was *very* pleased to hear that. They chattered on for a time. The weather, California, Vienna, then started to say good-bye.

"Oh yes," Morath said, "there is one more thing. I would very much like to have a word with Herr Kolovitzky."

"Naturally. Do you have the number of the Hotel Schoenhof?"

"I called there—he seems always to be unavailable."

"Really? Well, you know, that doesn't surprise me. An amiable man, Herr Kolovitzky, makes friends everywhere he goes. So, I would suppose he's in and out, being entertained, sitting in the pastry shops. Have you left a message?"

"Yes."

"Then what's the problem? He'll call you back, the minute he gets a chance. Then too, Herr Stevenson, the telephone lines between here and Paris—it can be difficult."

"Likely that's it."

"I must say good-bye, Herr Stevenson, but I look forward to hearing from you."

"Be certain that you will."

"Good-bye, Herr Stevenson."

"Good-bye, Herr Kreml."

They drove to Bratislava the next morning, where Morath meant to take the train to Vienna, but it was not to be. Chaos at Central Station, crowds of stranded travelers, all the benches taken, people out on Jaskovy Avenue, sitting on their suitcases. "It's the Zilina line," the man at the ticket window explained. All passenger trains had been canceled to make way for flatbed cars carrying Wehrmacht tanks and artillery, moving east in a steady stream. Morath and Balki stood on the platform and stared, in the midst of a silent crowd. Two locomotives pulled forty flatbeds, the long snouts of the guns thrust out from beneath canvas tarpaulins. Twenty minutes later, a trainload of horses in cattle cars, then a troop train, soldiers waving as they went by, a message chalked beneath the coach windows—*We're going to Poland to beat up the Jews.*

The town of Zilina lay ten miles from the Polish frontier. It would have a hospital, a hotel for the general staff, a telephone system. Morath's heart sank as he watched the trains—this was hope slipping away. It could be intimidation, he thought, a feint, but he knew better. Here was the first stage of an invasion—these were the divisions that would attack from Slovakia, breaking through the Carpathian passes into southern Poland.

Morath and Balki walked around Bratislava, drank beer at a café, and waited. The city reminded Morath of Vienna in '38—Jewish shop windows smashed, *Jew Get Out!* painted on building walls. The Slovakian politicians hated the Czechs, invited Hitler to protect them, then discovered that they didn't like being protected. But it was too late. Here and there somebody had written *pro tento krat* on the telephone poles, *for the time being,* but that was braggadocio and fooled nobody.

Back in the station restaurant, Morath sat with his valise between his feet, ten thousand dollars in Austrian schilling packed inside. He asked a waiter if the Danube bridge was open—in case he decided to drive across, but the man looked gloomy and shook his head. "No, you cannot use it," he said, "they've been crossing for days."

"Any way into Austria?"

"Maybe at five they let a train through, but you have to be on the platform, and it will be—very crowded. You understand?"

Morath said he did.

When the waiter left, Balki said, "Will you be able to get back out?"

"Probably."

Balki nodded. "Morath?"

"Yes?"

"You're not going to get yourself killed, are you?"

"I don't think so," Morath said.

The train wasn't due for another two hours, so he used a telephone in the station to place a call to Paris. He had to wait twenty minutes, then the call went through to the Agence Courtmain. The receptionist, after several tries, found Mary Day at a meeting in Courtmain's office.

"Nicholas!" she said, "Where are you?" She wasn't exactly sure what he was doing. "Some family business," he'd told her, but she knew it was more than that.

"I'm in Bratislava," he said.

"Bratislava. How's the weather?"

"Sunny. I wanted to tell you that I miss you."

After a moment she said, "Me too, Nicholas. When are you coming back?"

"Soon, a few days, if all goes well."

"It will, won't it? Go well?"

"I think so, you don't have to worry. I thought I'd call, to say I love you."

"I know," she said.

"I guess I have to go, there are people waiting to use the phone."

"All right. Good-bye."

"A few days."

"The weekend."

"Oh yes, by then."

"Well, I'll see you then."

"Good-bye, Mary."

The waiter had been right about the passenger train. It pulled in slowly, after six-thirty, people jammed in everywhere. Morath forced his way on, using his strength, smiling and apologizing, making a small space for himself on the platform of the last car, hanging on to a metal stanchion all the way to Vienna.

He called Szubl at his hotel, and they met in a coffeehouse, the patrons smoking and reading the papers and conversing in polite tones. A city where everyone was sad and everyone smiled and nothing could be done—it had always seemed that way to Morath and it was worse than ever that summer night in 1939.

Szubl handed him an envelope, and Morath used the edge of the table for cover and looked at the passport photo. An angry little man glared up at him, mustache, glasses, *nothing ever goes right.*

"Can you fix it?" Szubl said.

"Yes. More or less. I took a photo from some document his wife had with her, I can paste it in. But, with any luck at all, I won't need it."

"Did they look at your bag, at the border?"

"Yes. I told them what the money was for, then they went through everything else. But it was just the usual customs inspectors, not SS or anything."

"I took out the stays out of a corset. You still want them?"

"Yes."

Szubl handed him an envelope, hotel stationery. Morath put it in his pocket. "When are getting out of here?"

"Tomorrow. By noon."

"Make sure of that, Wolfi."

"I will. What about the passport?"

"Tell her your friend lost it. More money for Herr X, and he can just go and get another."

Szubl nodded, then stood up. "I'll see you back in Paris, then."

They shook hands, and Morath watched him leave, heavy and slow, even without the sample case, a folded newspaper under one arm.

"Would you go once around the Mauerplatz?"

"If you like." The taxi driver was an old man with a cavalry mustache, his war medals pinned to the sun visor.

"A sentimental journey," Morath explained.

"Ah, of course."

A small, cobbled square, people strolling on a warm evening, old linden trees casting leafy shadows in the light of the streetlamps. Morath rolled the window down and the driver took a slow tour around the square.

"A lady and I stayed here, a few years ago."

"At the Schoenhof?"

"Yes. Still the same old place?"

"I would think. Care to get out and take a look? I don't mind."

"No, I just wanted to see it again."

"So, now to the Landstrasse?"

"Yes. The Imperial."

"Come to Vienna often?"

"Now and again."

"Different, this past year."

"Is it?"

"Yes. *Quiet,* thank God. Earlier we had nothing but trouble."

8:15. He would try one last time, he decided, and made the call from a phone in the hotel lobby.

"Hotel Schoenhof."

"Good evening. This is Doktor Heber, please connect me with Herr Kolovitzky's room."

"Sorry. Herr Kolovitzky is not available."

"Not in his room?"

"No. Good night, Herr Doktor."

"This is urgent, and you will give him a message. He took some tests, at my clinic here in Währing, and he must return, as soon as possible."

"All right, I'll let him know about it."

"Thank you. Now, would you be so kind as to call the manager to the phone?"

"I'm the manager."

"And you are?"

"The manager. Good night, Herr Doktor."

The next morning, Morath bought a briefcase, put the money and his passport inside, explained to the desk clerk that he would be away for a week, paid for his room until the following Thursday, and had the briefcase put in the hotel safe. From the art dealer in Paris he had a new passport—French, this time. He returned to his room, gave his valise a last and very thorough search, and found nothing out of the ordinary. Then he took a taxi to the Nordbahnhof, had a cup of coffee in the station buffet, then went outside and hailed a taxi.

"The Hotel Schoenhof," he told the driver.

In the lobby, only men.

Something faintly awkward in the way they were dressed, he thought, as though they were used to military uniform. *SS in civilian clothing.* Nobody saluted or clicked his heels, but he could sense it— the way their hair was cut, the way they stood, the way they looked at him.

The man behind the desk was not one of them. The owner, Morath guessed. In his fifties, soft and frightened. He met Morath's eyes for a moment longer than he needed to. *Go away, you don't belong here.*

"A room, please," Morath said.

One of the young men in the lobby strolled over and leaned on the desk. When Morath looked at him, he got a friendly little nod in return. Not at all unpleasant, he was just there to find out who Morath was and what he wanted. No hard feelings.

"Single or double?" the owner said.

"A single. On the square, if you have it."

The owner made a show of looking at his registration book. "Very well. For how long, please?"

"Two nights."

"Your name?"

"Lebrun." Morath handed over the passport.

"Will you be taking the *demi-pension?*"

"Yes, please."

"Dinner is served in the dining room. At seven promptly."

The owner took a key from a numbered hook on a board behind him. Something odd about the board. The top row of hooks, he saw, had no keys. "403," the owner said. "Would you like the porter to take your valise up?" His hand hovered over a bell.

"I can manage," Morath said.

He walked up four flights of stairs, the carpet old and frayed. Just a commercial hotel, he thought. Like hundreds in Vienna, Berlin, Paris, anywhere one went. He found 403 and unlocked the door. An edelweiss pattern on the limp curtains and the coverlet on the narrow bed. Pale green walls, hushed, still air. *Very quiet in this hotel.*

He decided to take a walk, let them have a look at his valise. He handed the key to the owner at the desk and went out onto the Mauerplatz. At a newsstand he glanced at the headlines. POLAND THREATENS BOMBARDMENT OF DANZIG! Then bought a sport magazine, youths playing volleyball on the cover. A genteel neighborhood, he thought. Sturdy, brick apartments, women with baby carriages, a trolley line, a school where he could hear children singing, a smiling grocer in the doorway of his store, a little man who looked like a weasel sitting at the wheel of a battered Opel. Back at the Schoenhof, Morath retrieved his key and walked upstairs, past the fourth floor, up to the fifth. In the corridor, a heavy man with a red face sat on a chair tipped back against the wall. He stood when he saw Morath.

"What do you want up here?"

"I'm in room 403."

"Then you're on the wrong floor."

"Oh. What's up here?"

"Reserved," the man said, "get moving."

Morath apologized and hurried away. *Very close,* he thought. Ten rooms on the fifth floor, Kolovitzky was a prisoner in one of them.

Three in the morning. Morath lay on the bed in the dark room, sometimes a breeze from the Mauerplatz moved the curtains. Otherwise, silence. After dinner there'd been a street musician on the square, playing an accordion and singing. Then he'd listened to the radio on the night table, Liszt and Schubert, until midnight, when the national radio station went off the air. Not completely off the air—they played the ticking of a metronome until dawn. *To reassure people,* it was said.

Morath gazed at the ceiling. He'd been lying there for three hours with nothing to do but wait, had thought about almost everything he could think of. His life. Mary Day. The war. Uncle Janos. He missed Polanyi, it surprised him how much. *Echézeaux and bay rum.* The amiable contempt he felt for the world he had to live in. And his final trick. *Here, you try it.*

He wondered about the other guests in the hotel—the real ones,

236 • KINGDOM OF SHADOWS

not the SS. They'd been easy enough to spot in the dining room, trying to eat the awful dinner. He'd mostly pushed noodles from one side of his plate to the other, kept an eye on the waiter, and figured out how the downstairs worked. As for the guests, he believed they would survive. Hoped they would.

From a church, somewhere in the neighborhood, the single chime for the half hour. Morath sighed and swung his legs off the bed. Put on his jacket, pulled his tie up. Then he took the stays from the envelope Szubl had given him. *Celluloid.* Made of soluble guncotton and camphor.

He took a deep breath and slowly turned the knob on his door, listened for twenty seconds, and stepped out into the hallway. He descended the staircase one slow step at a time. Somebody coughing on the third floor, a light under a door on the second.

A few steps from the bottom—the reception area—he stared out into the gloom. There had to be a guard. Where? Finally, he made out part of a silhouette above the back of a couch and heard the shallow breathing that meant light sleep. Morath moved cautiously around the newel post at the foot of the staircase, entered the dining room, then the hallway where the waiter had appeared and disappeared during dinner.

Finally, the kitchen. He lit a match, looked around, then blew it out. There was a streetlamp in the alley, not far from the windows, enough light for Morath to see what he was doing. He found the sinks—big, heavy tubs made of gray zinc—knelt on the floor below them and ran his fingertips over the cement. Found the grease trap, realized he'd have trouble prying up the lid, and abandoned the idea.

Next he tried the stove, and here he found what he needed. In a cabinet next to the oven door, a large metal can that had once contained lard was now used to store the grease poured from cooking pans. It was surprisingly heavy, maybe twenty pounds of yellow, rancid fat, mostly congealed, with an inch or so of oil floating on top. *Sausages, butter, bacon,* he thought. *Roast goose.*

He looked around, saw an iron ring above the stove where implements were hung, carefully removed a giant ladle, and served up a heaping scoop of thick fat. Took a handful, and smeared it on the wooden countertop. Worked it onto the walls and the window frames and the doors of the cabinets. Then he laid the can on its side in one corner, sunk the corset stays halfway into the fat, lit a match, and tossed it in.

The celluloid caught immediately; a hot, white flash, then the fat sputtered to life and a little river of liquid fire ran across the floor and began to burn its way up the wall. A few moments later, he saw the ceiling start to turn black.

Now he had to wait. He found a broom closet by the entrance to the kitchen, stepped inside, and closed the door. Barely room for him in there, he discovered. He counted eleven brooms. What the hell were they doing with so many brooms?

He told himself to stay calm, but the crackling sound from the kitchen and the smell of fire made his pulse race. Tried to count to a hundred and twenty, as he'd planned, but he never got there. He did not mean to die in a Viennese broom closet. He threw the door open and hurried down the hallway through a haze of oily smoke.

He heard a shout from the guard in the lobby, then another. Christ, there'd been *two* of them in there. "Fire!" he yelled as he ran up the stairs. He could hear doors opening, running footsteps.

Second floor. Third floor. Now he had to trust that the Austrian SS guards changed shifts like everybody else. Halfway up the stairs to the fifth floor he started yelling, "Police! Police!"

A bullet-headed man in his shirtsleeves came charging down the corridor, a Luger in his hand. "What's happening?"

"Open these doors. The hotel's on fire."

"What?" The man backed up a step. *Open the doors?*

"Hurry up. You have the keys? Give them to me. Go, now, run, for God's sake!"

"I have to—"

Morath the policeman had no time for him. Grabbed him by the shirt and ran him down the hall. "Go wake up your officers. *Now*. We don't have time for monkey business."

That, for whatever reason, did it. The man shoved the Luger into a shoulder holster and went bounding down the steps, shouting "Fire!" as he went.

Morath started opening doors—the room numbers, thank God, were on the keys. The first room was empty. In the second, one of the SS men, who sat up in bed and stared at Morath in terror. "What? What is it?"

"The hotel's on fire. You better get out."

"Oh."

Relieved that it was only the hotel on fire. What had he thought? There was smoke in the hallway. The SS man trotted past, wearing candy-striped pajamas and carrying a machine pistol by its strap. Morath found another empty room, then, next door, Kolovitzky, struggling to open the window.

"Not like that," Morath said. "Come with me."

Kolovitzky turned toward him. He wasn't the same man who'd played the violin at the baroness's party, this man was old and tired and frightened, wearing suspenders and a soiled shirt. He studied Morath's face—was this some new trick, one they hadn't tried on him yet?

"I came here for you," Morath said. "I burned down this hotel for you."

Kolovitzky understood. "Blanche," he said.

"Are they holding anyone else up here?"

"There were two others, but they left yesterday."

Now they heard sirens and they ran, coughing, hands over mouths, down the stairs through the rising smoke.

The street in front of the Schoenhof was utter confusion. Fire engines, firemen hauling hoses into the hotel, policemen, crowds of onlookers, a man wearing only a blanket, two women in bathrobes. Morath guided Kolovitzky across the Mauerplatz, then a little way down a side street. As they approached, the driver of a battered Opel started his car. Kolovitzky got in the backseat, Morath in front.

"Hello, Rashkow," Morath said.

"Who is he?" Kolovitzky asked, later that morning, while Rashkow watered a tree by the roadside.

"He's from Odessa," Morath said. *Poor little Rashkow,* Balki had called him, who'd sold Russian railroad bonds and Tolstoy's unfinished novel and wound up in a Hungarian prison. Morath had gone to Sombor to get him out of jail. "He used to sell Russian bonds."

"The way he looks," Kolovitzky said. "He should come to Hollywood."

Rashkow drove on farm roads through the Austrian countryside. A day in July, the beets and potatoes sprouting bright green in the rolling fields. It was only forty miles to the Hungarian border at Bratislava. Or Pressburg, if you liked, or Pozsony. In the backseat, Kolovitzky stared at the Austrian passport with his photo in it. "Do you think they're looking for me?"

"Of course they are."

They stopped well short of the Danube bridge, in Petrzalka, once a Czech border point, now in the Slovakian Protectorate. Abandoned the car. Went to a rented room above a café, where all three changed into dark suits. When they came downstairs, a Grosser Mercedes with Hungarian diplomatic registration was waiting for them, driven by the chauffeur of one of Bolthos's diplomatic colleagues in Budapest.

There was a swarm of Austrian SS gathered at the border crossing, smoking, laughing, strutting about in their high, polished boots. But the chauffeur ignored them. Rolled to a smooth stop at the customs building, handed four passports out the window. The border guard put a finger to the visor of his cap, glanced briefly into the car, then handed them back.

"Welcome home," the chauffeur said to Kolovitzky, as they crossed to the Hungarian side of the river.

Kolovitzky wept.

A midnight supper on the rue Guisarde.

Mary Day knew the trains were late, crossing Germany, so she'd planned for it. She set out a plate of sliced ham, a vegetable salad, and a baguette. "And this was delivered yesterday," she said, taking a bottle of wine from the cupboard and a corkscrew from the kitchen drawer. "You must have ordered it by telephone," she said. "Very thoughtful of you, in the middle of—whatever it was, to think of us."

A 1922 Echézeaux.

"It's what you wanted?"

"Yes," he said, smiling.

"You are really very good, Nicholas," she said. "Really, you are."

ABOUT THE AUTHOR

ALAN FURST, who has often been compared to
Graham Greene and Eric Ambler, is widely
recognized as a master of the atmospheric spy
thriller. A journalistic assignment for *Esquire*
inspired him to write *Night Soldiers,* the first of
his highly original novels about espionage in
eastern Europe before and during World War II.
Born in New York, he has lived for long periods
in France, especially Paris. He now lives on Long
Island.

ABOUT THE TYPE

This book was set in Sabon, a typeface designed by the well-known German typographer Jan Tschichold (1902–74). Sabon's design is based on the original letterforms of Claude Garamond and was created specifically to be used for three sources: foundry type for hand composition, Linotype, and Monotype. Tschichold named his typeface for the famous Frankfurt typefounder Jacques Sabon, who died in 1580.